HOLD FAST YOUR CROWN

HOLD

—

FAST

—

YOUR

—

CROWN

Yannick Haenel

Translated from the French by
Teresa Lavender Fagan

OTHER PRESS / NEW YORK

Production editor: Yvonne E. Cárdenas
Text designer: Jennifer Daddio / Bookmark Design & Media Inc.
This book was set in Copperplate Gothic and Adobe Garamond
by Alpha Design & Composition of Pittsfield, NH

1 3 5 7 9 10 8 6 4 2

Library of Congress Cataloging-in-Publication Data

Names: Haenel, Yannick, 1967- author. | Fagan, Teresa Lavender, translator.
Title: Hold fast your crown / Yannick Haenel ; translated from the French by Teresa
Lavender Fagan.
Other titles: Tiens ferme ta couronne. English
Description: New York : Other Press, [2019] | Originally published in 2017 as Tiens ferme
ta couronne by Éditions Gallimard, Paris.
Identifiers: LCCN 2018037536 (print) | LCCN 2018049076 (ebook) | ISBN
9781590519769 (ebook) | ISBN 9781590519752 (paperback)
Classification: LCC PQ2668.A326 (ebook) | LCC PQ2668.A326 T5413 2019 (print) |
DDC 843/.914--dc23
LC record available at https://lccn.loc.gov/2018037536

Publisher's Note
This is a work of fiction. Names, characters, places, and incidents either are
the product of the author's imagination or are used fictitiously.

Part One

FILMS

1

THE WHITE DEER

Back then, I was crazy. I had a seven-hundred-page screenplay on the life of Melville crammed into a box. Herman Melville, the author of *Moby-Dick*, the greatest of all American writers, the one who, in launching Captain Ahab in search of the white whale, incited a mutiny of global proportions, and through his books offered dizzying prophecies I adhered to for years. Melville, whose life was a never-ending catastrophe, who constantly fought against the thought of killing himself and, after having wonderful adventures in the South Seas and great success telling about them, suddenly *converted to literature*, that is, to conceiving the written word as truth, and wrote *Mardi*, which no one read, then *Pierre: or, The Ambiguities*, which no one read either, then *The Confidence Man*, which, again, no one read, before holing up for the final nineteen years of his life in a customs office in New York, and declaring to his friend Nathaniel Hawthorne: "Though I wrote the Gospels in this century, I should die in the gutter."

Maybe I was crazy, but I had written that screenplay to express what inhabits the solitude of a writer. I knew, of course, that such a thing is impossible to portray. No one can truly represent the thoughts of someone else, because thought exists precisely beyond any external representation. However, that's what I had attempted to reveal in my screenplay: Melville's thoughts—that which populated his thoughts.

That population of thoughts is a world, and even the books Melville wrote and published aren't enough to convey the immensity of the world that inhabits the head of a writer like him. What's more, there is a line in *Moby-Dick* that describes that teeming immensity. Talking about the sperm whale: "the unique interior of his head . . . those mystical lung-celled honeycombs." Well, that's exactly what my screenplay was about: *the mystical honeycombed interior of Melville's head.*

When I talked to producers, I knew it would be a challenge to lay out the subject of my screenplay, and when, at a certain point in the conversation, one of them asked, "But what's it about?" I really enjoyed saying it was about this: "the mystical honeycombed interior of Melville's head."

Was it the word "mystical" or the word "honeycombed" that stunned them? No producer, of course, ever followed up. But I wasn't discouraged. When you act against your own interests (when you sabotage yourself), it is always out of loyalty to something more obscure which you secretly know is right. After all, what is most precious is as difficult to attain as it is rare.

What's more, back then, I wasn't really trying to please, or even to be recognized. What I was looking for was someone who wouldn't laugh when I told him about the mystical honeycombed interior of a head, someone who wouldn't look at me as if I were crazy (even if I was), someone who wouldn't tap on his phone or think about his next meeting while pretending to listen to me, someone who, if I said this to him, "the mystical honeycombed interior of a head," would simply smile, because what I said pleased him, or because he really understood what it meant. But that someone, if he exists, would have to have the inside of his head mystically honeycombed, as well.

Anyway, I was alone, and *The Great Melville* was on its way to joining the huge herd of abandoned screenplays. Somewhere there is a great plain covered with dust and bones, maybe a sky, or the moon, where exiled screenplays are piled up. It's possible they're waiting, already half-dead, for an actor, an actress, a producer, a director, to look at them, but in general their solitude is forever, and the dust gradually covers up any light they may have emitted.

Most of my friends thought the screenplay was nuts. They thought it was nuts for me to devote my time to such an *unbelievable* project. In their opinion, no one would ever consider making a film from that screenplay, no one would ever want to watch a film about the life of a writer who fails. What's more, my friends didn't want to see me fail because of it. They thought it would have been smarter to write a book about Melville—for example, a *biography*, but not a *screenplay*. Screenplays are the death of writers, they said. The moment a writer starts to dream about making a film is precisely the moment that marks his death as a writer. The signal of his impending ruin— for a writer, financial ruin, and above all moral, psychic, and mental ruin—is when he gets it into his head to write a screenplay.

But I had already written the screenplay, I had nothing more to fear. What ruin could I dread? I had written novels, I would write more—I had a thousand ideas for novels in my head, but first I wanted to pursue the adventure of this screenplay to its end. I was devoted to *The Great Melville*, I wanted to express the solitude of the writer and the mystical nature of that solitude, I wanted to reveal what is inside a mystical honeycombed head.

Because most people, and even my friends, consider writers to be mere raconteurs, possibly good raconteurs who possibly have unique ideas, even enthralling ones, about life and death. Except writing about a guy whose head is mystically honeycombed inside—they usually found that *a bit much.*

Anyway, back then everyone thought exactly that: that it was all a bit much. I did nothing to try to convince anyone otherwise, I had my idée fixe. Because of course *The Great Melville* was an impossible film, but that was the point, exactly. The "impossible" was the subject of the screenplay.

Basically, a writer—a true writer (Melville, and also Kafka, I said to myself, or Lowry or Joyce: yes, Melville, Kafka, Lowry, and Joyce, precisely those four, and I repeated their names to my friends and to the producers I met with)—is someone who devotes his life to the impossible. Someone who has a fundamental experience with written words (who finds in the written word a passage for the impossible). Someone to whom something happens that takes place only on the level of the impossible. And it is not because that thing is impossible that it doesn't happen to him: on the contrary, the impossible happens to him because his solitude (that is, his experience writing words) is such that that type of inconceivable thing can take place, and it takes place through sentences, through the books that he writes, sentences and books that, even if they seem to be about something else, are secretly only about that.

A writer, I told myself, I told my friends, as well as those rare producers with whom I managed to obtain a meeting to talk about *The Great Melville*, a writer (Melville, and also Kafka or Hölderlin, Robert Walser or Beckett— because I varied my list) is someone whose solitude reveals a relationship with truth, and who at every moment devotes himself to it, even if that moment comes out of minor tribulation, even if that truth escapes him and seems obscure, even insane. A writer is someone who, even if he hardly exists in the eyes of the world, is able to convey the beautiful as well as the criminal into the heart of that world, and who knows, expressing humor or desolation, the most revolutionary or the most depressing of thoughts, that it is essentially his destiny to do so.

I must say that when I uttered the words "destiny to do so," even my most well-meaning friends appeared disheartened. They probably considered it a presumptuous delusion, but what could be simpler (and more complicated, of course) than doing so? What could be more important than devoting your life to doing so, and to ensuring that each moment of your life engages with that dimension? Because then, not only do you have a life, you have an existence: you finally exist.

I told myself that a writer, at least Melville or Knut Hamsun or Proust or Dostoyevsky (I really tried to vary my list), is someone whose experience writing words coexists with his experience of being; and fundamentally, because he is permanently committed to words—to what comes out when he writes—he opens up his entire existence, whether he wants to or not, to that experience.

Whether the experience is illuminated by God or, on the contrary, by the death of God, whether it is inhabited or deserted, whether it consists of allowing itself to be absorbed by the trunk of a tree or by grooves in the snow, to be open to the excessive heart of an unknown woman, or to decipher the signs on walls, it carries within something limitless that destines it to be a world unto itself, and thus to change the history of the world.

I lost myself a bit in my presentation, but I did not lose sight of one thing, the most important thing for me. Through Melville's writing, we experience something about the destiny of being. The proof is that his head was mystically honeycombed.

I remember a friend who claimed that the absolute is only an illusion, a way of "getting all worked up," as Flaubert once said (she cited Flaubert). In her opinion, Melville, before possibly being the saint that I imagined, was above all an ordinary guy, with his routine, his weariness, and his outbursts: a guy leaning on a wall, who simply speculated on the existence of a hole in that wall. She was right, but for me, that speculation, that hole in the wall, even if it was tiny, was enough. It is enough to think that there is a hole in the wall for the wall itself not to interest me anymore, and for all my thoughts to be drawn to the hole. The man or woman who has one day seen a hole in the wall, or who has simply imagined it, is destined to live with the idea of the hole in the wall, and it is impossible to live with that idea of a hole in the wall without devoting one's life to it entirely, that's what I told my friend, and what I repeated to most of my friends, and to the producers who pretended to be interested in the screenplay that I had called *The Great Melville.*

And then one day I read something by Melville along these lines: in this world of lies, truth is forced to flee into the woods like a frightened white deer, and I immediately thought of that film by Michael Cimino, *The Deer Hunter.*

In that film about the Vietnam War, which has lengthy scenes showing a game of Russian roulette featuring Christopher Walken, suggesting that that absurd war was only mass suicide, the hunter, played by Robert De Niro, pursues a deer through a forest in North America; when he finally catches up to it, when he has it in the crosshairs, he doesn't shoot.

As in some legends, as in the story of Saint Julian the Hospitaller in which the great stag disarms the hunter, the deer spared by De Niro in Cimino's film is the survivor of a world ruled by crime, it bears witness to a truth hidden in the woods, to something that goes beyond the criminality of the world and which, in a sense, overcomes it: the innocence that escapes an America absorbed in its bellicose suicide. Because the deer, by escaping the slaughter, reveals all that threatens it: the world which has become the sacrificial prey.

That afternoon I said to myself: that deer is Melville—it's Melville-Kafka-Lowry-Joyce, or Melville-Hölderlin-Walser-Beckett, or Melville-Hamsun-Proust-Dostoyevsky—it is the destiny of literature, its mystical embodiment, maybe even its honeycombed head.

I was in my car, listening to France Culture on the radio, when I heard Tiphaine Samoyault, a writer I like, quote that line from Melville about truth that must flee into the woods like a frightened white deer. She explained quite brilliantly that this conception of truth was close to that of the Greeks, and to what Parmenides called *aletheia*, truth as veiling/unveiling. Truth is not an immutable concept, it appears and disappears, it is an epiphany, it exists only through the burst of light that makes it possible. I was absolutely enthralled with what I was hearing, and in my head, along with all the names constantly running around in it night and day and constantly *forming relationships*, now there was a white deer running through kilometers of forests, upon which my thoughts, night and day, were now concentrating (my head is a forest of names, which explains my fatigue).

While thinking of the deer that appears in Cimino's *The Deer Hunter* and which, in freezing opposite Robert De Niro, seems to expose the essential truth of human madness, I also thought of Rembrandt's *The Polish Rider*, which you can see in the Frick Collection in New York, probably because of the stark whiteness of the horse stopped in the middle of darkness, as if the war were suspended for a few seconds, and amidst the hecatomb, in a brief flash, there arises the light of truth.

But if I begin to tell you everything that comes to me, if I detail all my thoughts, and how and why they occur to me, if I tell you about their simultaneity, this story will go on forever.

2

MICHAEL CIMINO

A few hours later, around three in the morning, while I was wandering around my apartment looking for some remnants of vodka, opening and closing the refrigerator, cursing the fact that there was never anything to eat in my place, and that I was once again going to have to go out in the middle of the night to eat a Big Mac at the Porte de Bagnolet McDonald's, I realized, with a simplicity that even today seems incredible, that I had to get Michael Cimino to read *The Great Melville*.

Yes, it was essential that Cimino read my screenplay, that much was obvious. There was an absolutely crucial relationship, decisive, even, between Melville and Cimino. How had it not occurred to me before—Michael Cimino *had to* read *The Great Melville*, because he embodied in American film what Melville had embodied in American literature, he was the last great American film director. He may have been the only one in the past thirty or forty years to have revealed a world, an experience, the secret behind the founding of America—its criminal destiny—the genocide of the Indians, the insanity of military imperialism in Vietnam, and all the crimes upon which its democracy was ultimately founded.

Yes, through his films, *The Deer Hunter*, but also *Heaven's Gate* and even *Sunchaser*, Cimino explored the failure of the American dream, the way in which that nation made up of all nations, that land of emigrants which promised to become the land of all immigrants, a sort of utopia of minorities exactly like the one seen in Melville's novels, had turned against the very idea of universal emigration and had systematically crushed those who were determined to pursue the dream, i.e., above all, the poor.

I bit into my Big Mac, sitting on a stool in the Porte de Bagnolet McDonald's, and I told myself that Cimino, just like Melville, was one of the names, in a both bloody and immaculate history, of the deer. He was the American embodiment of it, he was the frightened white deer that runs by in the Hollywood forest that ends up in the crosshairs of all those for whom the very idea of a deer will always be intolerable.

Because Michael Cimino, after his worldwide triumph with *The Deer Hunter*, after winning Oscars and becoming the epitome, the embodiment, the future of American film, with his next film, *Heaven's Gate*, experienced one of the worst failures in film history, a true disaster that quite simply turned him into a pariah.

Like Melville, who had first known easy glory, then had sunk into failure from the moment he began to write *from the truth* (by making the frightened white deer speak through him), Cimino had approached the very truth there is in failure, and probably began to no longer separate failure from truth, to deal with truth only in relation to the failure that reveals it, like a frightened white deer that, unscathed, runs through that criminal forest called humanity.

Cimino's filming of *Heaven's Gate* "exploded" its budget, as they say in those cases, and the studios were even less forgiving since the film was a commercial failure. But I think that Cimino's banishment was for another, more profound reason. He was quite simply being made to pay for what he had revealed in his film, that is, the massacre of Eastern European immigrants by landowners in that young America.

Heaven's Gate is about the civil war of 1890 that erupted in Johnson County, Wyoming, and ended with the massacre of the poor, civilian populations from Poland and the Ukraine by militias paid for by the capitalists in the region. What Cimino's film was about was America, which after wiping out the Indians, continued to be founded on a systematic program of extermination; it was also about capitalism, which was not an expression of the dream of that young nation—rather, already, it was its nightmare.

It was obvious, at least to me, that Michael Cimino would certainly listen to me talk about my screenplay without tapping on his phone, or thinking about his next meeting, and that he was the only one, when I would speak about Melville's head, of the mystical honeycombed interior of that head, who would not burst out laughing. Because he, himself, Michael Cimino—I suddenly understood this while drinking a glass of the vodka I bought at the twenty-four-hour store at the Porte de Bagnolet, and smiled to myself at the thought—he, himself, Michael Cimino, was undoubtedly someone the interior of whose head was mystically honeycombed.

From that night, I regained all hope. Instead of telling everyone I met about my screenplay, I stopped talking about it, and began trying to find out how I could get in touch with Michael Cimino.

I quickly found out that he had disappeared from circulation. He was said to be penniless, ill, no one wanted to produce his films anymore, and he had turned to writing literature. He lived on a farm in Montana, or in a cabin, it wasn't really clear which. It was also said that he never got out of his pool, and that for more than thirty years no one had seen his eyes, which, unfathomable, were masked behind sunglasses, as if that screen over his face, worn with a constancy reflecting the most extreme brooding (a mythological brooding, like that of Achilles), was proclaiming the fact that there is precisely nothing left to see, that there are no more films, that the screen is henceforth dark, and that such a revelation is true both for film and for life. But those dark glasses, whose strangeness was mentioned in every article ever written about Cimino, since he had a particular way of wearing them, a way of expressing himself *from* his sunglasses and *from* the suppression of the visible that haunted his films, those glasses perhaps above all signified the importance of barriers in his life; they summed up spectacularly, like a theater curtain that is drawn in protest, the multiple barriers he had experienced throughout his life, while at the same time attempting to overcome them. Barriers between himself and others, of course, but above all a barrier between the delicacy of his dreams and the millions of dollars he was blamed for losing, a barrier between poetry and money, a barrier between the sexes (because in his films, men were feminine and women masculine), a barrier between America and its failures and the Europe he pondered.

Anyway, Cimino, they said, spent his time in solitude, in that desert that had grown in him, and which no vision challenged because the desert is the very end point of sight. Had he gone completely crazy, or on the contrary, had he achieved wisdom? In a sense, madness and wisdom are the same thing, and reason seeks only to hide the fine line between them. In any case, like the hero in Kafka's *Amerika*, a book which was initially going to be called *The Man Who Disappeared*, he had slipped far, far away, into the hidden heart of that American land, revealing, as Melville had done before him, the huge pool of blood upon which the country was founded.

His disappearance made sense to me: hadn't he been forced to escape into the woods like the white deer? I watched his films again, one by one, taking notes, and the more I watched them the more obvious it became that not only would Cimino understand *The Great Melville*, but that in a sense, in each of his films, he had *already* produced my screenplay.

3

POINTEL

I've mentioned that at the time, I was crazy—let's just say I was possessed: names, books, films, lines from books and films, were teeming, alive, inside my head, they planned bacchanals together, and there was nothing I could do to pull them apart. I was literally inhabited by that flood of names, quotes, book and film titles whose giddy movement gradually took over my breathing and my nerves.

It never calmed down: who was it who said that names, since Christ, are like the morning breeze and are like dreams? In my experience, the morning breeze is overrated, my dreams are huge, raging fires growing through the night. They wake up the names, other names, all the names that talk amongst themselves.

So there you have it. My sickness, as my friends would say, my madness, was this: the perpetual motion of names. Each one came with the wind, together they formed a herd, like wild horses roaming in a valley. Each name illuminated another, it was never-ending. I spent my days reciting lists to myself, little snippets of phrases, quotes, and everything was related, and opened up exponentially, like a land without borders, like flames of happiness that rose up out of an extinguished world.

Of course, one might have thought I was sick, but that life of names I was in charge of made me strangely lighter, as if at any moment Melville's white deer was going to appear before me. That's it: I was living in the midst of a procession of white deer, and in a way, that was my madness, but it was also my glory, because in the procession that passed by in my head, I was welcomed. Existing among the names gave me wings.

One morning in March, after weeks of searching, of strange meetings, depressing phone calls, someone gave me Michael Cimino's contact information. I was in the office of a film producer on rue Notre-Dame-de-Nazareth near the Place de la République. That day, the guy I was talking to about my screenplay, Pointel, thought I was completely nuts, he said no one would want to put money behind such a project. Pointel had stopped producing "ambitious" films, as he called them, some time ago; in his opinion, the age of great cinema was over, there was only TV now, and he was content to produce series for French TV channels, sagas: "shit for grandmothers," he said.

But this sixty-something man, whose face was as weathered as an ancient mariner's, and who had a distinctly loony smile, really liked American literature. He had spent his childhood in San Francisco, still lived half the year in California, and started talking about beaches, mainly Big Sur, where he had a little house, really a cabin, he said: he had built it himself, and was very proud of it.

Several times Pointel quoted a line from Kerouac: "The absolute innocence like of Indian fashioning a canoe all alone in the woods." And he started in on a monologue on American literature, which, as I mentioned, he adored: Melville, Whitman, Faulkner, and for him, what was most beautifully written on "war and love" (I'm quoting him), on "hope and disappointment," on "politics and horror"—all of that had been written over there—and American films, in his opinion the best in the world, were only the heirs of American literature, which was the best in the world.

So, when Cimino's name came up, and I said that he was the only one who could do a film like *The Great Melville*, because his life wasn't unlike Melville's, Pointel looked at me for a long time without saying anything, like he was trying to figure out if I was serious, as if, all of a sudden, the possibility that my screenplay might be worth something had just occurred to him: "Michael? He's a friend of mine. Here, I'll give you his number. Tell him I told you to call. You'll see."

He handed me a yellow Post-it note, got up, walked me to the door, and shaking my hand said: "If you manage to wake up Michael: jackpot! Keep me posted," and he smiled, patting me on the shoulder.

Wake up Cimino—what could that possibly mean? It was perfectly clear, I said to myself while I was going down the stairs, that the telephone number was fake, Pointel had fed me bullshit, he was as nuts as my screenplay, and what's more, he was pulling my leg: at that very moment, without a doubt, he was on the phone with a producer friend (a guy he went sailing with, or some shit like that) and was telling him how he had had a crazy French writer in his office who wanted to do a film with Michael Cimino, and both of them, undoubtedly, were busting a gut laughing, like the alert and sad vultures they had become, and which these days almost everyone had become in France, and probably everywhere in the world.

It was time for me to stop this insanity, to forget about these stories of a white deer and of a mystical honeycombed head. To tell the truth, it wasn't really fun anymore, I had quite simply become obsessed. These past few years, I hadn't paid attention to what was happening to me, much less to what was happening to others, I had slid into a disturbing solitude, a solitude that I thought was glorious, but which was only a sordid isolation; my life, which I considered an adventure, revolved around my computer, in front of which I sat for ten hours a day, my fridge, which was constantly empty, and a few bars near Gambetta or Belleville, where I went to get drunk while talking about anything to anyone. All because I had an idée fixe, all because I read Melville, the great Melville, and had discovered in his books, in his life, and in his thoughts, something that seemed essential to me, something for which I had insanely abandoned my friends, my joy, the novels I was writing—in fact, life itself.

Walking around aimlessly that day, in front of the Pompidou Museum I ran into Agathe, a young woman I had been in love with a few years back, who had become a filmmaker. She was gorgeous, the white and purple flowers blooming around us like clusters of grapes seemed drawn to her aura; it seemed those flowers had opened only to shed their purple glow on her beautiful pale face, and to add their sparkle to her red-and-white-checked dress, inviting you to share in her silky, childlike lightness, sparkling reflections that seemed like snow in the middle of March, flakes that caressed your cheek, as if that flowery snow were the promise of a soft kiss, and you were perhaps not alone in the world because that young woman was smiling at you and she seemed to have all the time in the world for you. But her phone rang, she immediately answered, and as she walked away, she blew me a kiss with her fingers.

4

PHONE CALL

I didn't do a thing for several weeks. Computer, fridge, vodka. I heard the voices of lucid, sad vultures everywhere, people belly-laughing, giving each other phone numbers.

I said to myself: a cabin in Big Sur, that's what I need, or even a cabin in the Finistère, a cabin in Pas-de-Calais—anywhere, as long as there's an ocean and I can forget those wild voices, forget all those names rattling around in my head, that glorious procession that had led me to a dead end.

Sure, even a decrepit shack on the shores of a forgotten sea, provided I don't hear anything anymore, not vultures or deer, and that I finally wake up, as Pointel had said about Cimino. Then, out loud, I said: "If I manage to wake him up: jackpot!"—and I burst out laughing.

One morning, around eleven o'clock, while tapping out Michael Cimino's phone number, the one Pointel had written on the Post-it note that I had kept in my jacket pocket all this time, which I had kept with me as I traveled to the Port du Croisic, to the home of the Ricoeurs, a couple of friends who had invited me to "rest up" at their place, I expected to get a wrong number, or maybe get Pointel, who would then burst out laughing, and with that horrible laugh tell me my film was a completely worthless subject, but I didn't give a shit: I was calm, I needed to make this call once and for all.

I tapped that phone number so I could be done with it. To rid myself of *The Great Melville.* To wake up. No one was going to answer, or I would hear a laugh—and then, finally, I could go on to something else, as my friends in Croisic, tactfully and kindly, had begged me to do, encouraging me to resume my life as a happy novelist, to enjoy my talent rather than waste it, and to stop seeing film as a possible fulfillment of literature: because literature didn't need any other fulfillment than itself: they kept repeating this to me during the two weeks I stayed with them, on the seashore, during daily walks on the beach, and they were right.

Someone answered, and at that precise moment, I realized that I had forgotten the time difference: it was 11 a.m. in France, but if this number was American (and looking at the numbers it did indeed appear to be American), what time could it be over there? Even before introducing myself, I apologized and asked, "What time is it?" The guy answered, "Three in the morning." I said I was terribly sorry, I was calling from France and had forgotten the time difference. The guy said it wasn't a problem because he never slept. I asked if it was possible that I was speaking to Michael Cimino, and he told me, laughing, "I am Michael Cimino."

So Michael Cimino listened to me jabber on for a few minutes in English about Melville, Herman Melville, and about failure as the truth of being (I said that to fail was to be right, historically); and Cimino answered me very cordially in French (in a French that was about as good as my English), saying that Melville was without a doubt a magnificent writer, and he had read a lot of him, and Dostoyevsky, he said, and he pointed out that the end of *Heaven's Gate*, on the boat, when Kris Kristofferson is standing in his cabin, full of *illusions perdues* ("lost illusions"—he had said those two words in French with a sort of rascally refinement, as if he had become a character out of Proust), the ending was an homage to the author of *Moby-Dick*, but that he had been working for years on another screenplay, an adaptation of Malraux's *La condition humaine*; "be that as it may" (that's what he said), he would be delighted to meet me to talk about literature ("about Melville, Malraux, Dostoyevsky," he said), delighted to meet a French person, because France was the only country where his films were really understood, and maybe Poland (but Poland was an "imaginary country," he added mysteriously). Anyway, he was currently in Los Angeles, but would be in New York for a few days in mid-April "to buy some books," he said, and if I'd like, we could meet there. I answered yes, of course, New York—what day? And Cimino said: "How about April 17, in the afternoon?" "Perfect," I said, "absolutely perfect: the seventeenth, I'll be there." We agreed on the exact hour and place of the meeting, then he thanked me for calling.

I was dumbstruck. In my head, the white deer was galloping again, the forest of names was rustling with new confidence. Something mystically honeycombed was increasing my joy once again. I laughed out loud, and I drank a big gulp of vodka in honor of Cimino.

Excellent—I had woken up. I was going to meet Cimino, I was going to talk to him about *The Great Melville*. To be done with this story didn't mean being rid of it, but fulfilling it *in reality*.

I called my Croisic friends to tell them the good news. They were really happy for me, and at the same time a bit worried because this story still wasn't over, and in their opinions, it threatened never to be over, but they realized I was going to meet Michael Cimino (they had seen his films, too) and that that was a true adventure.

While drinking another shot of vodka, I thought of Pointel: he hadn't been pulling my leg, and in a way he had given me my chance. "If you manage to wake up Michael: jackpot!" I repeated that while laughing. From this moment on, I told myself, I was going to do only that: wake up Michael Cimino, wake up the great Melville, and finally wake myself up. No more vodka, no more empty fridge, no more spending the night in front of the computer. Discipline. Absolute discipline. Awake. Jackpot!

A few minutes after the call to Michael Cimino, the phone rang, and it was him: he had hit the "call back" button on his phone. Since we were seeing each other in New York soon, could I bring him a book on Malraux from Paris that he couldn't find there, not in Los Angeles or New York, a book by the philosopher Jean-François Lyotard, a book that was probably not translated into English, a book he absolutely needed for his screenplay, a book he believed contained absolutely essential information, information that might even change everything in his screenplay, change all his ideas about Malraux up to now, and therefore about Malraux's novel, *La condition humaine*, a novel, it was clear, he told me, that was absolutely secretly a philosophical and even mystical treatise on the meaning of revolution and suicide (and also, of course, he added, on the absence of meaning in them, because fundamentally, he told me, *La condition humaine* is above all a book on the strange *relationship*—strange and decisive, he told me—between revolution and suicide: one might say, Michael Cimino told me, that *La condition humaine* is both a book on the suicidal nature of revolution and a book on the revolutionary nature of suicide, because in a sense, Michael Cimino told me, revolution, for Malraux, is a form of suicide—a necessary suicide, of course, a great and beautiful suicide, he said while emphasizing those two adjectives—and at the same time the suicide of some of his characters, and in particular that of Kyo, is ultimately a political act, the most beautiful, the greatest of political acts, that is, an absolutely revolutionary act, of course)—in short, would it be too much trouble if I looked for the book in Paris (and it would probably be easy to find in Paris), and bring the book on Malraux to him when we met in New York?

"No problem at all," I said, "It would be a pleasure. I'll be happy to bring the book on April 17."

I was thrilled by the idea that Cimino would ask me to do something for him, because that *confirmed* our meeting, gave it substance, made it *real*, because after all, how could I be sure that on April 17, at 3:00 p.m., Michael Cimino would come to meet an unknown Frenchman who had written a screenplay on Melville? How could I be sure that he would make the effort to be there, the man who had gotten the world used to him no longer being there at all? Now that there was this book, I was almost sure that he would come to the meeting, I was sure that he wouldn't forget it, or, at the last moment, try to postpone or cancel it, or quite simply put it out of his mind.

I started looking for the book on Malraux by Jean-François Lyotard, and I found it right away in the Gibert bookstore, then for a plane ticket to New York. There were no more seats available *around* the seventeenth (I hadn't realized that the seventeenth was in three days), but there were some on the seventeenth itself: there was even a half-price offer for a roundtrip ticket on the same day.

A day in New York, a single day: leave the airport, see Cimino, go back to the airport. Fly to New York just to see Michael Cimino. The idea really pleased me. So what if I wouldn't be able to see the sights. I wasn't really interested in urban sightseeing. So I decided to grab that offer, arrive in New York on the seventeenth in the morning and leave on the seventeenth in the evening.

5

THE POLISH RIDER

At 3 p.m. on April 17, as planned, I was standing in front of Rembrandt's *The Polish Rider*. I was having trouble concentrating on the painting, because I kept watching for Cimino to arrive. I kept repeating the words he had spoken on the phone to set our meeting: "Shall we meet at the Frick Collection? It's a museum right across from Central Park."

I had been delighted by the coincidence, because it's in that museum that Rembrandt's *Polish Rider* is exhibited, and because, as you know, I associate that painting with Melville's frightened deer of truth. I told Cimino not only that I agreed, but that I was delighted, and suggested we meet in front of that painting, which I particularly liked. He said, simply, "Wonderful." But now that I was in front of Rembrandt's *Polish Rider*, I wondered if he had actually understood, if it was clear to him that it was in front of this painting, precisely in front of it, that we were to meet.

Maybe he understood something else, maybe he thought that we would meet randomly in the museum, and that I had mentioned Rembrandt's *Polish Rider* only to let him know that I knew the museum: the museum that held Rembrandt's *Polish Rider*.

What to do? I had been waiting for a half hour, and now if I left this painting to go look for Michael Cimino in the rest of the museum, he might, while I was gone, appear in the *Polish Rider* room and, not seeing me, leave. The best idea was not to move: even if he hadn't understood that we were supposed to meet in front of Rembrandt's *Polish Rider*, even if he thought we would meet "randomly" in the museum, at some moment or another he would necessarily come into the room with Rembrandt's *Polish Rider*, and we would then meet.

Because I was standing in front of that painting, in clear sight, constantly glancing around me, turning to look at the entrance to the room, watching for Cimino to arrive, the guard kept catching my glance. Each time, she stared at me, and over time, her look became harsher; she wasn't exactly expressing disapproval (that would be excessive), but slight, wary questioning: what was I doing there, standing for more than forty minutes in front of a painting, when I wasn't even looking at it (I was too preoccupied by Cimino's imminent arrival), constantly looking around me—that's what the guard's look was expressing (and I couldn't blame her).

So that Michael Cimino would find me right away, I was armed with the book by Jean-François Lyotard on Malraux, which I was holding straight up, in front of my chest, as if I were trying to sell it, which, I could see, added to the bizarreness of my appearance, thus to the suspicions of the guard, who seemed increasingly nervous.

I then realized (I had been waiting almost an hour) that I didn't know what Michael Cimino looked like today; I had an idea of his face, but that face was probably the one he had had at the time of *Heaven's Gate*, at the height of his glory, which went back more than thirty years: each time I turned toward the entrance, I expected to see that Michael Cimino with the round cheeks of thirty years ago, whose image I had seen everywhere at the time, appear wearing a cowboy hat and Ray-Bans.

But I was confident—confident about whom: Cimino? Me? I smiled as I stared at the Polish rider's face. He, too, seemed confident, and in spite of the apocalyptic, threatening sky weighing down on him, in spite of the darkness that seemed to absorb the warm colors, red and brown, that enveloped him, you sensed in the rider's stance, in his noble reverie, an expectation that was stronger than the ruins; you sensed that the darkness in which he was immobilized with his horse was only the prelude to something, something unknown for the moment, which would change everything. Rembrandt's *Polish Rider* was watching over a new era, over a new silence.

There comes a time when the absurdity of a situation seems like a victory, like a sort of masterpiece: it is enough in itself. And in this case, the hope that inspired me was so excessive (there was also the jet lag) that I had reached the point, standing in front of Rembrandt's *Polish Rider*, of forgetting all my concerns, forgetting the very reason for my being there, forgetting that I was waiting for Michael Cimino.

I put the Lyotard book on Malraux back into my jacket pocket and sat down on the velvet bench in front of the painting. I felt good here alone in New York. The afternoon light was shining through one of the windows, it was soft. With it, with its spring rays, the dark colors of *The Polish Rider* took on a peaceful hue, and while checking to make sure the guard wasn't watching (but since I had sat down on the bench she had stopped being suspicious of me), I took out a small bottle of vodka that I had bought in the duty-free shop in Roissy-Charles-de-Gaulle airport to endure the plane trip, and taking little sips, slipping into a pleasant torpor, I polished off the bottle.

I must have fallen asleep, because suddenly the guard was standing next to me, she was shaking my shoulder while talking into her walkie-talkie. "We're closing," she kept saying.

Outside, the sky was pink, and all the green in Central Park was glimmering like a softly burning bush. I breathed in the scent of wisteria, of the honeysuckle that climbed along the main door of the museum, and all the petals flew around, little yellow and purple words in the dusty and saturated story of the New York air.

I lit a cigarette and sat down on the steps of the Frick Collection. My return flight was just before midnight, it was now 5:30 p.m. Since I had some time to kill I thought I might go sit on a bench over in Central Park and watch the trees, the sky, and the young women whose light, early spring dresses were awakening other desires in me than those that had been flooding my head for months, clearer, more fluid desires—desires that were increasing. What was that line in Fitzgerald's *The Great Gatsby* about New York? Ah, yes: "the old island here that flowered once for Dutch sailors' eyes—a fresh green breast of the new world." I, too, felt green and fresh. I had crossed the ocean, and voilà: I was awake.

A woman was sitting on one of the steps and was watching the visitors coming out of the museum. She was surrounded by bags of books from the Strand, was wearing dark glasses and a cap with FUCK written on it, and was chain-smoking cigarettes while tapping on an iPad. She noticed that I, too, was carrying bags of books from the Strand, and we smiled at each other.

It's funny, I wasn't even disappointed. Michael Cimino hadn't come, but in the end, it made sense. Hadn't he become a sort of ghost? Like the Polish rider, he was living along a dark line, a line from which one perceives the beginning and the end of things, and, for the one who manages to understand that line intimately, it induces a frightening clarity, but also a sort of innocence that today everyone has lost.

I thought back on our phone conversation. Had I dreamt it? Sometimes there are faceless figures in our heads that represent portents when we need them; they are like specters that infuse our speech, helping us out when necessary.

I lit another cigarette. I wanted some vodka. I closed my eyes. I had arrived very early that morning, around six. I hadn't slept on the plane, and the whole day, while waiting to meet Michael Cimino, I had wandered around the city, walking up Manhattan from the Brooklyn Bridge. I had stopped at the Strand, and, like that woman, I had bought a bunch of books that I was now carrying around. I was going to continue wandering around the city for a few more hours, then I would go lie down in the Kennedy Airport waiting room with my bags of books until my plane departed.

So, I had come to New York to see a painting by Rembrandt and to buy some books. That's what I should have told the immigration officer at Kennedy Airport that morning when he asked me why I had come to the United States: to see a painting and to buy some books. Instead of what I had muttered: "To speak with somebody."

The guy had looked up and stared at me curiously, as if what I had said deserved special attention. "Who exactly?"

I hadn't really understood his question, he had to repeat it several times (and of course, making an immigration officer repeat something often turned a simple formality into an incident).

Anyway, when I had understood that he wanted to know the name of the person I had come to New York to meet, I don't know what came over me, I said, like Bartleby, Melville's character: "I would prefer not to." The guy didn't understand: "What?" he said. And then I had to repeat what I had said several times until he understood, and he probably thought I was being insolent because he gestured to the policemen who were waiting on the other side of the line who then came over. It was clear that when I was asked, "What is the reason for your trip?" I should have answered something like "business," or "sightseeing."

They took the bottle of vodka out of my bag and examined it with disgust, then *The Great Melville* screenplay, which I had had printed in red. Clearly, that color disturbed them. One of the cops asked me what it was. A screenplay, I said, a screenplay about Melville, "the author of *Moby-Dick*." And I pointed out, absurdly, that Melville had in fact worked in customs in New York and that, in a certain sense, he was their colleague.

I was about to leave the Frick steps when the woman wearing the FUCK cap came up to me. She asked if I was the person she had a meeting with. I said no: I had a meeting with someone who hadn't come, I had waited for him for several hours and now I was going to catch my flight home. Then the woman held out her hand, smiling, and said to me in French that she was really sorry, she was very late because of another meeting, and when she had arrived, a half hour ago, they wouldn't let her into the museum because it was about to close.

I didn't understand. Then she asked me how *The Polish Rider* was doing today. We both smiled, and I took the book on Malraux by Jean-François Lyotard out of my pocket and handed it to her. "I have some books for you, too," said Cimino, and we headed for Central Park.

The air was soft, light, and we couldn't stop smiling. There were bursts of blue coming from the leaves of the elm trees, and something else seemed to shine from tree to tree, a truth that did not just belong to the spring, a sort of glow that, while appearing fragile and uncertain, enchanted the hearts of children on the paths and those of the couples lying on the grass; that glow gradually erased the shadows, and like Fitzgerald's "fresh green breast of the new world," it seemed capable of erasing the void, of conquering the horrors and of carrying this late afternoon into the joy of perfect moments.

We walked for a long time, up to the Hudson River. Cimino pointed to a bench, and we sat down. He took out a bottle of vodka, which we sipped while smoking cigarettes.

We talked. Night fell, pink, red, bluish, with a bit of wind that made the gulls spin around. Cimino showed me the books he had bought at the Strand, and I showed him mine. The books went back and forth, and we laughed at recognizing books we liked, or others that we had always wanted to read, then we exchanged some, and in the end, Cimino gave me a special book, wrapped in gift paper. He asked me to open it later, when I had returned to France.

We looked farther out at the Statue of Liberty, and I reminded Cimino that in Kafka's *Amerika*, when Karl Rossmann arrives by boat from Europe, he sees the statue holding not a torch, but a sword, the one that would continuously cut off his path, the one that wanted his death. Cimino said, "I'm Karl Rossmann." Then we calmly finished the bottle of vodka, looking even farther out at Ellis Island, where, Cimino said, for each one of us everything begins and everything ends.

6

SABBAT

Five months later, I received a text from Pointel. It was September 23. I remember it distinctly because it was my birthday. I was in the middle of celebrating the event as was appropriate, by drinking a six-pack of beer in bed watching Francis Ford Coppola's *Apocalypse Now*, when the message appeared on my phone.

Since I had gotten back from New York, I felt certain I was holding on to something. Something absolutely crucial, something awesome. Maybe it only barely existed, it might not even have had a name, but that thing kept jumping up in front of me; and like a howling beast that fear has kept cowering in the back of its cave, it emerged out of the darkness and bared its teeth *every time I watched a movie*.

Yes, I was crazy enough to believe that a secret traveled through films, crazy enough to imagine that you could grasp it and even be enlightened by it. I had looked for this secret in the films of Michael Cimino, and now the search had widened, because truth is like the huge body of a goddess: it is there and not there—you see it and you don't see it.

But I saw it. Was it that Milky Way where golden rays sparkled? Or that rotten hole where green skulls rolled around? By following Melville around the world, by hunting with him not only a whale that had taken the place of God but also a flood of shadows and horror, and glimmers of adoration, and the joy of the labyrinth, and the sinking into the abyss, and the red eyes of crime, and the stormy and serene possibility of love, I had discovered that a spark is lit in the heart of destruction like an arctic crystal; and that this spark was enough to set the world on fire. That fire is white, believe me. It is the opposite of devastation. We burn in it without being consumed. And don't laugh, that is exactly what I see: an immaculate fire.

That's why all I did at that time was watch films. I had spent all summer watching three or four films a day, lying on my foldout bed, in front of the large flat screen that my neighbor down the hall, Tot, had found on eBay. He considered it a heresy to watch films on a computer screen, as I had been doing for years, and in exchange for the large screen, the unlimited enjoyment of which he had given me, I took care of his Dalmatian when he was away. Tot played poker. He would leave suddenly for a tournament anywhere in the world without saying when he would be back. So I often took care of his dog, whose graceful body and almost childlike playfulness I really liked.

In the beginning, the Dalmatian, whose name is Sabbat, stayed in Tot's apartment, and I simply took him out three times a day onto the patch of grass in the inner courtyard, as Tot had instructed me to do. I would also feed Sabbat, following the instructions Tot had stuck on his fridge in capital letters: IN THE MORNING, FILL THE GRAY DISH WITH FRESH WATER, THE RED DISH WITH BIO "SPECIAL DIET" KIBBLE, AND THE BLUE DISH WITH A POUND OF DICED RED MEAT, which every evening I took out of the freezer and placed in the sink for the next day; IN THE EVENING, FILL THE RED AND BLUE DISHES WITH "CANINE DIET" DRY FOOD (AND GIVE SABBAT A DRIED BEEF TREAT).

In general, I would watch my first film around noon, then a second around 2 p.m.; and after taking care of some business, i.e., going to the Franprix market to replenish my stock of beer and vodka, then buying cigarettes at the Tabac on rue Pelleport, I started a third film in the evening. It was usually longer, aesthetically more ambitious, one of those films that assume you think along with them, that is, that you are putting your thoughts to the test, and that those thoughts agree to change; one of those films that expect you to be open to the possible fire that consumes them and that you, yourself, might possibly catch on fire:

a film that responded to my research, and whose flames brought rays of light.

In order for me to get my bearings in the forest of all those films, the white deer had to appear at one moment or another: not the deer, in person, nor any animal shape fleeing through the woods, but an event that such a flight announced, that voice of the sacrifice that travels through the ages and unveils the truth beneath appearances.

And, of course, the deer doesn't appear on demand; it doesn't gallop through every film, even if it is tempting to think so. In a sense, nothing is rarer than its appearance. That's why I watch for it so intensely, that's why I devote all my time to it. I don't want to miss the epiphany of the white deer of truth.

And so that summer I watched dozens and dozens of films, and among them dozens and dozens of bad films, sometimes even real duds, without coming across anything that even slightly resembled a reflection of my deer. But it took only a detail, three seconds of a glimmer, the echo of an echo of a voice lost in the desert, a trace of blood on the edge of a sidewalk, for what I was waiting for to appear, what I was hoping for more than anything, that thing that my desire, constantly, was on the verge of inventing: a sign, a portent.

Around one or two in the morning, I ended with a final film, sometimes the same film, and I would write down the dialogues I had liked in a special notebook. I'll talk about that notebook later. Since my encounter with Michael Cimino, I had put *The Great Melville* aside, and that notebook, in a certain sense, had replaced it.

Yes, the lines in *The Great Melville*, those I had printed in red, those that had gone through customs in New York and which Michael Cimino had read in their entirety, from the first to the last, while punctuating his reading with grunts of satisfaction, pointing with his finger at scenes he liked, those lines now needed me to give them the freedom they required, a horizon toward which each one of them was leaning like an impatient animal.

I remember a herd of wild horses in Malcolm Lowry's *Under the Volcano*—gorgeous animals with lush coats, constantly galloping toward a violently hued light that illuminated the peaks of the Sierra Madre; the movements of that herd through the book created an ever more distant prairie, one fashioned by endless desire. And it is perhaps that furtive vision full of joy, rather than his mescal, that the consul, a prisoner of himself, endlessly drinks in.

For me, the lines in *The Great Melville* were similar to the uninterrupted galloping of Lowry's horses; they evoked the same scarlet happiness, the one that comes to us from the greatest hopes. That happiness bursts open when the horizon is torn apart: our thirst opens a passage in it, and even if the galloping is more distant, the sound fainter and fainter, its existence alone constitutes a promise that touches our lives.

Rather than continuing ad nauseam to rework the text of my screenplay, I decided to give it a break: perhaps it would become better by itself; perhaps, by distancing itself from me, it would discover what made it so strange to others, and would manage to be a bit less so, or no longer be strange at all—to finally please (but I didn't have any illusions; my screenplay was tenacious, even stubborn, and in truth I didn't want it to change: abandoning one's desire is the same as acceptance, and isn't acceptance the enemy of art?).

So I had placed those bound pages into a metal box, a red cookie box, long and flat, like a little coffin, and I set it on my bedside table, under the protection of the stuffed swallow that presides there. I'm extremely fond of that swallow—it's a goddess. In the *Odyssey* doesn't Athena appear to her dear Ulysses in the form of a swallow with blue-gray eyes? My swallow also has that shiny gray, slightly mother-of-pearl, in its eyes, the reflection of the perfection of silence. Whenever I was feeling unmoored, between two films, I would talk to her: "One more time, Athena, love me as much as possible."

It was pleasant to think that the object of my desire was within reach, shut in a container that protected it and endowed it with sacred value: beneath the rows of papyri that hung along the wall to the left of my bed, that little box sat like a reliquary. When you have written something you think is important, even if it's only three lines, those lines continue to live through your thoughts, and without your knowing it, they transmit their discoveries to you. It sometimes seems to me that it is they, on a very secret level, that live instead of us, thereby sparing us the trouble of finding a solution to our lives: the lines exist; as for us, we don't matter.

And so, while I watched a film sipping a beer or doing shots of Absolut (that vodka whose translucent round bottle and the transparency of its name I loved), I had only to glance slightly to my left to see the altar made up of the papyri, the swallow, and the manuscript box. I then felt I was favored, as if life were smiling down on me.

Between each film, I took Sabbat out. Most of the time, I just took him down to the little patch of grass where he shook himself for a few minutes and peed against the trunk of the plane trees. When he pooped, I had the unpleasant task of scooping it up and throwing the bag out in the garbage can. Tot had given me a stash of little bags, and I would get one ready as soon as Sabbat assumed the defecating position. This was always a delicate moment, and I knew—and Tot himself had confirmed this—that it is ill-advised to interfere with a Dalmatian who is taking a shit: the moment the Dalmatian shits he travels back to his origins, to his royal instincts, to the memory of his throne. No one should disturb such a dream, at the risk of driving the Dalmatian crazy and causing irreparable damage to him and perhaps to others.

Indeed, one evening, when I had interrupted the nth number of intense viewings of *Apocalypse Now* to take Sabbat out, and he had trotted up to his favorite spot, a damp corner alongside some acacias, a corner where he managed to re-create the world that favored his relaxation, the concierge, Mme Figo, had appeared, furious, holding up I don't know what sheaf of forms relating to the packages I constantly had delivered to me and that I never came to get from her *loge*. Not only did she have to waste her time with delivery men who insulted her, but what's more she had to hold on to the mountains of boxes in the tiny space of her *loge* when in fact nothing obligated her to do so.

Even before I was able to respond that every time I went down to get my packages the *loge* was closed, Mme Figo noticed the Dalmatian who was doing his business under the acacias. She scolded me for leaving dog droppings everywhere on the property, an accusation which I immediately protested; my neighbor, Tot, the owner of the dog, had given me ample little bags into which I scooped the excrement. That I had perhaps neglected one or two turds on the grass of our respectable property unfortunately seemed possible, and I was completely ready to confess to that, because it happens that Sabbat sometimes shits at night, and the yard is only dimly lighted, but on the whole I scrupulously respected the guidelines for public hygiene, and so it was uncalled for, even wrong, to accuse me.

Why didn't I take my dog into the street like everyone else? shouted Mme Figo. The question itself was legitimate, but I pointed out that it wasn't my dog and that I was only following the instructions of my neighbor, Tot, who knew what was best for his dog, because in fact this concerned *his* dog, not mine, and what was more I imagined, pure speculation on my part, that the grass on the property was probably a more attractive place for a dog to take care of its defecating needs than the cold, impersonal gutters of Paris streets.

Since I was lighting a cigarette, Mme Figo seized the opportunity to rail against my smoking: not only did I flick my ashes here and there on the flower beds of this yard for which she was responsible, but I also dropped my butts in them, too. This new accusation was even more unfair than the one before, because I never dropped any butts or even hid them by shoving them underground as some do, I said, but always put them in the bag where they joined Sabbat's excrement. I was innocent, I said to Mme Figo, and maybe even irreproachable.

Our dialog reached maximum intensity, and as I feared, that intensity upset Sabbat: he leapt from his thicket and jumped on Mme Figo, who fell down into an acanthus bush, cursing us, me and my stupid dog.

———

After the afternoon walk, before I plunged back into the
thrilling hell of *Apocalypse Now,* in which I observed a cata-
basis that, far from describing the American miring in the
Vietnam War, involved the sacrificial situation of us all,
Sabbat and I went back into Tot's apartment and I kept the
dog company for a few more minutes, since he didn't like to
be alone. Sunk down in the club chair in the living room,
legs stretched out on the coffee table, while Sabbat, mad
with joy, brought me a stuffed animal or some chewed-up
Barbie doll, I looked out the window at the passing of the
light through the leaves of the tall plane trees. Sabbat soon
stretched out on top of me, his front paws on my shoulders,
his mouth up against my neck, his big Dalmatian heavy
stomach comfortably resting against my abdomen, and his
back paws stretched along my legs; he sighed great sighs
of pleasure and closed his eyes, reassured, as if we were
going to live this way, together, for weeks, months, years,
an entire lifetime.

I like looking at the plane trees in the yard. The view
from Tot's apartment was essentially the same as the one I
had from my bed, but each nuance of light modified the
color of the trees, and it took only a bit of wind, a cloud, a
slight cooling for the shape of the branches and the leaves
to appear new.

I'd like to go into every apartment in the building and
follow the light throughout the day to see all the metamorphoses. A moment ago, around 6 p.m., when the sky had

been clear all day, and the afternoon was still, when the colors were inflamed, first they wavered, uncertain, and the grass, the acacia bushes, the little clumps of bay trees, seemed red, almost black. That redness climbed, and then the plane trees and the chestnut trees in the inner courtyard were filled with a reddish glow that was thrown on the bay window, on the ceiling, on the walls of the apartment building. In moments like those the world takes on the color of hot sand, and bursts of orange and yellow sparkle in the corners of the windows. The reflections tremble a bit, folded in the mother-of-pearl, purple and red, bluish. A knife should be plunged into the matter of days, slicing off the fat, sparing only that which amazes you: do we need anything other than vertigo?

7

TOT

Tot's trips abroad usually didn't last more than eight to ten days, but I hadn't heard from him in more than three weeks. He had taken a plane on September 1 for a tour of casinos in North America, and it was now the twenty-third. Since Sabbat hated to be alone, and my visits were no longer enough to stop his whining, I had ended up keeping him at my place; I liked that dog, but I had perhaps taken my role too seriously. I had the impression I was spending my days feeding him, taking him to the little yard so he could do his business, playing ball with him like a child; I couldn't think calmly anymore, my solitude was falling to pieces: it was critical that Tot return.

Even Anouk, his girlfriend, didn't know when he was getting back; and since he had neither a cellphone nor email, we had no way to reach him. Furthermore, even when he was home, he was unreachable. His passion for gambling brought him into contact with shady characters, and he sometimes became entangled in unsavory money problems; then he would shut himself up for weeks and live like a fugitive, his shutters closed—"playing dead," as he called it. When that happened, it was I, always and forever I, who took the dog out.

I never really understood the basis for our agreement (I probably didn't want to think about it). Exchanging dog care for a television screen seemed a bit much to me, and moreover, had I asked for this? Nothing, I had asked for nothing. You live alone, and now you're invaded, first it's a dog, then comes the rest, like the proverbial snowball.

The first time I had seen Tot was on the landing. I was coming out of the elevator, a guy was looking at me from his doorway. He was tall and thin, barefoot, wearing a red silk kimono embroidered with fire-breathing dragons. I immediately figured out that the fire was his own. He looked like a man who had been pulled out of a fire before the flames completely roasted his body. And then there was something about him that made him seem like a mercenary or a savage: an emaciated face, sharp eyes, short hair, like a former soldier. I learned later that he had joined the Foreign Legion, and had spent five years in a camp in Djibouti, then in Abu Dhabi. I learned that he had fought on various fronts, during operations in Chad, Mali, as well as in Lebanon. I also learned, from Anouk—because he said nothing, was usually silent, and opened his mouth only to give orders—I learned that while he was scuba diving off the coast of Djibouti, he had cut his leg on some coral, and a shark, attracted by the blood, attacked him. Tot's body was, it seems, entirely covered with scars, remnants of that terrible battle, but the shark was dead. Tot had torn it to pieces.

He asked me in a low voice, a lugubrious, muffled voice, if I had seen his dog. I had in fact just seen in the little yard of the inner courtyard a Dalmatian that was urinating against the plane trees. That's him, he said. Did I think he would come back up? I shrugged. Knowing what a dog is thinking wasn't really my area of expertise.

A bit later, someone knocked on my door. It was him again, bare feet, with his kimono and crazy eyes. He had an abscessed tooth, and had to see the dentist right away, down on Place Édith-Piaf. His gums were bleeding and he just wanted to pull his teeth out, one by one, with pliers. Furthermore, I remember this very well, at that very moment he slid his hand into the pocket of his kimono and took out a little set of metal pliers that he immediately rammed into his mouth. I thought he was going to pull out a tooth, right there in front of me. I already imagined the bloody hole. But then he asked me if I would take care of his dog while he was gone.

It's impossible for me to describe my relationship with Tot. I'll start with this story, whose labyrinthine nature, believe me, is involuntary. I would have liked this narrative to be clear, but it seems that clarity is always only a phase: its perfection comes out of the inability to see what is beyond the horizon.

And also, nothing is ever complete. If I tried to reduce Tot to his despair, I would fear his vengeance—we were connected by an almost frightening understanding.

Most of the time, Tot was on edge, aggressiveness seemed to be his natural state. He seemed always ready to fight. Had he killed someone? He clearly had an over-whelming desire to. That desire is ambiguous: it beckons you, like thirst. It is probably impossible to escape such a desire because it is constantly growing and soon overcomes your very breathing: once the idea of committing a crime enters you, not only can you no longer rest, but your death becomes clearer—*you are living with your death.*

For most people, death doesn't exist, they lose friends, they lose a parent, they suffer from that, but their own demise remains distant. Nothing in the world can get them to visit their own grave. They close their eyes while the knife slowly pierces their heart.

Tot, on the contrary, was a creature of sacrifice. The fevers that struck such a vigorous being and put him in bed for entire days came from that sacrificial hold. Tot's calm then came from the fact that he was burned from head to toe. Such a burning protected him from the ruin to which most creatures succumb, because they fear for what they've built.

That was his strength. Tot in no way sought to be recognized. He existed alone, with nothing that could chain
him down, except his fevers, whose tenacity were night-
marish. Whether he was empty or profound was of no
importance—Tot was above all dangerous, and that danger provided a certain consistency to his life. He probably
didn't conceive of a truth other than that of his vices. Their
immensity, their rigor were his breath of life.

In between his poker tournaments, Tot went hunting.
I even accompanied him on one of his nocturnal expe-
ditions in the forest (it's not yet time to tell about that
outing). His apartment had the same layout as mine, the
same bay window, the same obscure color. No décor. It
was like a hideout, with found furniture and computer
parts piled up in the corners. In the bedroom/living
room, where I had put my TV, he had installed a gun
locker. It contained all sorts of whitish-colored weapons,
whose blades shine in my head when I write these lines,
in particular a hatchet that he used the evening he invited
me to dinner. And there were three shotguns. One afternoon when we were drinking beer at his place, he took a
key out of his pocket, opened the gun cabinet, took one
out, cocked it, pointed it at his dog, abruptly raised the
weapon, and held it out to me.

Was it Tot who introduced me to hunting? I don't think
so. Such a passion, when it declares itself, has been simmer-
ing for a long time. But if for me hunting mainly took place

in my head, for Tot it was a real activity. He had to pursue a physical shape to its death.

His rapid, precise movements were those of an expert. He would go in a second from coldness to fever, then the reverse, exhibiting a self-discipline that is lacking in muddled hearts.

The shotgun he had placed in my hands was German, a Haenel, according to him the best for trackers. The Haenel assault rifles, he explained, were what the Wehrmacht used. And ever since World War II, the Haenel company had specialized in custom-made weapons. This one, a semiautomatic assault rifle with a straight buttstock, had been designed especially for him to follow prey through a forest and shoot while he was moving. Because in hunting, said Tot, tracking the prey is what matters. When the moment comes to aim, to shoot, to kill, the hunt is already over. Hunting, said Tot, does not consist of adjusting the crosshairs of a scope, but of pursuing a prey until nothing separates you from it. To truly experience the hunt, it is essential that your fatigue equal that of the animal you are tracking. The breathing of the hunter and the hunted must be in sync, and, in a sense, become as one; it isn't true that in hunting the hunter and the prey are substituted for each other, he said, rather, they become one. A true hunt, a *successful* hunt, means you have conquered the animal even before shooting it, that is, you have confronted it with yourself throughout an entire night, and by pursuing

it through the forest you have emptied yourself of what separates you from it. The true hunter, he said, is the one who
continues to breathe when his prey is out of breath. The
true hunter exhausts his prey, which, giving up, collapses at
his feet. Then, as the animal turns its eyes toward you, its
look consecrates the animal that was in you. The panting
that travels through your two bodies destroys the distance.
In hunting, Tot said, there is no pity. The one who has
exhausted the other is then able to finish him off. That is
when, he said, one discovers one's teeth. I like to kill, said
Tot, and the hunters who say they don't are lying.

I should admit something, which is probably not unrelated
to my problems with Tot. One evening, Anouk knocked on
my door. Was it July or August? She was looking for Tot. I
told her he had left for a few days. That was a lie, Tot was
there—he was playing dead. He didn't want to see anyone,
not even Anouk (especially not her, he had told me).

It's not that I wanted to protect Tot, but the hold he had
over Anouk disgusted me, she was losing her charms day
by day. She was in Tot's hands, he only had to close his fist
and she would be crushed.

She was surprised he hadn't told her. She looked as sad
as a little girl who has lost her doll. I invited her to come in.

Anouk was around twenty (I would guess twenty-four).
I had met her two or three times when she and Tot were

strolling in the neighborhood. She was beginning her doctorate in philosophy, focusing on Wittgenstein, on a little text by Wittgenstein devoted to *The Golden Bough*, and more generally on the connection between logic and mysticism. She taught philosophy in a suburban high school, in Deuil-la-Barre. It was her first year, she was still in training, and already teaching seemed nuts to her. She was brilliant, and her passion for a man as impenetrable as Tot was, in my opinion, a real waste. I imagined her groveling in front of that mute owl. That image was torture.

I had just begun the nth number of viewings of Cimino's *Heaven's Gate*, and asked if she'd like to watch it with me. It's a film about the criminal founding of America, I told her, a film that shows how the rich eliminate the poor, how, around the end of the nineteenth century, in a county of Wyoming, the landowners, supported by the government authorities, had drawn up a blacklist of immigrants to eliminate and paid mercenaries to do the deed. I really liked this film because it tells of class struggle, as in Flaubert's works, through the flickering lens of ceremonies. And there's sex, dancing, and death. What's more, as she would find out, there's the vastness of blue skies that crush the characters, there are the Rocky Mountains, those of Colorado and Montana, with their snow-covered peaks where the white deer of truth shines out amid the rest of the herd, there are endless prairies traveled over by convoys of immigrants that get stuck in the mud, and there is the golden light that gives the tragedy the color of hope.

When she walked into my room, she recoiled a bit. At night, my room resembles a tomb. She said, smiling, that it looked like that of a pharaoh in his pyramid. She sat down in front of the papyri and stroked the throat of the swallow with her fingertips. Her movements were so delicate that they seemed invisible. She had a reserve of silence that I really liked—I was so used to being alone that talking seemed unnatural to me.

I was already a bit drunk. I poured her a shot of vodka, she took off her aviator jacket, put her hair up in a bun that revealed a neck scattered with beauty marks, sat on the sofa bed, drank the vodka, and immediately asked for another. Rain was pattering softly against the bay window. Anouk seemed as determined as she was absent, with the stubborn and empty look that young women sometimes have. Her gray eyes, her baby face, made her look like a squirrel. Her earrings were the shape of tears.

She stretched out on the bed next to me. She said she would wait here for Tot to return, we would hear his key in the lock. I held out the bottle of vodka, and she drank a big gulpful; we started watching *Heaven's Gate*, smoking a joint.

It was nice to watch a film with someone—is there a better definition of peace? In the dark, while on the screen the Wyoming landscape unfolded its skies of fire and the mountains contemplated the lives of the characters with the distant calm of gods, I caught a glimpse from time to time of Anouk's face in the light of the screen. I thought she would look sleepy, but she was concentrating. When she lit a cigarette, a little red glow lighted the piercing in the corner of her nose. I took advantage of the light to look at the line of her lips, sculpted by the shadows.

And while the rain continued to beat against the bay window, the rustling leaves of the trees in the courtyard seemed to enter with the storm into my room. The huge skies filled with the white mountains in *Heaven's Gate* merged their blinding brilliance with the claps of thunder, whose sound frightened Sabbat. The night was orange and red. It's pleasant to be sheltered when the deluge strikes. Anouk was leaning against a pillow; I could sense her smile. It was a perfect night.

She loved the long scene of the party, when the immigrants, before they are massacred, are dancing on roller skates in a barn in Heaven's Gate, that door to paradise which will ultimately not be another name for America. Nor would it be a Promised Land, only a poor party room covered in red light where, dancing to the bittersweet rhythm of Cajun music, the herd of the eternal sacrificed of History are gathered.

The film runs almost four hours. I suggested we pause it. Anouk asked if she could take a shower. While she was in the bathroom I made some spaghetti *all'arrabbiata* and opened a bottle of white wine that I had in the fridge.

She came back in with a towel wrapped around her, wet hair, smelling like lemon and orange flowers. She lay down next to me, smiling. Little drops ran down her shoulders. Her toenail polish was orange.

Had I heard Tot come in? No, no sound, no one.

When she brought her face closer to mine to kiss me, she untied her towel. Her breasts were tiny, her body soft and frail like that of my swallow. It seemed, while I was bringing my mouth down to taste her, that I could have crushed her little bones with one bite.

It had been several months since I had made love, and alcohol doesn't really help. In general, I feel heavy, sluggish, it's difficult to get erect. But Anouk took me in her hand gently. It was warm, almost burning, and her long fingers with painted nails gripped me with damp vigor. "No penetration," she said. Little lights twinkled in the room and we kissed so passionately that a bit of saliva ran down our bodies and dampened Anouk's breasts, which I was kneading like a madman. I went down on her, for a long time. It was a joy to play with her lips, to lick all that juicy pulp and open with the tip of my tongue the lovely folds of her vulva. My mouth was on fire, I was drooling, I couldn't control myself. She clutched my hair, groaning, pressing my head against her so my tongue would go farther in. She began to tremble, her shoulders shook, and she cried out. Her pleasure pierced the night. I thought of Tot, behind the wall, who must have heard.

Sabbat woke up, frightened, and jumped on us. He bit my ass, then jumped onto the middle of the bed to lick Anouk's face, whining.

I stood up, my face dripping. She got on her knees and took me in her mouth. Her look was the color of the storm, but she already seemed absent. The night enveloped us like a velvet handkerchief. In spite of the pain in my buttocks, under Anouk's fingers I felt myself becoming entirely fluid. Perhaps beatitude begins here, when the hand of a woman brings you out of weightiness. Sabbat began to bark. I put my penis against Anouk's cheek and came onto her face, crying out my pleasure, in turn. She burst out laughing, and so did I. I opened the bay window, and we stretched out on the bed. The smell of the rain blended with that of sex and lemons.

8

SACRIFICES

So, on September 23 I gave myself the gift of another viewing of *Apocalypse Now*, which I had been watching continuously all summer long. At 3 p.m., just as I received Pointel's text, I was in the middle of the second viewing of the day.

With this film, I was getting closer to the key. I was sure of it. The white deer of truth runs through films, and that's why I didn't stop watching them. But ever since my encounter with Cimino, it was Francis Ford Coppola's *Apocalypse Now* that I watched almost daily. It seemed that this film completed Cimino's oeuvre. In a sense, it constituted the continuation of it, because in *Apocalypse Now*, one went even further in an exploration of the hells into which the world was endlessly falling.

In that film, more than in any other, one goes at any moment from life to death and from death to life. The mission of Captain Willard, whom the American military authorities order in the middle of the Vietnam War to go up the river and look for Colonel Kurtz, in my opinion doesn't take place in Vietnam, or in Cambodia, or in any region of Southeast Asia, but in a place that doesn't exist on any map. It is carried out at that frightening—sacred— point where life and death meet.

Because the film really isn't about Captain Willard setting off to eliminate a dangerous element of the American army. It's about him getting close to the monster. In fact, Colonel Kurtz, in no longer obeying the orders of the high command, in abandoning his command to lead an army of Montagnards who worship him as a god, did not just cross the lines that military order imposes, he shifted into an unknown dimension in which crime, in assuming religious significance, is no longer important.

Cimino's soldiers, those in *The Deer Hunter*, were only puppets whom the war used and destroyed. They fell one after the other into the absurd trap of Vietnam, became prisoners in a bamboo cage in the middle of a rat-infested river where, already half-dead, they could have drowned at any moment, and were released by their jailers only to be forced to gamble on their fates through Russian roulette— to be exposed to the suicidal caprice of chance. And, as in the *Iliad*, where ten disastrous years behind Trojan walls served to erase the lineages of the heroes, the end of the relentless sinking into the Vietnam nightmare seemed only to be to offer American soldiers the gift of death.

But the journey recounted in *Apocalypse Now* was situated in a different realm of sacrifice. It was the *moment after*, the one when chance no longer exists, the one when time itself is no longer anything but crime. If, as the film's title suggests, the apocalypse is now—and the seals are broken—then the nature of acts changes. Not only do they no longer have any meaning, but they become foreign to the universe that contains them. They are voices that debate, gestures that conjure, wills that blind.

What I had written in my screenplay was precisely related to the end, to the idea that the end has arrived, that it is already here, and that in a sense we are living *after the end.*

Yes, since my passion for Herman Melville had obliterated everything in its path, my days unfolded in the delight of a revelation whose subject was the end, the idea of the end, the watermark—inside every moment—of an interminable end that reframes the world.

The fact that this end does not just come out of devastation, but also, mystically, from the morning dew—that it freshens the world—Melville, like all great writers, had known this. His books are secretly, mainly about resurrection.

Before describing my next meeting with Pointel, I must tell you about the first time I saw *Apocalypse Now.* It was when the Islamic State was beginning to show its beheading videos. It was at the beginning of an August. Lying on my sofa, I was sweltering. The air was humid and dirty, like that of the little islands infested with cannibals around which the *Pequod* turned, off the coast of Sumatra, when Captain Ahab, at the height of his fury, was getting close to the whale. Sabbat was howling wildly in the apartment next door. His cries echoed in the inner courtyard, where the neighbors, their nerves frayed, were constantly complaining. And I was slipping into depression. Even if you're able to conceive of your solitude as glorious, even when you reign over a land of nuances in which the merest detail opens rays of light, where the coat of a Dalmatian protects you, where the starry flowering of a head of papyrus crowns you, it's nevertheless true that this land exists only for you—and, some evenings, it doesn't even exist at all.

In short, things weren't looking so good. I was forty-nine years old, I lived as a recluse in a cramped studio and spent my days watching films and drinking. Of course, I was devoting myself to a task that to me seemed essential, almost sacred, that type of activity that touches on the absolute, which even perhaps comes from a vocation that forces you not to be concerned with social niceties or success (and I never missed an opportunity to repeat those very supportive words: "absolute," "vocation," "sacred"). But some days I would doubt that such a pastime could give meaning to my life, because even while thinking, with a lot of self-indulgence, that I could consider myself a hero under the pretext that I was seeking the white deer of truth that appears in films, nothing really distinguished that heroism from the pathetic life of a loser.

I could indeed recite my eternal mantras out loud: Melville-Proust-Joyce or Dante-Flaubert-Beckett or Shakespeare-Rimbaud-Faulkner. But it had become impossible, some evenings, not to recognize that I might be completely deluding myself. I didn't know if the white deer shivering over there, under the branches of a pine tree, really existed, or if it was only a mirage. Or, when I recited the names of poets in the night, I didn't know whether I, myself, was a poet, or quite simply a clown.

With the heat, the alcohol was making me dizzy. I have often written lying on a bed, feverish, half-drunk. And in that state I've even achieved a clarity that has decided my life. In such cases, I try to make the night last. But it isn't easy to know if your life is going to pieces or if you are going toward what is most alive. That evening, I found that neither films, nor Melville, nor even my altar of papyri were enough. There comes a moment when anguish twists your stomach—then, *nothing is enough anymore.*

And so I went to have a drink at the Petits Oignons, a café in the Twentieth Arrondissement, near where I live. And within a few minutes, while chatting, laughing at the bar with Walter, the owner of the café—a tall, thin guy with a gray beard, an "Elvis fan," as he said—with Anouk, Ferdinand, Chiara, and Rachid, I came back to life.

The walls of the Petits Oignons are red. The dim lighting gives the place the feeling of an aquarium; our words, our laughter, floated like fish that swim among the coral of the underwater prairies. Thus it is that processions of whales come, couple after couple, swimming in the most secret part of my mind, and bring terror, prayer, and deliverance. That is how my desire progresses: if I begin to drink, I have to swallow the whole aquarium, I must empty the ocean—open up the floodgates of the world.

There was a regular at the bar, Gloriot, a guy who wrote detective novels, with horn-rimmed glasses and short, salt-and-pepper hair, a very funny guy who drank only Pernod and always talked about the devil. According to him, Satan had been there from the beginning, and it was because of him that time had been invented to crush us one after the other. Satan was as bored as a fat cockroach. That was Gloriot's expression—and the more he *has*, he told Walter, the less he *is*, because, precisely, Satan is nothing. That's why he wants us, he wants us to work for him. And most of the time he's already figured it out. We don't make a move without that soul-eater being involved. Our lives, Gloriot said, are *privatized by Satan*.

That evening, we talked only about the assassination of an American journalist by that as yet little-known group of jihadists, the Islamic State. The video of his beheading had been posted on the Internet, and from what Gloriot was saying, since he had seen it, it was an abomination: the man's hands had been tied behind him, he was wearing orange, he was on his knees in a desert in Iraq or Syria. And standing behind him, a guy wearing a black face mask spit out in English a curse against America, then took out a knife and slit the man's throat. Black flags then flapped in the desert, covered with white inscriptions in Arabic. The orange-clad body was shown lying in the sand, its head resting on its stomach.

There were others who had watched the video, and some who, out of ethics or disgust, had refused to watch it (ethics and disgust sometimes seem indiscernible). Rachid, a tall guy with an emaciated face and a shaved head, who managed the Phone Call store on rue Orfila, thought it was sickening that anyone could watch such a video. Watching it was playing the jihadists' game. It was voyeurism. In his opinion, Gloriot enjoyed that pornography of crime. Gloriot defended himself: "I'm staying on top of the news," he said, "and not only am I staying on top of the news, but I'm getting prepared. I don't want horror to get the better of me, I want to stand up to horror—and triumph out of the terror through which evil believes it is weakening us. I don't watch it out of fascination," said Gloriot, "but, on the contrary, to conquer the fascination it inspires in us."

The knife of the jihadist, who appeared to be English, didn't just cut the throat of a man, it declared spiritual war. People need to know the end as much as the beginning— in a sense, they *want* the end. Nothing enthralls them so much as the moment of their death, nothing excites them more than death throes, said Gloriot. Thus, the sacrifice of this poor man opened a breach in our well-fed Western comfort, and his immolation, by tearing off the cloth that covers our eyes, perhaps makes us understand that we are living in a world that is constantly putting an end to its days, a world that, while hiding its emptiness behind spectacle and merchandise, has already swallowed each one of us, and is forever bogged down in the inessential.

Then there were grumblings of protest. Rachid and Ferdinand protested vehemently, and even Walter, who usually was quiet, went so far as to assert that it didn't take a massacre to know who we are and what we want. Sacrifices teach us nothing. Torture is always too much, it only enhances injustice.

A rather bizarre guy defended Gloriot. He was a tall black man whom everyone called the Baron. He had a beret with a little feather on it stuck on his head, enormous eyes, a martial elegance. He was completely drunk, trembled while holding his beer, but spoke with assurance. In his opinion, we would all end up kneeling in a desert, our throats slit by God's verdict. And it didn't matter which god it was, even the idea of god didn't matter. The religious bullshit that frightened us didn't matter. We had lost touch with our own existence. We were perhaps the impious, but were above all the miserable, weakened, blind, servile. He no less than anyone else, he stressed. And if weakness were a fault (and in his opinion it was), our fault necessarily called for a revolution. It had become crucial that we change our way of life and start thinking again, because the absence of thinking leads to the abyss. And it was precisely the absolute absence of thinking among Westerners, as well as the absence of thinking among jihadists, that had led to the most primitive scene in the history of humanity—the beheading of a man in the desert.

The wine and whiskey were clouding my head. After being isolated in my room watching films for so long, I had become unused to others. All this agitation, this flood of words, was suffocating me. I was quietly drowning in the red of the walls that was dripping in our glasses.

And while an exasperated Walter turned up the music so Elvis's voice would drown out all the talk, I was slowly drowning in a flood of little lights. Faces trembled in my glass; the sky melted, fruity, between my lips. It was a bath of scarlet stars with dripping words that Elvis's voice caused to sway. Anouk and Ferdinand were dancing, holding their drinks in their hands, singing at full volume the lyrics of "Suspicious Mind." And behind his counter Walter was mimicking the way Elvis moved during his 1970 concert in Las Vegas, with the arm movements of a crooner in a white jumpsuit, the parodic nature of which, far from destroying the show, added a distancing dimension to it, as if the clothes and the tender gestures, by coming together, had opened onto an indecipherable truth: the gods who make fun of themselves are the most powerful.

———

I couldn't shake the image of the beheaded man dressed in orange whom Gloriot had described. While I leaned against the wall of the Petits Oignons, the head was watching me, like that of a stuffed animal. Out of its mouth there flowed a green-and-black lava, as if in dying it was spewing out all the visions it had endured. Then I heard, I read on its lips, this cry: "*the horror!*"

The head turned me around, I held on to the bar. In my drunken state, intensified by the orange filters of the setting sun, by cut-off heads floating on the water, there appeared the face of Colonel Kurtz: the bald head, shining in the humidity, of Marlon Brando at the end of *Apocalypse Now*.

He is lying on his pallet in the darkness of a temple, in the middle of the jungle—and is sweating. The darkness is green. The palm trees are filled with bodies hanging from the branches. The cut-off heads are piled on the steps that lead up to Colonel Kurtz.

It seems to me that the mud is dead saliva. It seems that I am swimming in that mud, in the direction of the temple, in the direction of Kurtz, who is turning toward me and throwing me a package covered with rags. I catch it, it's heavy, sticky. I open it: it's my head. Colonel Kurtz says, "The world ends like that."

———

That apparition terrified me. As I was going to the toilet, I caught my reflection in the mirror above the sink, but it wasn't me. Of course, there was a resemblance, the face I saw wasn't unknown, but I couldn't say that it was mine. The features were dry, the cheeks hollow, the eyes closed. How is it possible to see one's reflection with closed eyes? I got closer. Not only were the eyes still closed, but the skin of the face was blue. I was looking at a dead person. It wasn't unpleasant, it was even interesting. But what gripped me, more than my dead person's head, was the sudden desire, and more than the desire, the need, the urgency, to find words. Looking at my dead man's head, I absolutely had to say something—it seemed that I had never experienced such an imperative need for language. Not only did I sense that words existed, as if I were witnessing their birth, but I was one with them. There was no longer any difference between them and me. Three words were on the verge of escaping from my head, and I was those three words.

With a black felt-tipped pen, I quickly scrawled three little empty rectangles on the mirror, the first two where my eyes were reflected, and the third at the level of my mouth. While saying each name, I filled the rectangles:

ISAAC   MOBY DICK

COLONEL KURTZ

Then the dead person was gone. In his place there was me, eyes swollen by fatigue and alcohol, grunting a frozen laugh. I had *returned*.

I quickly left the café. In the street, Anouk and Ferdinand were smoking. Anouk touched my arm: was I okay? I started running. A car almost hit me. The night, on avenue Gambetta, was red. And in that red the trees burned all along the front of Tenon Hospital. When you light a fire, the transparency of the air is clouded. Very quickly, the smoke dissipates the darkness, and now, with flames, with their orange and blue crests, a passage is opened. My mouth was full of fire. I was running, I was carrying flames—I was myself the passage. I ran into the Baron, who was pissing against a wall. He raised his fist and cursed the sky. I burst out laughing. The colors of the fire laughed with me. Yellow, red, blue—they sparkled in the sky like Christmas lights.

Hurtling down the avenue, drunk, my head full of laughter, I was still inside my screenplay, I was swimming in its lines. Through the terror it created in us, the cut throat of the American journalist spoke to us in a whisper: *The ritual is never interrupted*, that's what the voice reminded us.

Behind me, the Baron started running. I accelerated. It seemed he was calling me, and several times I thought I heard my name being carried through the night: "Jean!

Jean!" I didn't want to turn around. I had to speed up, get to the Place Gambetta, where there would be life, noise, people—where I would be saved.

The sound of his steps, like those of a killer, got closer. I was sure he wanted to kill me. Despite my drunkenness, or perhaps thanks to it (to the relaxation it produces), I understood that every moment harbors a crime. I *saw* it. It happens that humans carry out obscure acts that are the equivalents of such crimes. Then the horror washes over us, and in a flash of lightning, *we see*. But this involves something else. While listening to Gloriot, Walter, and the Baron back at the bar, I had understood that there is a scene that no one can see, a scene that doesn't take place anywhere, one that secretly determines each of our actions; a scene that, in a sense, is worse than a beheading in the desert—worse than any representable infamy. It was that scene that I looked for every day while watching films.

I reached Place Gambetta. It was absolutely deserted. I turned around, out of breath. The Baron had disappeared. I wasn't worried about crazies, or assassins, I told myself. Only the night and its laughter mattered to me. I believe that at that moment I was happy. The joy that burns in some hearts is located beyond what a bunch of drunken revelers perceives. I looked at the old Paris sky. I, too, heard the stars cry out. The entire life of the dead depends on a true thought. The voice of the lamb is both a fire and a breeze.

9

GUY THE COBRA

When I woke up, a single thought popped into my head: watch *Apocalypse Now* again. It must have been noon, the sun was flooding into the room. I had a bit of a headache, but not too bad. For a whiskey hangover, I considered myself lucky.

I rushed over to my computer to download the film, but I couldn't get it to work. So I thought of Guy the Cobra. He had to have *Apocalypse Now* in stock, and his store was only five minutes away. I didn't wait for the elevator and raced down the stairs.

I had slept in my clothes, and in my excited state I went out just as I was, without even washing my face. Outside, the weather was glorious and the light was warm, blue-yellow, with the sharp and violent scent of great summer days.

When I got to the corner of rue de la Py, I felt dizzy and leaned against one of the fruit-and-vegetable stalls of the "Paris Garden" on Place Édith-Piaf. Bunches of grapes, oranges, pears, apples, figs, were glistening in the sun, and looking at all that fruit did me good. They looked sweet and fresh—exactly what I needed. It had been a long time since I'd experienced such sweetness, such freshness. Solitude is good, but my life was probably excessively arid (a bit of sweet, fresh comfort would have been welcome).

I bought a bottle of Efferalgan tablets at the pharmacy, and I swallowed one right away with water from the Wallace fountain. Then I took some money out of the ATM. I only had twenty euros left in my account. I wasn't surprised. Even though I bought almost nothing, the small amount on which I had been living since I had sold my car had melted away. Clearly, I should have done something about it, made a few phone calls, filled out some forms—but I didn't have the energy. Once I had had some money, some of my books had even sold well, or fairly well, but I had spent everything. For several years, I had let my life roll along. I was confident, and at the same time I didn't care. Was I depressed? I don't think so. My negligence was, rather, the result of a sort of happiness, a crazy happiness—an extravagant happiness. You probably have to be crazy to experience such lack of concern when you're staring into the abyss. I've always felt like Ishmael in *Moby-Dick* when he says (I'm reciting Melville's text, which I know as well as my own screenplay): "amid the tornadoed Atlantic of my being, do

I myself still forever centrally disport in mute calm; and while ponderous planets of unwaning woe revolve around me, deep down and deep inland there I still bathe me in eternal mildness of joy."

And so, I am someone who doesn't confront the universe; the universe swims in me.

I was lucky since I was no longer paying rent. The management company was going to sell the apartment I was living in. I was supposed to leave by October 1, and since I had been living there for twenty years, they offered me two months rent-free, "to give me time to find other housing." But I wasn't worried. There would always be an article to write for some newspaper, or a box filled with old dishes I could get a hundred euros for, I just had to go scrounge around in the basement.

I had vaguely counted on *The Great Melville* to bail me out, but, setting principle aside—not allowing my head to be swelled with the oh-so-seductive, so gratifying idea of the "misunderstood masterpiece"—I had to acknowledge that by simply writing what I wanted, I had set out, as Melville admits bitterly about himself, "to write the type of books about which it is said that they are failures." And in fact *The Great Melville* was a failure, a formidable failure. No one, not even Pointel, had really read it, no one would ever read it, except for me, I, who, some evenings, stinking drunk, recited pages from it with the thundering lyricism of a Flaubert howling out *Madame Bovary*.

But in the end, what does a failure really mean? I didn't *believe* in failure. Melville's was proportional to the demands that motivated him: it indicated a secret glory. Society slaps the label of failure on anything that doesn't respond to its demands. It denies success to anything that surpasses its set criteria. I wasn't really impressed with society's idea of literature. What does it know about it? Nothing. Everyone thinks they know what literature is, but no one knows anything. And that morning, with my twenty euros, my vertigo, my mild hangover, and my irrepressible desire to see *Apocalypse Now*, that morning and every morning of my happy and crude existence, as well as every evening and every night, not only did it seem to me that I knew what literature was, but that in a sense I *was* literature.

Yes, I was that absurd hero who, doubting everything, believed in his star. I was that smiling middle finger. I was that light that glitters between a swallow, a row of papyri, and a single man's bed. I was that sleepless night, as dark as it is comical, during which are proclaimed what must indeed be called revelations.

With my twenty euros in my pocket, I ran to the little video shop on rue des Pyrénées owned by Guy the Cobra. He was sitting on a bench next to the tables where discounted DVDs were displayed. An orange, ochre, very warm light was reflected in the leaves above his head. His legs were crossed, and he exuded that nonchalance that I like in him. Guy the Cobra was rolling a joint.

He earned his name from the tattoo on his left arm. He's a tall guy who looks like a worn-out rock and roller, wears all black, and knows the history of film down to its minutest details. If you're looking for an obscure French western starring Jean-Pierre Léaud, not only will he tell you it's *Une aventure de Billy le Kid* by Luc Moullet, he will certainly have seen it and will provide you an analysis that will make you salivate with impatience to see it. But what's more, he will find you a copy, and if you don't have enough money on you, which was often my case, he'll lend it to you.

Guy the Cobra also lived in a world made up of names. As soon as he said the name of a director, he would launch into a comparison with another, whose films in turn called for a series of comparisons. New names then germinated passionately in his mind, most often at top speed, so that in a few minutes that universe of references had taken the place of what is called reality (it had probably been a long time since *that* had existed for him).

Was the inside of Guy the Cobra's head mystically honeycombed? I'm not sure. Behind a life of names, there is sometimes the name of God, but most of the time there's nothing. The names talk to the names, that's the beginning of joy.

When I told him that day that I was looking for *Apocalypse Now*, he started to frown. Guy didn't like Coppola.

In general, he didn't believe in his madness, and so not in his poetry, either. The rich, he said, can't be poets. In his opinion, it was better to have the limitless craziness of a Werner Herzog. Had I seen Herzog's films? I really had to see *Fitzcarraldo*, he said, offering me his joint. It's that film where Klaus Kinski wants to construct an opera in the jungle. He tries to drag a boat up to the top of a mountain in Peru. According to Guy the Cobra, the film was a "completely underrated" masterpiece, "scandalously ignored by critics." Its metaphysical dimension, he said, was similar to that of the greatest quests. "It's a crazy Grail," he explained. In *Fitzcarraldo*, even more than in *Aguirre*, Klaus Kinski—the greatest actor of all time, he said, much better than Marlon Brando—achieves Shakespearean acting and *attains the sacred*: "He is both king and the one who assassinates the king."

Great, I said, but I was looking for *Apocalypse Now*. Guy had to find me a DVD of *Apocalypse Now* right away. I had dreamt of it during the night, the film had something to tell me, a "specific message," I told him—did he or didn't he have a copy of *Apocalypse Now*?

Of course, he said, and he went over to the van parked in front of the shop, opened the back, and took out of a box a copy of the extended version of *Apocalypse Now*. Coppola, Guy pointed out, had been forced to shorten his film for distribution, and had cut out some crucial scenes, but with this version you could finally see the film in its entirety.

The filming in the Philippines was overshadowed by constant madness—according to Guy, one of the most demented filmings in the history of cinema. Two hundred thirty-eight days of paranoia, drugs, illness, accidents, and even a typhoon that wiped out the set, and a war that blocked the roads in the country. And that avalanche of destruction had in turn destroyed Coppola's mind. Every night he rewrote the end of this endless film on white notecards that he gave to Brando, who, without even having read the Conrad book *Apocalypse Now* is adapted from, with his shaved monk's head and his three hundred pounds, had ultimately discovered how to incarnate a mountain, alone, how to give a voice to that mountain, and how to destroy it. Yes, Brando, during an incredible monologue, improvising in a single take the "testament of the Western world stuck in the quicksand of nihilism," as Guy said, had, in his opinion, become both Sinai and the Tablets of the Law, rather an "anti-Sinai" carrying a "counter–Tablet of the Law."

I went home, triumphant, with the DVD of *Apocalypse Now*. Seeing me go by in the lobby, Mme Figo came out of her *loge* like a dervish. With people like me, she said without even saying hello, it was impossible for her to do her work right. She accused me of never opening my mailbox, the mail was piling up so that now it was "stuck," she

said, and she couldn't put any more mail in. It so happened
that I no longer had my mailbox key, I told Mme Figo,
for whom this latest negligence on my part was scandalous. "In that case," she said, "you should have informed me
immediately! You can't treat people like that. I'm going to
file a complaint with the board!"

Complaint about what? I wondered. I have the right, I
told Mme Figo, *not* to open my mailbox.

"Everyone opens their mailbox," she replied. "You're not
normal, are you?"

"You're right, I don't *want* to be normal, I don't *want*
to open my mail, I'd be happy if everyone just forgot
about me."

"Well, *they* haven't forgotten you," said Mme Figo, with
the nasty smile of someone who is about to deal the fatal
blow. She held out an envelope on which I immediately
recognized the words DEPARTMENT OF REVENUE.

"That's impossible, I'm tax-exempt."

Mme Figo shrugged her shoulders, she was savoring my
defeat.

"Everyone pays taxes."

"Not me, I don't have any money. You see, I simply
don't earn enough money to pay taxes."

She seemed slightly annoyed, but now there was something in her look, a hint of contempt, the contempt one
shows for the poor.

Opening the envelope, I saw they were billing me for eight hundred euros. It was a lodging tax. I don't know what came over me, but while Mme Figo was waiting for me to react, while she was waiting to find out the amount I owed, and was hoping I'd be upset, even desperate, I held the DVD above my head, and, holding it very high, with two hands, like a banner: *"Apocalypse!"* I shouted— *"Apocalypse Now!"*—and I rushed off before Mme Figo could even open her mouth.

10

THE END

When I watched it that morning (I say morning, even though it was already afternoon, because I had gone back to bed with a cup of coffee, I had drawn the curtains to keep the light off the screen, and Sabbat was sleeping next to me, stretched over the manuscript box), when I watched *Apocalypse Now* that August morning, my eyes were burning, as if I were moving fast over the levels of Kabbalah. While I'm writing these lines, far away, very far away, in a forest where my solitude opens me up to an anticipation that has replaced fear, that burning continues: it gives this book its heartbeat.

We're in the jungle. Helicopters are flying over a forest of palm trees. The palm trees catch fire, the forest is burning, children are burning, water buffaloes, goats, tigers are burning. The sky is consumed by huge red flames. Orange-and-black smoke covers the screen. Jim Morrison's voice rises up, accompanied by the sound of the helicopter blades: "*This is the end, my only friend, the end.*"

It's a voice from beyond the grave floating over the chaos, the voice of a great priest reciting a mass for the end of the world. The service begins, we enter into a sacred world. "The End" is the title of a Doors song. "The End" is the message.

Then, superimposed on the battlefield, you see the head of a strung-out man raving in a hotel room, his eyes bugged out, a bottle of whiskey in his hand. The sound of the ceiling fan in his room blends with that of the helicopter blades above the jungle. One element fills everything, destruction is everywhere. The world is dying both in the forest that is burning and in a burning head.

We're in Saigon in Captain Willard's room. He's performing karate moves in slow motion, in his underpants, in front of a mirror. He's staggering, feverish, dead drunk. The fever is a mask of death. Captain Willard's suffering numbs him to any sensation, as if he were a prisoner of a nightmare. He is waiting to be given a mission. He can't stand Saigon, he wants to go back to the jungle. Jim Morrison continues to sing his black prayer: "*And all the children are insane.*" Captain Willard punches the mirror, and collapses, crying, on the bed, which is now covered with his blood. His whiskey-drenched crying calls for no consolation. When one survives the ritual that extracts you from other men, you face the abyss.

Two American soldiers knock on his door. Willard opens it, he thinks they've come to arrest him. The two soldiers see the blood on the sheets, the bottles of alcohol, the shards of glass, the crazy mess in the room, but they don't seem shocked. One of them reads Willard a summons from high command. Willard is to go to Nha Trang, to ComSec Intelligence. They have been ordered to escort him there. Willard says he isn't feeling well, and collapses on the bed.

I wanted a mission, he says in voice-over, while the two soldiers drag him to the shower, and for my sins, they gave me one. I was going to the worst place in the world and I didn't even know it yet. Weeks away and hundreds of miles upriver that snaked through the war like a circuit cable plugged straight into Kurtz.

I was blown away—I still am. Every time I see the beginning of *Apocalypse Now*, it seems I am witnessing a lamb being sacrificed. The sky is torn apart and flooded in blood. My veins are on fire, as if poison were burning in them.

Ever since I first watched it, I always rewind and rewatch the first ten minutes of the film, in which a hidden liturgy seems to be seeking a follower. Does the path that passes through crime exist? The silent path that goes beyond massacre and leads you to innocence?

Sometimes at night the devil is sleeping on my lips. If I open my mouth, he starts nibbling on my teeth. If I don't react, he will swallow my tongue. I must as quickly as possible find a word, the right word, the one that disarms the evil, the one that cuts through the darkness and offers clarity again.

I continued watching. I need to describe *Apocalypse Now* for you in detail. The meaning of the story I'm trying to tell depends on your knowing this film. Some days, the story threatens to consume me.

Captain Willard is taken into a bungalow guarded by armed soldiers. Three men—a young colonel, played by Harrison Ford, a general, and an empty-eyed civilian—greet him, and inform him that he has been chosen to carry out a delicate mission. His colleagues in intelligence have approved the choice—hasn't he already led obscure operations on his own? Hasn't he already killed several people for the CIA?

They explain that an officer in the Special Forces, one of the best that the country has ever produced—Colonel Kurtz—has gone crazy. His ideas, his methods, have become unhealthy. He went into Cambodia and took over an army of Montagnards, who worship him as a god.

A battle, the general says, is fought in the heart of every man between the rational and the irrational, good and evil, and good doesn't always triumph, sometimes the dark side wins; every man, says the general, has a breaking point—you and me, he says to Willard—and Kurtz has reached his: he has obviously gone insane.

They play a recording of Colonel Kurtz's voice for Willard. It is then, while the sound recorded in the jungle crackles and Marlon Brando's nasal voice fills the space, that *Apocalypse Now* sends me the first sign. It is always at that moment that I really understand that Willard's initiation is also mine. When the voice of Kurtz/Brando is heard, the head of a deer appears.

What's it doing there? We're in a command post of the American army, on the front lines of a horrifying war, and a stuffed deer head is observing us. In its glassy eyes shines the memory of forests; its velvety antlers express the spirit of the hunt, just as if, beyond eras and continents, the rocky caves of Lascaux and the vaults of the Chauvet grotto were sending us a signal. As if time itself was reminding us that at any moment a torrent of large deer might break through the darkness, and that the ochre, charcoal, or blood-red pigments have since the beginning of time drawn permanent figures projecting and reproducing on our retinas. It is as if we were being secretly invited to see a cross stuck in the hollow of a tangling of antlers. As if, behind the infantile and monstrous spectacle of war an immemorial ceremony was unfolding, that of a sacrifice which, through its ritual, conjures death while its actions cause it. As if that deer head, hanging on the wall of a makeshift command post, has been watching us forever. As if it was going to start talking, interrupt the babbling of the soldiers, and invite my solitude to enter into the mystery.

HOLD FAST YOUR CROWN

Yes, another story is being told there, lying in wait behind the fury of war. An even more terrible story than the one showing the bombardments that destroy the forests of Vietnam, a story that addresses your soul—that summons it.

Every time a deer appears, I see the hunt. And in hunting, it is not simply a matter of pursuing the prey in order to kill it, nor even of reenacting the original act of predation. It's not about immersing one's sensations in a lost, damp forest, nor even reconnecting with the world of teeth or confronting beasts, danger, death.

The hunt is spiritual. In it there unfolds a world apart, similar to that lightning that draws sexual desire, capturing lovers only to isolate them. Through their nakedness a sacrament is replayed, that through which the hunter and his prey, removing themselves from the restrictive world, summon the signs that enable them to no longer be what they are, and to belong to the knife, to the shine that strikes the blade, to the throat that cries out, to the artery that is torn, to the blood that flows.

During the hunt, you are delivered, there is no longer anyone in you. You are the knife and the prey, the throat, the panting, you are the wound. You are the furtive light that shines on the blade, where the smile of the goddess is reflected before you succumb.

Even if he is hunting a poor hare with the cruelty of a drunken moron, the hunter, without even knowing it, is pursuing a nakedness. Over there, in the distance, in the underbrush, a light is shining toward which he runs; the game is only an alibi for his desire, and even if he happens to encounter the desired animal—the one that increases his strength and turns him into an indefatigable killer—through every boar, every deer, through the pursuit that becomes a trance, he seeks only one thing: to fall upon Diana, to uncover the forbidden body of the goddess.

Because through the shiny eyes of the stuffed deer in *Apocalypse Now*, it is Artemis who is observing, it is Diana who is plotting a meeting with his death. The frightened white deer of truth that is wrapped in your words, that protects you and that you protect, is also a predator.

Colonel Kurtz's voice is slow: he says he was watching a snail crawling on the edge of a straight razor. That's my dream, he points out, it's my nightmare: crawling, slithering along the edge of a straight razor, and surviving. After a few seconds of silence, he resumes: but we must kill them, we must incinerate them, pig after pig, cow after cow.

The colonel played by Harrison Ford stops the tape, says to Captain Willard: "Your mission is to proceed up the Nung River in a navy patrol boat, pick up Colonel Kurtz's path at Nu Mung Ba, follow it, learn what you can along the way. When you find the colonel, infiltrate his team by whatever means available, and terminate the colonel's command... You understand, Captain, that this mission does not exist, nor will it ever exist."

I like that the itinerary that leads Captain Willard to Colonel Kurtz is related to the Buddhist *bardo*—that initiatory state that leads from life to death, and vice versa.

Ultimately, nothing exists outside that state. We believe we're living, loving, we imagine we're exulting in a reconstructed universe, but we are only passing through the illuminated lands of a *bardo*.

Within the *bardo*, we encounter the dead. Some give us direction, others lead us astray. We must continue to move toward the light, even when it is completely extinguished, because darkness takes advantage of our slightest distractions. It wants to live in our place, and when it achieves this, it drives us out.

The darkness waits for us to lose the light; but it takes only a glimmer, even the smallest, the poor spark of a match head, for the path to be revealed. Then, the current is reversed, you *go up death*.

It's night, I'm holding my breath. Do we ever find what we seek? The thing we most want is also that which we most fear. It's not yet time to say what I was confronting at the time. I was alone, and solitude is populated with monsters. In the Apocalypse of John there is a half-hour silence that follows the opening of the seventh seal. In my madness I was there, in the heart of the silence. Then, evil turns toward us, it says: "You haven't understood me," and that is, perhaps, right.

11

NAPALM

So it was 3 p.m., September 23, when I received Pointel's text. The telephone vibrated on my desk, waking Sabbat. He was lying down, stretched out over the cookie tin that held my manuscript, as if he were protecting it. To read me, you had to get through the dog, I said to myself, smiling. Like the garland of papyri, like the invisible flight of the swallow, like the films whose inexhaustible content was offered to me every day and night, Tot's dog belonged to the circle that the room drew around me, to that careful layout that I had created during the summer and which, now that all has disappeared, continues to illuminate my movements.

A scent of cut grass came through the open glass doors, it filled me with its freshness like a gift from the ocean. I felt as if I were on the South Seas, on the deck of a whaling ship sailing among the islands that smelled like pepper, surrounded by a cloud of swallows weaving their joy around the main mast.

The text said: "Jackpot?" I thought Pointel was wishing me a happy birthday. "Jackpot?" was perhaps a subtle way of asking if turning fifty was a victory. Then I realized that Pointel couldn't know I was fifty today, nor that September 23 was my birthday.

I smiled when I remembered what he had said: "If you manage to wake up Michael, jackpot!" It had been five months since I returned from New York, five months of a long summer, and even if I had just, as usual, revolved around the three great poles of my existence—computer, fridge, vodka—even if I had only honed the two main skills of a single person—drinking and wasting my time—it seemed that that period had been crucial, and that through the films I had watched over and over, this huge summer had opened up like the branches of the fir trees when the frightened white deer goes by.

Pointel and I hadn't seen each other since that momentous month of March when he had given me Michael Cimino's phone number. I hadn't kept him up to date about anything. Why would I? I have the habits of a single person that might appear harsh to some people. I never answer the phone, and for a long time no one has called me. I had friends, a few lovers, too, but one day, for no reason, the most ordinary gestures appeared empty. You realize while walking on the little path of life that *there is nothing behind the hedge.*

In short, I was one of those people for whom receiving a text amounted to an event.

I immediately answered, "I met with Cimino." Pointel wrote right back, "Let's have dinner." Then he added, "Tonight, 8 p.m. at Bofinger's?"

I agreed, got out of bed, and picked up the dozens of beer cans that were scattered around the room. It was a beautiful day: blue sky, bright sun, light wind—the ideal day for getting out of bed.

It happens that sometimes you forget about the heart of a tiger that pants under the skin of the ocean. We perceive the sea as a flowery land and, as Melville says, *a sad sweetness, a bit mystical, rises into the rose-colored air.* And so this September 23 seemed like the day of a party. Today, my solitude seemed light, maybe I was actually going to feel happy.

I got dressed, put on my favorite shirt, the pearl-gray one, which I reserve for big occasions (I was wearing it when I met Michael Cimino). Then I slipped on my old charcoal-gray coat, the one I've had for around twenty years, in which I envelop myself, summer and winter, when adventures are afoot.

It was around 3:30, and I was ready—my mind focused on the evening. I smiled. What was I going to do now? I still had more than four hours before meeting Pointel. My plan was to take Sabbat out in an hour or two, feed him for the night, then take my time walking to Bofinger's. It was beautiful out, walking would do me good, and between here and the Bastille, going through Père-Lachaise cemetery, it would take less than an hour.

I hadn't gone out to dinner with anyone in weeks. In general, the idea of a prolonged conversation with someone seemed too much for me. And I like my days to be completely free. Even if I don't do anything, they must stay available, mornings, afternoons, and evenings have to stay open. When I have plans to meet someone, the desire to cancel the meeting becomes increasingly irresistible as the hour approaches, because the entire day is focused on that point, which ends up compressing it, the angles close in, and it is no longer possible to think of anything else, there is no more solitude, you suffocate.

But that day, I wanted to see Pointel, I wanted to pick up the thread of the story. If he suddenly wanted to know how I was doing, wanted to see me six months after essentially laughing at me in his office, it wasn't to talk about my screenplay.

No, what Pointel wanted was for me to talk about Cimino. He was curious to know what had happened between us. How was it possible that Michael Cimino would meet with just anyone? Because, though Cimino continued to receive worldwide acclaim for his work as a filmmaker, without having done anything in over twenty years, though the most outrageous rumors about his health were circulating on the Internet—some American sites claimed that the multiple plastic surgery procedures that had reshaped his face were hiding a sex change—no one, not even Pointel, was certain he was still alive.

Instead of continuing to watch Apocalypse Now in bed, I sat in the armchair, like a guest. I poured a bit of beer, lit a cigarette, and instead of continuing the film, I pressed the Fast Forward button on the remote. Since I couldn't stop thinking about tonight's dinner, it was impossible to concentrate on another complete viewing of the film, but I could relax while watching a scene just for pleasure.

I found the one that Tot immediately remembered when I had told him about my obsession with the film. Like everyone, he had seen *Apocalypse Now*, but it was above all this scene that had stuck with him, and in particular a line spoken by a completely crazy officer. He was right, that line was incredible, it was the most insane line in the film, and also the funniest—the funniest because it was the craziest. I needed to relax. Watching that scene, listening to that line, would do me good.

It happens that darkness doesn't hold anything. It's the emptiness that appears to us when we look someone in the eye. You then plunge your gaze into a night that absorbs bodies and minds, that envelops the visible. It's the night of

the world that appears to us. And sometimes, I think like
Tot that that night is incredibly funny.

In a great mood, I pointed at the TV and said to Sabbat, "Just wait and see!"

He raised his head and looked at the big screen where
the helicopters were flying through flames.

Was it a hole they made in the sky? First, you don't see
anything, a screen of black smoke has taken the place of the
world. In the background you hear the dying. When the
world experiences its end, there is no more blue, no more
green, the water and the sky have lost their colors, there is
only mud. A mud over which shouting is superimposed, on
the earth, in the sky, everywhere.

A helicopter lands on a beach where shells are exploding in all directions. The village is burning, it's frightening
chaos. Marines jump out of the helicopter shooting rounds
from their automatic weapons. And while bullets are flying
everywhere and everyone is lying in the mud, here comes
Colonel Kilgore, played by Robert Duvall: chest puffed
out, nonchalant and triumphant as a Roman emperor,
wearing Ray-Bans and a cowboy hat.

He adjusts his Stetson with the golden crest of the cav-
alry on the front where two sabers are crossed, and walks
along the battlefield, a yellow scarf tied around his neck.
They tell him that one of the men in his company is Lance
Johnson, the famous surfing champion. He immediately
forgets the battlefield and starts to talk surfing with the

young surfer: "I've admired your nose-riding for years," he tells him. "I like to finish operations early, fly down to Yung Tau for the evening glass."

The copters fly in the direction of Yung Tau, to the sound of Wagner's "Ride of the Valkyries," music that is used to frighten the "slopes."

To secure the coast and open up the waves to the great surfer, Colonel Kilgore orders pilots to bomb the entire area: "Bomb them into the stone age, son!"

A curtain of flames lights up the forest, the effect is enormous, it's as if the earth were catching fire. And then comes the moment Tot loves most of all: while the palm tree–covered hill is consumed in a black sky, and the waters of the river are crushed by the impact of the bombing, Colonel Kilgore crouches down, calm in the midst of the chaos, relaxed as a cowboy riding on a prairie in Oklahoma, and in a steady voice, as precise as a music lover, he says this line that makes Tot cry laughing: "I love the smell of napalm in the morning."

12

TWO VISITORS

My phone started vibrating on the coffee table. It was another text from Pointel. I now knew that he wasn't going to leave me alone—my solitude was over. But even before I had time to read his text, my doorbell rang. That was too much. Absolutely nothing happened to me for five months, and within a few hours not only was I getting an onslaught of text messages, but now someone was knocking at my door. I was completely overwhelmed.

What was more important, answer the text or open my door? I was paralyzed. The prospect of going out to have dinner with someone involved quite a bit of effort (if I had my way, I would rather throw myself into a fountain or go running into traffic on the expressway). I was already having trouble concentrating on the upcoming evening, so now, having to deal with someone knocking on my door was traumatizing.

What if it was Pointel? But he didn't know my address. Unless I had written it down on his copy of the screenplay. But no, there's no way he would come over here. And why would he have invited me to a restaurant if he was going to come over and knock on my door?

A line came back to me, a line from that notebook I mentioned before, a line I think of when things aren't going so well: *follow along stealthily the thin wall that separates me from myself.* I really liked that line, and despite its terrible implications, there is something comforting in its thinness. You have the impression that you just have to say it for it to happen. Yes, while repeating it out loud, I was truly following along stealthily the thin wall that was separating me from myself. I was discovering an enigma and at the same time I was continuing to approach it. I was entering that obscure realm of endless calm.

With the help of that line, which I chanted like a mantra, I was able to approach the door. I looked through the peephole. There were two guys, with a lot of black hair and mustaches.

I held my breath. Was it an optical illusion? They looked the same, the same hair, same outfit, same mustache. I was Captain Willard, whom they were coming to get in his hotel room to be sent to hell. But these two were more bizarre than a couple of soldiers ordered to arrest you. They seemed to be both Jehovah's Witnesses, whose amazing tolerance for rejection exasperated me in advance, with the relentless rigor of bill collectors, and possessing another type of madness, a more convoluted, even more noxious one that was exuded from their symmetry, their fixed smiles, and the incongruous white of their suits. They rang again. Staring out the peephole, I thought, seething: what do these two assholes want? And how could they have escaped the vigilance of Mme Figo? I thought, absurdly: they reek of spiderwebs, be careful of spiders, especially those that are at your door. I had no intention of opening it. The best thing was to play dead.

The third time they rang, they kept pressing the bell, one of the mustached guys kept his finger pressed on the doorbell without letting up, and Sabbat began to bark. In a few seconds, his barking changed into yelps of rage. I didn't recognize him anymore. He was wild, there was foam on his lips, and he was hurling himself against the door as if he wanted to break it down. His howling sounded like that of a wolf. The two guys weren't afraid, on the contrary, encouraged by the presence of a dog, they started knocking on the door so violently, so *madly*, that, horrified by the din, and to make it stop, I threw the door open, allowing Sabbat to run between the two guys and race toward the stairs.

I was wrong, the two guys didn't look alike. True, they both had mustaches, but they were different: one mustache, whose tips pointed upward, looked like that of a carnival barker; the other one was thicker, and seemed to be consuming the man's upper lip. Both were very black, like the men's hair, and their suits seemed fake. They probably wore them just to come and ring my doorbell, but what for? What were they supposed to be disguised as? I was just about to ask them when I noticed that their outfits were a bit different: the jacket on the guy on the left had all sorts of folds, pockets, buckles, and buttons that made it look very practical, but you couldn't say what it was for. And there was something else: the guy on the right, the one who spoke first, was carrying one of those repulsive little leather totes called a "one-night-stand bag."

Yes, they seemed to be disguised, or let's say dressed up, and their mustaches could even have been fake, but if I had tried to pull them off, they would probably have been real, and the men would have shouted out in pain.

"Are you Tot?" asked the guy with the elegant mustache.

"No, I'm me."

"You aren't Tot?" repeated the second mustache guy, somewhat hostilely.

"No, I assure you."

"So who is Tot?"

"He's the other guy."

"What other guy?"

"The other door," I said, pointing to the apartment behind them.

"There's no one in there. You're Tot."

"I'm telling you I'm not Tot: he's on a trip. What do you want with him?"

"A trip where?"

"I don't know. Listen, I have to go get the dog," I said, taking a step toward the stairs.

"That's not his mutt?" asked the first mustached guy, also moving toward the stairs.

"Yes," I said, exasperated, "I'm watching him. I'm watching Tot's dog."

I turned around: while I had been talking to Mustache #1, Mustache #2 had gone into my apartment, and was already calling from inside:

"Carl, come see this!"

I was furious and ran into the apartment, followed by Carl/Mustache #1. Mustache #2 was standing in front of the large screen where you could see, close up, the breasts of a woman. I had paused the film, and while I was shouting at the two weirdos to get out, Mustache #2 was pointing the remote at the screen, and the film started up: a pretty girl with blond hair was babbling on while a guy was undressing her. He had almost unbuttoned her flowered blouse completely, she let him, her breasts were white, heavy, superb.

"He was watching porn!" cackled Mustache #2, as if I wasn't there.

"Not at all. It's *Apocalypse Now*," I said.

It was the scene with the Bunnies. To boost the morale of the troops the American command invite strippers over. They arrive in a black helicopter with the Playboy Bunny logo on it, and set down on a makeshift landing spot, half-naked, to the sound of a rock-and-roll hit. The performance degenerates: jumping down from the bleachers, the overexcited GIs invade the stage, the girls jump back into the helicopter, which takes off, later catastrophically crash-landing from lack of fuel in a remote corner of Cambodia, on the banks of the river where Captain Willard and his men end up making a stop.

Without even being aware, I had sat down on my sofa to fully appreciate this crucial moment of *Apocalypse Now*. As crazy as it may seem, I had immediately forgotten about the two guys and had plunged back into the film.

This scene of *Apocalypse Now* might appear minor, given the weight of the insane encounter between Captain Willard and Colonel Kurtz, but every viewing deepens the inherent cruelty, and while watching it again I understood that behind the masquerade of a striptease for the soldiers, while Miss October and Miss May are prancing in their high heels, one dressed as an Indian, the other as a soldier, lurks the immemorial feeding frenzy to which the women are exposing themselves in the heart of the war massacre.

In my opinion, it was obvious that this scene in *Apocalypse Now*—which is above all a masculine film—was fundamentally important. It revealed that putting people to death would never end because the concupiscence of men leads women to the sacrificial altar.

I had completely forgotten that the two clowns were there. Were they, like me, drawn into the film, or had they taken advantage of my distraction to inspect my apartment? Honestly, I can't remember.

Because every time I see the Bunnies' helicopter stuck in the jungle sludge, my thoughts fly off: I think of *Moby-Dick*, I think of Noah's Ark. And while I'm writing these lines, doves are flying in the forest around me. In the middle of a war, the ark is waiting to be put back in the water, and out of the windows, you see naked women. Is this where metamorphoses take place? I think that something even more obscure, more timeless, occurs which comes out of the trafficking between men and the gods, that is, from the madness of tales.

To really understand this scene in *Apocalypse Now*, you have to know that in exchange for two barrels of fuel, Willard negotiated two hours with the Bunnies for his men. The soldiers climb into the beached helicopter, wild with excitement, and then, through a blond light that seems to cut an island of heat where green, yellow, and red parrots are flying around, the women allow themselves to be undressed. In the middle of the mud their bodies seem to be a land of delights.

That's where I was in the film when the two guys rang my bell, and that's where we picked it up again. The young blond woman with heavy breasts is crying, saying: "Being Playmate of the Year is the loneliest experience I can imagine…and there's this glass wall between you, this invisible glass…They make you do things that you don't want to do." Another girl, brunette and buxomy, performs an act with trained birds, and when one of the soldiers puts his arms around her, the parrots fly around his shoulders: "You kiss like a bird!" she says; then the two of them are rolling around in the mud making little sounds; a suitcase opens; there's the body of a man inside.

I really like this scene because the orgy hoped for by the soldiers darkens in the melancholy of the suitcased sacrifice. The bird sound that the Playmate utters replaces no orgasm, it is substituted for the very existence of orgasm. It is a poor death throe. In this world of perdition, there are only victims.

In fact, the two Mustaches had sat down and weren't missing a second of the striptease. For a few minutes, I didn't react: maybe peace really did exist. I felt good; it was the same sense of well-being you feel when, having pulled off a scab, a wound reopens: the blood is freed.

For a second there I was going to start discussing the film with them, offer them something to drink. Such passivity shocked me. It often happened that I would expose myself to unpleasantness. I needed to get a grip.

I stood up abruptly, as if I was coming out of a trance. "What the hell are you doing here?"

They were strangely sheepish, and smiled. They looked like children who had been caught doing something naughty.

"We're not hurting anything."

"What do you want?"

"We told you, sir, we're looking for Tot."

They were now looking around, but halfheartedly. They might have been armed, but mainly I could tell they were tired. I sensed they would have been very happy to stay there and rest.

"Who are you? Cops?"

"Why do you think we're cops? Are you doing anything illegal?"

"That's it. Get out of here."

Who were those two guys? Why did they seem fake? The prospect of the evening with Pointel had made me so nervous that reality itself was torturous: I sometimes feel the knife that is advancing toward my throat; I then know I shouldn't move. The slightest gesture dissipates the vision. I have to close my eyes, and then my thoughts create the hand that is holding the knife.

It's a scene that was taking place that day, on a fourth-floor landing in an apartment building in the Twentieth Arrondissement in Paris, and yet, in my madness, it seems that it has been happening for millennia. I'm climbing a mountain with a load of wood on my back. The sun is a rock. The sand under my feet absorbs my silence. I head toward the place where the light tears the rocks, where its huge clarity trembles with sparks. I can't see anything: that's where I'm going.

Is there a veil? While the knife is getting closer to my throat, I get closer to the veil. Up to the last moment—up to the next to last—I stare at the glow that is shining on the blade: does the knife have to plunge into my throat for the veil to be torn?

Abruptly, in this endless comedy that my life had become, something was happening. I couldn't turn back. In a sense, being at a brick wall is an opportunity. Just as the two Mustaches opened the door to the stairs to leave, a current of air blew through, and the door to my apartment banged shut behind me. I was on the landing, without my keys. I cursed those two imbeciles who had put me in this mess and quickly went down the stairs to look for Sabbat, who was sniffing his piss in the bushes in the little courtyard.

Part Two

PROBLEMS

13

IN FRONT OF THE DOOR

I arrived at Bofinger's at 8:00. It was Saturday, and the restaurant was packed. I told the man at the entrance that a table had been reserved in Pointel's name. The maître d', a prematurely balding, nervous young man, almost a double for Emmanuel Macron, answered that indeed, M. Pointel would be dining there that evening, under the glass dome, at his usual table, but not with a dog.

"What dog?" I said.

The maître d', sensing a problem, simply pointed at Sabbat, who was calmly listening to us, his tongue hanging out.

"That's not a dog," I said. "His name is Sabbat, he's my friend."

The maître d' was unflappable.

"Tell your friend that we're very sorry, but he can't come in unleashed."

I was about to tell him the whole story: the two Mustaches, the door slamming shut, the key inside, and Sabbat, who had run down the stairs, but I thought better of it; if you want to go into a place whose entrance is barred to you, it is never a good idea to play on sympathy. And if, in addition, you admit that in fact a door has just closed on you, it becomes absurd, even unseemly, to hope that another will be opened.

"We didn't have time to grab the leash," I said.

"Think about it, sir, your friend is wearing a collar, I'm sure you'll find a solution."

I went to smoke a cigarette on the sidewalk across the street. Sabbat watched the pigeons. He was sitting, calm, and his head brushed against my left leg. Why worry? Pointel would get there soon, he would fix everything. And I felt good on the sidewalk. There was a soft light in the trees, green everywhere, blue, and a light wind in which desires float. How long had it been since I'd gone out? The streets became wider, a light emotion moved from face to face; passersby patted Sabbat's head and smiled at me. There was a clear joy that was spreading like drunkenness up to the Place de la Bastille, where the light-bearing angel held up its broken chains, thrusting forward the golden hues that lighted this early evening.

At the entrance to the restaurant, laid out on a bed of ice, there were oysters that were making me hungry. Their shells sparkled, like little lights stuck on a cliff. Mother-of-pearl encourages sparkling. It is said that an oyster secretes a pearl from where it was hurt. And so the wound is desirable, it greets the zest of the lemon that, while I am writing these lines, is making my mouth water. I am going to drink at those lacy edges, I am going to suck down the pearl. Yes, a watering mouth, everything comes from that, the world exists only to create desire.

I was leaning against the wall, next to a luxury shoe boutique, where a wall of ivy mixed with beautiful purplish clusters formed a sort of fresh barrier; it was wonderful to feel the softness of the leaves and smell the sweet perfume of the wisteria. And while coveting the oysters over there sparkling on the ice on the other side of the street, I thought of a passage in Shakespeare's *The Tempest* that describes the birth of pearls. I had cited it often in *The Great Melville*, because in it I saw one of the secrets that Melville had discovered, and now I was reciting it just for pleasure:

Full fathom five thy father lies,
Of his bones are coral made:
Those are pearls that were his eyes.
Nothing of him that doth fade,
But doth suffer a sea-change
Into something rich and strange.

While I was reciting them, those verses wound around the wisteria, and I felt a whole vine of lines, green and fresh like the ocean where drowned fathers were lying, growing in me: "Of his bones are coral made," I said to myself, "Those are pearls that were his eyes"—and I saw the underwater immensity filled with skeletons where long, red minerals were growing, similar to hard algae that through the darkness were beckoning to me. They were telling me that it is good not to turn away from the abyss because it is there that bodies change into pearls; it is there that death is transformed into hard, red life; it is there that time is crystalized.

The depths of the seas are populated by a memory that waits to be awakened. And now, while reciting these lines, my body wound in the wisteria, entirely covered with ivy, I plunged in turn into the depths of the waters to gather the single and rare thing that was intended for me. Nothing is hidden, I told myself. *Everything is still there.* There is no veil. The mystery contained in Shakespeare's verses implies the metamorphosis of all the lives that have passed and the secret of their resurrection through our desire. Because nothing and no one ever dies completely, every spark of life waits to be recognized by those among us who frequent the abyss. We always think that fathers are dead, but when someone dies, pearls, coral, and all other possible treasures are born in their place and wait for us to find them.

That "something rich and strange" that Shakespeare is talking about—that idea of a treasure only waiting to be found—I have never given up on it. Somewhere, on the other side of the world, on an island inhabited by deer, in the heart of the Rocky Mountains or of a prairie illuminated by the embraces of immigrants, in a desert of snow, a ghetto in Poland, a group of undocumented workers, a room covered with messianic books, or even here, on the corner of a sun-filled Paris street, through the orange and green reflections of the windshield of a salmon-colored Mercedes parked in front of me, in the scented freshness of honey on a wall of wisteria, in the excitement of a Dalmatian gleefully chasing pigeons, on rue de la Bastille, I know something is waiting for me, something rich and strange—a treasure.

And that treasure consumes my thoughts. All that I do, all that I desire, all my thoughts, even the most frivolous, even those that seem to distance me from the essential, are devoted to it. When one devotes one's life to deciphering an invisible message, one must expect to encounter obstacles, to lose oneself in the useless, to fall prey to multiple spinouts. But even the most aberrant skidding off the road is still part of the path. Yes, when, last April, I had found that line of Melville's about the truth forced to flee into the woods like a frightened white deer, I saw on the distant horizon of my adventures, rather my misadventures—because my days, as you've noticed, have that slightly screwy hue that gives them the air of a comedy—the opening up, in spite of zigzags, and sometimes thanks to them, of a direction, a path, a road.

———

It was 8:15. Still no Pointel. I watched Macron, who was greeting each customer with an obsequious and ironic majesty. From time to time, he glanced over at Sabbat and me, as if we were bums who needed to be kept at a distance. I had at first taken him for one of those psycho-rigid employees who apply the rules to the letter because the slightest transgression drove them crazy. But no, that guy was paid to sort out the chaff, he repelled pariahs the way the cops working with the customs officers on Ellis Island could at first glance, from among the immigrants who came to seek their fortune in America, detect the presence of a possible outlaw, and who, if they didn't find one, would pick one out randomly. This evening, I was the pariah.

Shouldn't I text Pointel? But I was afraid that he would see my text as a sign of impatience. So I decided to wait another five minutes.

With all my ruminating, I had completely forgotten my keys problem. That afternoon, after having found Sabbat in the little yard, I went to find Mme Figo. I knew she kept a spare key, but as usual there wasn't anyone in her *loge*. I waited half an hour in the lobby, Sabbat was walking around me, I was afraid he would take a piss on the artificial flowers, so I slipped a note under Mme Figo's door in which I explained my situation. Would she please call me so we could figure out the best way to solve this problem?

Even better, would she—and it would be wonderfully kind of her—put the spare key in my mailbox (and of course leave the box open) so that this evening, after my work meeting, I could get into my apartment?

I hoped, but only halfheartedly, that she would find that note before the *loge* was closed for the night, and especially that she would get in touch with me. But while I was waiting on the sidewalk for Pointel to arrive, I had still not received a call from Mme Figo, and she would probably not call me, forcing me to sleep outside all night. In a way, my situation gave her the opportunity for revenge, and, what was strangest, I found that funny.

I was in an amazingly good mood. I enjoyed walking across Paris with a Dalmatian, and now my place was here, on this sidewalk lighted by the last rays of the sun, wrapped in wisteria and ivy in a glorious solitude. And even if the meeting with Pointel were to bring me only new unpleasantness, it didn't matter. I had the wisteria, I had the ivy, I had my solitude. Today was my birthday, and at fifty years old I was giving myself this gift: to live in an adventure novel.

Suddenly I began to have doubts. Had I understood correctly what Macron had told me? Because thinking about it again, in confirming that Pointel would dine there this evening (information that I, myself, had given him, and that he had simply validated with the neutrality of a professional), he had not specified whether Pointel was actually there or not. Suddenly I realized that I had no assurance that Pointel wasn't *already* there. Indeed, Macron had said: "M. Pointel will dine here this evening, under the glass dome, at his usual table," and I hadn't paid attention to what he had said. It had seemed perfectly clear. But now, when thinking about it again, it took an equivocal turn. His statement spoken in the future tense ("M. Pointel will dine") was perhaps hiding a different meaning. There was undeniably ambiguity in what he had said, I would even say a shimmering, and it was possible, given the ironic nature of the man, something that I would call cunning. Yes, a cunning shimmering meant to hide whether Pointel was in fact inside the restaurant. Because now, I was sure of it, Pointel was in fact waiting for me at his usual table, under the glass dome, and out of respect hadn't informed me of that. He was graciously allowing me the possibility of being late. Yes, that was it. I thought I was early and now I was late. I needed immediately to text Pointel. If he was inside, he would invite me to join him, and then I would tell him about the problem that was keeping Sabbat and me on the sidewalk across the street. And if, on the contrary, he hadn't arrived yet, I would quite simply continue to wait for him.

Pointel immediately responded to my text. He was very sorry, a meeting had run longer than expected, he was on his way but the traffic was bad, I could go in and wait for him, a table was reserved in his name.

I didn't dare tell him that in fact I couldn't enter the restaurant. The best thing was to continue to wait outside, watching the entrance, so I wouldn't miss his arrival. My plan was simple: the moment Pointel arrived, at the precise moment when the maître d' took a few steps from the entrance to greet him and warmly shake his hand, as is done with good customers, Sabbat and I would cross the street, I would call out to Pointel with a large smile, he would turn around, also smiling, and that big smile would win over the maître d', who would open his arms to Pointel, Sabbat, and me, in the same spirit of conviviality, and that's how we would finally get into Bofinger's.

There was a flurry of text messages. Pointel told me he was going to be seriously delayed. I could go ahead and order something while I waited, oysters, whatever I wanted—it was his treat. He had alerted the restaurant, the waiters were aware, they would serve me a bottle of his favorite wine—a well-chilled pinot noir—he had placed the order, he asked me to drink to his health and let him know what I thought of the wine.

I walked over to the restaurant with Sabbat, who was yelping with excitement. When he saw me, the maître d' assumed a haughty air.

"M. Pointel would like me to wait for him inside," I said. "He called, everyone knows, they are already serving the wine, I really must go in."

He looked at the dog coldly, gestured for me not to move, went into the restaurant and came back out with a tie that he held out to me without saying a word. It was a mauve silk tie, the color of lilacs, I would say. I thought it was vulgar, but I wasn't going to make any more of a fuss. I tried to tie it around my neck, but it was clear I didn't know what I was doing.

The maître d' no longer hid his exasperation.

"It's not for you, it's for the dog. You don't have a leash, hold on to him with the tie, I don't have anything better to offer."

I quickly slipped an end of the tie into Sabbat's collar. He allowed me to do it with the patience of a saint. Tot had trained him really well. I had walked across the Père-Lachaise cemetery with him, walked up the rue de la Roquette, and crossed the boulevard de la Bastille without his ever leaving my side. When he happened to move away slightly, he constantly looked around to make sure I was still there. And before every crosswalk, he even sat down to wait for my signal.

"This way," said the maître d', and Sabbat and I finally went in.

14

A FRACAS

We made a solemn entrance. Sabbat raised his noble head high, and I, leading him with his mauve silk leash, forced myself to appear haughty, yet relaxed, like an aristocrat. With my dusty espadrilles, my old coat without buttons, and my hair that hadn't been cut in six months, I'm not sure I passed. But after all, even Louis II of Bavaria, taking his white greyhound hunting, sometimes looked like a madman.

When Sabbat and I went in, preceded by a waitress (a young blond woman who looked like a teenager), to whom the maître d' had passed the baton, we were led into the main room where the noise of clattering dishes blended with conversations. Everyone turned to look at the bum who was walking a creature out of a Walt Disney movie. I had a moment of panic: when you enter a public space alone, you become a prey.

Discomfort leads to excess. I stared at the nonplussed diners with the insolence of a maharajah. The nobility of Sabbat encouraged me, and hadn't I gone to the trouble of wearing my pearl-gray shirt? I felt invulnerable when I wore it.

The moment I entered the room I felt the names beginning to seize me. I was going from one name to another, faster and faster: that happened to me every time I crossed a threshold, and if most often I managed to control the frenzy, that evening, with the pressure the maître d' had put on me, then the anxiety that all these people caused me, I feared it was going to be more difficult. There couldn't have been a worse moment to decompensate. I had to contain myself with Pointel, especially since I still hadn't paid the lodging tax, and with a little luck, as he had promised me in March during our meeting, he might have some work for me, proofreading screenplays, that type of thing.

The waitress indicated the banquette that was right under the glass dome, in the middle of the restaurant: "M. Pointel's table," she said. She pulled out the table so I could sit down, but Sabbat, used to Tot's soft sofa, leapt up majestically and stretched out on the beautiful Bordeaux leather on which little glimmers of light, the elegant light of the last day of summer, were shining.

My dining neighbors gave us disapproving looks, and the waitress quickly requested that Sabbat get down. I had to make sure he stayed under the table, at my feet, I might even have to tie him up.

The glass dome was made of little yellow, red, and blue panes of glass, which depicted a folkloric scene in Alsace where village women in black hats with large bows and red skirts were dancing with fellows in their Sunday best. It diffused a milky light, a bit sickening, that floated in the air with the mushy weight of jellyfish.

In a few minutes I had completely lost my composure. Just being squeezed behind this table which the waitress had methodically pushed into me was enough to feed my anxiety. I was dripping with sweat, but there was no way I was going to take off my coat. I've been wearing it for years and always, in difficult situations, it has come to my aid. Knights have their armor, I have my coat. When I wear it, I am protected. Inside it there is my notebook, one or two books, and something to write with. There's my phone, a few lucky charms, and a flask of vodka, everything I need to survive. I like knowing that I have the essential on me, that I can last a long time, anywhere, without asking any-one for anything. And, in case things take a turn for the worse, it's good to be able to leave right away, without going to the coat check.

Even more than the people watching me, even more than the heavy weight that in this restaurant anchors you to your plate and your silverware without you knowing what to do with your hands, it was the light that bothered me the most, a sticky light that was made heavy by the smell of cooking. And so I put on my dark glasses. If you could disappear in the folds of your coat, disappear in the air like the ashes of a volcano, life would be tolerable.

The waitress came back with a bizarre guy, very tall and hunched over, who was wearing a black wig shimmering with blue reflections, like the wings of a crow. I thought he had come to kick me out, but he opened a bottle of vintage pinot noir, sniffed the cork, and while pouring me a glass, specified that it was from "M. Pointel's personal reserves."

I tasted the wine and nodded, as was fitting, thinking that it must cost a fortune. The waitress placed the bottle in the silver bucket filled with ice and I waited for her to go away to guzzle down the entire glass. It did me good. I wanted to drink another right away, but the bucket was too far away, and even by leaning over the table, which I had begun to do, I wasn't able to reach it. Impossible to push the table without upsetting my neighbors on either side, and without knocking over the bucket.

And so I waited for the waitress to return and asked her if it would be possible for the bucket to be placed on the table, because I was very thirsty, I said, the wine was excellent, I anticipated drinking a lot of it, and since M. Pointel still hadn't arrived, I could at least pass the time enjoying this very good wine.

She attempted a smile, tiny but sufficient so that, in my solitude, I saw an ally in her. I'm one of those people who would like to participate in the drunkenness of the sky, but the weight crushes me. What would happen if we really felt the earth turning? Sitting in this bourgeois restaurant, I finally understood that I was horribly alone. Spending all those days doing nothing but watching and rewatching the same films, I had isolated myself to the point of absurdity. This evening, I had to make an effort. In a sense, this dinner with Pointel was an occasion to open myself up.

I continued to drink while watching platters of seafood go by. Out of the windows of the restaurant you could see the silhouette of the angel of the Bastille that was perpetually taking flight, as if it were urging us to leave this poor world and enter a void where the light re-creates the earth and the heavens. I thought of all those angels in the Paris sky that recount a fairy tale of annunciation. Those of Notre-Dame, with their long white wings, which, resembling the elect in the four winds, have been blowing their horns from one extremity of heaven to another; the one that stands on the top of the Sainte-Chapelle, that colossal angel, made of lead, whose stony gaze cuts through lies, and which holds a processional cross; then all the Victories with gilded wings that hold out crowns of laurel; the one, half-naked, on the roof of the Petit Palais; the one that is meditating, seated, exhausted, at the top of the arc du Carrousel: I can imagine their conversations, and the inconceivable tale that every night, from mouth to mouth, is woven out of their joy. Sometimes, in between two films, around three or four in the morning, smoking a cigarette at the window of my room, I think that if the world doesn't completely fall into the abyss, if it seems vaguely to still turn on its axis, it's because that tale, woven each night on the rooftops, weaves a fabric as solid as it is ungraspable, and is the guarantor of time.

While I was sipping the pinot noir (and I could already tell I was going to drink way too much of it), a line came back to me, a wonderful line from Kafka whose simplicity I have always liked: "I had a friend among the angels." Was it in *Amerika* that I had underlined it? I took out my notebook to check: yes, it was in *Amerika*, it was in that completely crazy book by Kafka in which the Statue of Liberty welcomes you, on the first page, holding a sword instead of a torch, in which the idea of the Promised Land takes the shape of an enormous big top, a moving circus where everyone sees his hopes dissolve, where hope and disappearance become the same, swallowed in that comedy that seems to have replaced the world, as if an indecipherable prophecy had opened on the American horizon, and on the entire planet, onto the universal future of that clown show.

Kafka, angels, America, clowns: all of that took hold of me. I went from one idea to another, from one name to another, from one line to another. I knew it wouldn't stop, I knew that I was going to inundate Pointel with my babbling, and completely drown our meeting in a flood of names, anecdotes, quotations, and once again waste an opportunity to have a true exchange (but perhaps a true exchange, on the contrary, implies that everyone gives free rein to the names that come to him...).

How could I do it? I drank down another glass of pinot noir. Maybe once I was drunk the names would leave me alone. Do names dissolve in alcohol? Frankly, I didn't think so.

In the middle of the restaurant there was a large aquarium with green plants on top, in which the rays of the glass dome were reflected in bursts of mother-of-pearl that sparkled on my wineglass. I could see little rainbows whose chiaroscuro danced under my fingers when I brought my glass to my lips. If I managed to slip under that bow of colors, to slip among the rings of the prism, if I left my place on the banquette to plunge into that miniature ocean, I would surely be delivered. Delivered from what, I had no idea—but ultimately deliverance has no object, what it promises is itself.

The aquarium was filled with huge green-and-blue fish that swam among lobsters whose pincers were held closed by elastic bands, and all sorts of shrimp and crabs that moved around among the algae and moss. The pack had moved to the glass wall and was staring at me.

It's when you're at the very bottom that deliverance arrives, everyone knows that, but personally I felt that I wasn't *yet* at the very bottom. Granted, a trap door had opened and I was falling through it, but it was obvious that my trials were just beginning, I was going to fall even farther, because there were not only all those little glass pieces whose faded color had been nauseating me since I had arrived, but now I was being attacked by the creatures in that aquarium which I hadn't immediately seen, and which, when my situation was just about to stabilize (Sabbat had fallen asleep under the banquette and the red wine was beginning to have an effect), rose up in front of me. The restaurant was already floating in a disturbing light, with jellyfish that were splashing around in the soup and rainbows that were unfolding on glasses, and now horrible shellfish were climbing in the mud *to make me suffer.*

I emptied two more glasses of wine one after the other, under the watch of the waitress who, it seemed, had been given special orders to keep an eye on me. The bottle was now three-quarters empty. I was sweating even more, but there was no way I was going to take off my coat. Or look at the lobsters. Don't think about being stuck behind the table. Forget how close everyone was to me, forget Macron who, over there, in the entrance, was watching me. Keep repeating this phrase: "When you have fallen to the bottom I will come and pull you up." I think it was God who said that. It's in a midrash. He is answering Israel, who asks him: "When will you come to pick us up?" That phrase, which was one of a thousand and one phrases written in my special notebook, the one I had on me, tucked in the outer left pocket of my coat, speaks above all of the Messiah, and that evening, while repeating it to forget the offensive of the crustaceans, I realized that the figure of the white deer of truth, the one that had led me to Michael Cimino and had guided me throughout the summer, had something to do with redemption. Is it really possible to achieve redemption, a bit drunk, all alone, the evening of one's fiftieth birthday, between an aquarium filled with crustaceans and Emmanuel Macron's double? Such things fall within the realm of mystery.

I had, however, decided that that evening everything would be fine. I wanted to have a normal conversation with someone normal (even if Pointel was not a model of normalcy, either). And then there was still time to flee. After all, I was free to extract myself from this dinner, free to talk to no one, to continue to watch movies all day, all night. Moreover, I had been outside for more than five hours, and I was already missing my room. I suddenly had a mad desire to watch *Apocalypse Now*, or a Cimino, or even *Twin Peaks*. I had recently started watching the David Lynch series, and I had already seen the entire thing three times. It was incredible. In particular, I would have really liked to have rewatched, right here, right now, the scene in "One-Eyed Jacks," a brothel filled with red curtains, where the intrepid Audrey Horne, played by Sherilyn Fenn, makes a knot with a cherry stem in her mouth. But I remembered that I had left my keys inside my apartment, and that thought was enough to deflate me.

Sabbat came out from under the banquette and began to whine and to give me little taps on my thigh with his paw. That's all I needed. He was hungry. I hadn't given him anything to eat since the morning, and in a few minutes he was going to be uncontrollable.

I managed to get the waitress's attention and asked her if it would be possible for my dog—who was, however, not really *my* dog, I watch him when his master is away, and he was with me this evening only because the master still hadn't returned from a trip abroad—in short, I asked her if it would be possible to give him something to eat.

The young waitress seemed taken aback, and soon I saw Emmanuel Macron reappear.

"We don't serve food to animals," he said, in his exasperated tone. "You haven't understood: *animals are not allowed.* I made an exception only because M. Pointel vouched for you."

The red wine had completely gone to my head. I brazenly insisted. Macron said I was out of line, he threatened to call the manager.

The alcohol was making my head spin. It was spinning as if I had set off on a whaler. Sabbat, when the maître d' had raised his voice, actually leapt from his hiding place and started to jump on him, his tongue hanging out, and it wasn't clear if he wanted to play or to attack. It was then, looking around me with shame, because everyone was looking at the dog jumping higher and higher, that I noticed, sitting in front of a platter of seafood, the two Mustaches.

I jumped up and shouted, "You over there!" followed by Sabbat who, quite happily, started to bark. I ran over and threw myself on one of the Mustaches, knocking him off his chair, upsetting the waiter who was pouring him wine.

"What the hell are you doing here?" I shouted. "You're following me, huh?"

While the Mustache I had knocked over was wrestling with his chair, the other had gotten up from the banquette, his napkin tied around his neck. He shook his fist at me, calling me all sorts of unrepeatable names.

When he was standing up, the Mustache I had attacked (and who I saw was Mustache #1, the one with the pointed mustache) jumped on me and began to punch me. Just as I was about to hit back, the waiter grabbed him from behind, and Mustache #1 couldn't protect himself from the punch I delivered to his nose. Both men fell backward, and collapsed on the table next to them, causing the people dining there to jump up, aghast.

I shouted out, "They're cops! They've been following me everywhere, they even barged into my apartment!"

Of course, no one reacted, and I was aware of the absurd stupidity of what I was saying: if they were cops, then what had I done?

Macron ran over to subdue me, helped by two waiters, and they had begun to escort us to the door, me and my satanic dog. They were already shoving us out the main entrance, the one we had had so much trouble entering barely a half hour earlier, when Pointel, leaning on a crutch, appeared.

15

THE EYE OF THE DEER

Pointel took care of everything. The maître d' accepted my apologies, I swore I would remain calm, Sabbat was served a dish of meat on the sidewalk, which he devoured while I watched, and Pointel, who didn't really understand what had happened—or who didn't give a damn—continued to answer phone calls leaning heavily on his crutch. He had a huge cast, covered with inscriptions written in red felt pen, which went up his leg to his thigh. And he gesticulated vehemently, he spoke loudly. With his long, slightly tow-colored hair that brushed his shoulders, his face covered in scars, a four-day beard and an extinguished cigar stuck on his lower lip, he was unrecognizable. Granted, when I had met with him six months earlier in his office on rue Notre-Dame-de-Nazareth, he had given me the impression that he enjoyed a certain amount of bizarreness, and that he was even a bit crazy himself. But at that time everything about his appearance, including his carefully maintained tan, shouted out "businessman." This evening, on the contrary, he looked like a bum who had just been beaten up, especially since he had cut the leg of his pants in order to put them on over the cast, and the two strips of fabric floated around his leg absurdly, like rags.

"You look like Captain Ahab," I told him.

"Huh?"

"Your leg, did a whale grab it?"

While limping over to our table, accompanied by Sabbat, who, with a full stomach, had calmed down again, Pointel told me that he had recently been in a car accident. It had happened one night in Poland. He was returning from the famous film school in Łódź, where one of his old friends, Jerzy Skolimowski, the director of *Deep End* and *Moonlighting*, who had recently adapted Gombrowicz's *Ferdydurke*, had just held a master class. The road Pointel had taken went through a forest. He was driving like a bat out of hell, and then suddenly a stag with huge antlers burst out of the dark. The animal threw itself onto his car, as if it had wanted to commit suicide. It hit the bumper very hard before coming down on the hood like a clap of thunder. At that moment, while the car was moving into the underbrush and crashing against a fir tree, he had seen the deer rise up in the air; it was an almost mystical vision, Pointel told me. Such an enormous beast projected in the black sky of Poland, surrounded by fir trees, it could have been an apparition.

Pointel was still amazed by it, and yet, he said, standing right in the middle of the large Bofinger's dining room—while Macron was growing impatient because we were impeding traffic in the aisle and I was trying to avoid the looks of the diners who had witnessed my outburst—it wasn't really his style to take these stories of animal annunciations and other catechism bullshit seriously. But something had really happened to him, a sort of miracle, he noted. Because after flying into the air, the deer, falling back down, had shattered the windshield, and its antlers were pointed directly at him, like the banderillos of a torero, and he could already see his entire body pierced through, he could see his eyes crushed, he said, he saw himself *dying through his eyes*. But the banderillos dug into the seat around his head, a few millimeters from his face, and when he could focus again, he couldn't move at all: not only did the prongs of the antlers form a cage around him, but the huge deer, crushed against his chest, had completely immobilized him. Pointel was a prisoner in his car, in the middle of the night, in a forest in the bowels of Poland, and the worst thing was that he didn't know if the animal that was emptying its blood on him was still alive.

Macron abruptly interrupted Pointel's narrative, taking his arm so he would get to his table as quickly as possible. We had to keep moving, we couldn't stand there right in the middle of the restaurant, especially since Sabbat had begun cleaning himself, and a Dalmatian licking his genitals was not an appropriate spectacle for people trying to enjoy their dinners.

As I was walking by I glanced over at the table of the two Mustaches, who had disappeared. Sabbat slid under the banquette. The waitress was busy adjusting Pointel's chair. I poured him a glass of wine, poured myself another, the bottle was empty now. Because of his cast, he couldn't sit down, so we toasted standing up, under the annoyed looks of our neighbors, who were fed up with all the hubbub.

"To the deer's eye!" said Pointel.

The sommelier with the black wig brought another bottle of pinot noir, which he let Pointel taste, and while the waitress was placing a stool at the end of the table so Pointel could rest his leg on it, we were already drinking another glass.

They say that at the moment of death, you see the film of your life flash by. As for Pointel, during the first night he spent trapped in his car, he couldn't stop staring, horrified, at the eye of the deer that was shining in the darkness. The eye seemed alive to him, so he feared the animal would wake up. He was afraid that in disengaging itself the deer would pull his head off with its antlers. So he started to watch for the slightest shudder in the beast, without realizing it was dead. Because in that eye which was only a few centimeters from his face and which continued to remain open, there was only the emptiness of the night, the emptiness of the forest, the emptiness of Poland, where—and he cursed himself for his decision—he had

come to die. In his anger, he cursed himself a thousand
times, and he cursed cinema, directors, the race for money,
the madness of making films... because in the empty eye
of the deer, it was ultimately the emptiness of his own life
that was reflected back on him, an abysmal and aberrant
void, he told me, the nothingness of a life that had never
been anything but a long devotion to secondary, useless,
absurd pursuits, each one of which was only a slave to his
obsession with never stopping.

To end up trapped inside his own car seemed like a maca-
bre joke to him, but also a fitting end, because he never got
out of that car, which he had turned into his office, spending most of his time on the phone while racing through the
nights on the highways of Europe, doing business from Paris
to Rome, from Rome to Geneva, from Geneva to Berlin,
always going from meeting to meeting in that car which had
become, he now realized, literally a cage.

"In the end," Pointel told me, "I have always lived in
a cage, and maybe we all live locked in our cages. No one
really wants to escape. Living in a cage satisfies us because
we have neither courage nor imagination. We want nothing to happen to us and so nothing happens to us. To tell
the truth, we don't really live, we spend our time observing
an eye and we convince ourselves that we are watching that
eye, when it's not only that eye that is watching us, but
what's more, that eye is the eye of a dead being. That's it,"
Pointel told me, "we're living under the hallucinatory yoke

of the eye of a dead being." That's the conclusion he had come to while he was stuck in his car, while the deer was emptying its blood on him.

The first rays of daylight arrived, and no one came to his aid, no one had noticed that car crashed against a fir tree in the forest. Not only did very few cars go by on that little road in the middle of Poland, but when one did go by, he could hear the sound of it only in the distance. Pointel realized that it was impossible for him to be seen because his car had traveled pretty far into the woods. Covered by the branches of the fir trees, it was in fact no longer visible.

He tried to cry out, but there was only silence. He was buried in his tomb, buried in the middle of a forest, with the skin of a deer covered with blood for a shroud.

He began to shriek, he shrieked for hours, never had he shrieked so much, he told me. He shrieked with the despair of the death row prisoner. And then he started to fear he would be eaten by wild beasts attracted by the odor of the dead stag. The day went by, he was thirsty, his teeth were chattering, and in the night, the deer's eye continued to stare at him. Why had it come to crash against his car? He vaguely remembered that legend in which a large deer, its forehead bearing a cross, comes to curse the hunter that massacred its family. But what had he, Pointel, ever done?

It had been twenty-four hours and he hadn't been able to move his legs or arms, and he struggled in vain to move them, but now he felt nothing except cold, hunger, and thirst. From watching it so long, he had believed he had found in the deer's eye a passage. He had entered inside that eye, had crept along it as in a hallway, but nothing opened up, the hallway never ended. There was neither door nor window, no light, no life.

Flies were buzzing around the stinking deer cadaver, and, Pointel said, during the second night, he felt he was buzzing like a fly in his own gullet. He saw himself already dead. "Imagine, I started thinking about Montaigne," he said. "I don't think I had read him since lycée, and yet lines from his writing kept coming back to me. It was when he falls from a horse and thinks he is witnessing his own death. Of course, it's impossible to experience one's own death, no one has ever returned to tell someone he was dead and had lived the moment of his death, but Montaigne says something like that: *I thought of preparing myself to see whether, in that moment of death, so short and so brief, I could perceive the release of the soul.* I don't remember the line very well anymore," said Pointel, "but the expression 'release of the soul,' I'm sure about. That was exactly what I was waiting for while I was watching in the deer's eye the reflection of my own fading face. I can tell you that the moment of death is neither short nor brief. On the contrary, it lasts, it never ends, you go out slowly, and a sort of hallucinatory torpor took me over. I was delirious since I hadn't eaten or drunk anything and was cold, and then I sensed that my strength was fading, too. Things were leaving me, minuscule things, and my soul itself was going to be released from my body which I already no longer felt. Montaigne was right to talk about the 'release of the soul,' the expression was exact. Stuck in the car, with flies in my eyes, mouth, nose, I regretted not having read Montaigne more closely. We never prepare enough for death, but reading Montaigne would have at least given me something to think about, I could have mobilized my reading memories, and since I had spent my life reading screenplays, that is, lines that are erased, I had nothing to mobilize. Except for that little line from Montaigne, which I wasn't even sure was exact, I was completely empty.

"So I spent a lot of time with that little phrase, I rolled it on my tongue like a seed, I was infused with it, to the point that several times during the second night, while the slightest sound in the darkness around the car terrified me, I thought that I was entering into that sort of ultimate trembling that Montaigne mentions—I thought that *my soul was being released.* And I experienced a crazy sort of joy. It was the strangest thing that had ever happened to me in my life. I abandoned myself to it.

"How long did that abandonment last? I don't know, but it opened a breach in my head, a void. And believe me, nothing can get in. It is the place of abandonment. Have you ever abandoned yourself—really abandoned yourself? It happened to me; and that's how I died, that's how my soul was released.

"The rest is anecdotal." He poured himself another glass of wine and drank it down in one gulp. "The second day, when the sun was already high in the sky, and I couldn't salivate anymore, an old man appeared. He looked like an owl. He was barefoot, had a sheepskin jacket and a long, dirty beard. His eyes were crazy, and he walked toward me with his rifle aimed at me. I thought he was going to shoot me. He poked the deer with the barrel of the rifle, then he began to talk to me. His words were strong, as if he were barking. And I, too, *wanted* to talk, but no sound came out of my mouth. The guy took out a knife and began to cut up the deer. I thought: when he finishes with the deer, he's going to take my meat. He got closer, the blade of the knife shone in front of my eyes, and I think I fainted. Then all of a sudden my chest was freed, I took in a deep breath, I felt like I was smelling things for the first time, the smell of the forest, the sharp perfume of the heather, the damp earth, the huge freshness carpeted under the burning sun, with the sort of headiness that comes from the sap of the fir trees. At that moment, I realized I couldn't move. I shouted. Or rather a shout came out of me—a cold shout. The old man got me out, I couldn't feel my legs anymore. He carried me to the edge of the road where he set me down. I can't really remember: did he stay with me to wait for a car? I see myself lying in a van, then there's the hospital. The cast—just a leg broken... it was miraculous. And later, in a tow truck in the forest to extract my car. And the eye, forever, in my head. That is how," he said, "I am alive."

16

PLATEAU PRESTIGE

Pointel suddenly stopped talking. His phone rang, and he raised his glass:

"To Michael Cimino!" he said.

We clinked our glasses, and he asked me the question he had asked in his text, a question to which I hadn't been able to respond because of the appearance of the two Mustaches on my landing: "So, just like that, Cimino became a woman?"

"It's much more complicated," I said. "Neither man nor woman."

The phone kept ringing, he had to answer it. He excused himself and slowly got up, leaning on his crutches.

I was once again alone with the aquarium, the glass dome, and the looks of the other diners. After listening to the long story, I felt naked. I was hungry. If I continued to drink like this without eating, I was going to fall under the table. Already it seemed impossible to get my bearings. I had set off, and if, for the moment, the sea was calm, the waves announced a storm that would take out the stars. New diners were arriving, Macron kept coming and going, and every time he went by our table, he gave me a dirty look. And Sabbat? I leaned under the table—he had fallen asleep.

I opened the menu. Pointel and I absolutely had to order. They had "sauerkraut of the sea," the expression made me laugh. It seemed to be pretty hearty: monkfish, salmon, haddock, dumplings made with squid ink, prawns, and roasted potatoes. But I really wanted oysters. After all, I didn't get to eat them very often, whereas sauerkraut, even a "sauerkraut of the sea," I figured, rightly or wrongly, was more common, and even a bit vulgar. Oysters, that's what I needed. According to the menu, Bofinger's guaranteed they would be "firm, hearty, soft or meaty." I liked those four adjectives, they were promising, especially since the menu offered all sorts of varieties, though I didn't really know what they were. The special *grands crus* from Normandy no. 2, the special Sélection Bofinger no. 3, the *fines de claire* no. 2 and no. 3 (those looked good to me), then the special Gillardeau no. 3, as well as an enigmatic and enticing *Casting d'huîtres*, which I guessed consisted of a mix of the preceding ones. That's it, the Casting was what I wanted.

I smiled to myself, happy the way one is after making a good decision, and poured myself another glass of pinot noir and drank it down.

Pointel's story was amazing, and at the same time, it seemed familiar to me, like an allegory to be deciphered. Why had he told it to me? We hardly knew each other. As he was going deeper into his story, I had sensed he was uneasy. Do you talk about your own death with just anyone? But that was it exactly. For him, that unease made the plunge into the inadmissible irresistible. It's because that experience was upsetting to him that he had told it to me. He probably didn't know himself what he was passing on. And through his story he was seeking, in a sense, to return to its intensity. The constellations that are extinguished for us shine in the final leap of an animal. "Open your eyes," it says.

Pointel had read—let's say skimmed—my screenplay, which, itself, spoke only of death. So maybe he had figured he could tell me his story. He was right: through that story I recognized the epiphanic animal of the films I spent my days watching, I found the deer that Robert De Niro has in the crosshairs in Michael Cimino's *The Deer Hunter*, and above all I saw the return of the eternal figure of the white deer of truth.

Wasn't it toward that deer that all my adventures were directed? If I had been floating in a vacuum for so long, one that had gradually cut me off from society, it was to be ready when the deer emerged—it was to be able to welcome it.

I could imagine, without too much exaggeration, that Pointel's story had been intended for me. It is true that I had already had too much to drink to reflect on the truly karmic nature of that story (and thus on Pointel's role as messenger), but there it was: the deer was getting closer—through that story, it was sending me a sign, and I knew that a deer never comes alone. With it, the entire history of the world bursts forth.

The deer's antlers, which had almost pierced Pointel's head, were reconstructed in mine, along with the names. An antler was being written in my mind. I now reached my hand out to it.

And there was something burning in my veins, something Pointel's story had ignited, something that was also familiar to me: an anger. In my darkest nights, when despair is the same as a love of life, when I think at the same time of suicide and of the future, I feel I could attack. The wild animal wanders in the woods the way the irascible circulates in our veins. That's what I was thinking while I waited for Pointel. Of this exact line: "The wild animal wanders in the woods the way the irascible circulates in our veins." Who was I, really? Sometimes the ritual is illuminated; you know you're on the way. You sense your hand burning. It is possible that the kingdom belongs to the violent, but if violence precedes revelation, the final gesture challenges it. It will be enough, at the very last moment, to bend down and pick a flower.

When he returned, Pointel told me he was looking for financing for the next film by Leos Carax. It was an incredible pain in the ass, Carax had a great idea, a story in which international finance and cloning came together. Carax's idea was that there is a relationship between genetic manipulation and financial speculation. According to him, what happens in biology and what was happening to the economy come from the same plan to destroy the human species.

"Ultimately, what interests Carax," said Pointel, "is capitalism as perversion. He wants to portray stock market speculation as a game made up by Satan. And since it is tricky to represent the devil in a human form, he wants to film viruses.

"Film itself is a virus," he said. "The notion of a virus is represented in film, with its planetary images, its trailers that appear on computer screens at the speed of light. Ultimately, there's no longer any need to make films," he said. "Coming attractions are enough, those are viral. They constantly create desire, and our desires are no longer our own, but those that the film industry has dictated to us, and because of those images that they assume are their desires, people run to a movie theater or are glued to the Internet."

In any case, said Pointel, Carax's film will cost billions, and since he has to avoid repeating the financial catastrophe of *Les Amants du Pont-Neuf,* which had completely burned Carax, Pointel, to be forearmed, was in negotiations with Qatar, and would I please excuse him if the phone rang

during our dinner, in Qatar it was still 5:00 p.m., though
when it was a matter of money the offices never closed.

"Of course," I said, completely soused. And his phone
rang, didn't stop ringing, he went out, limping to the front of
the restaurant, returned, the phone rang again, he left again.

But we did manage to place our order. Macron himself, with obsequious zeal, insisted on taking the order.
Pointel chose the Plateau Prestige, which was made up of
a half–American lobster, a half-crab, three pink shrimp,
two scampi, gray shrimp, six whelks, and a dozen oysters
selected from among the varieties on the menu (a sort of
Casting, in fact).

It's for two, Pointel said, but he invited me to order one
for myself, because he didn't want to share. He could usually eat the whole thing himself.

But I was still drawn to the Casting of oysters. Pointel
immediately objected. The Plateau Prestige was a better
choice, because not only were there as many oysters as in
the Casting (which Macron confirmed), but in addition
there were all sorts of shellfish, which he would be happy to
eat if I didn't want them. It was really a better deal, he said;
and since he was the one paying, I also ordered a Plateau
Prestige.

While biting into the flesh of an oyster, I felt myself
losing it. I had drunk a lot, but it wasn't the wine that
was making my head spin. In seeking the life that leads to
absolute space, I get drunk. But I always stay on the edge

of the mystery. No, this evening I was losing it out of pleasure because the flesh of the oyster is a delicacy that makes you shiver. You might say it is the treasures of the mother-of-pearl sparkling on your tongue. And that oyster, which the waitress had told me was a *grand cru* from Normandy, melted in my mouth like a dissolving sea jewel. Eating oysters is a sacramental act, I told Pointel, who grunted. He swore only by the lobster.

17

THE GREAT CIMINO

Then Pointel turned off his phone. While breaking open his half-crab with a shell cracker, he asked me how Cimino was. Had I been able to get him to read my screenplay? "Cimino reads everything he is given," he told me. "He spends his time reading, he's looking for the pearl, the absolute screenplay, the one that 'attracts God in its pages'" (that expression surprised me because it was a line from my own screenplay, a line that I had used regarding *Moby-Dick* in *The Great Melville*, and I was happy that Pointel was citing it, happy that it came out of the text and entered into the conversation). "Cimino," Pointel insisted, "had himself written dozens of screenplays, he was first a great screenwriter before becoming a very great director. Have you read his novels?" Since he was no longer directing, that is, for some twenty years, Cimino had become a writer, and although he of course wrote his novels in American

English, he published them only in translation. "You've read *Big Jane*, I imagine," Pointel asked me. "Well, that novel doesn't exist in America. It was written in English, but Cimino refused to publish it in that language. *Big Jane* can't be found in the U.S., which says a lot about Cimino's relationship with his country."

When Pointel and I went outside to smoke a cigarette, accompanied by Sabbat, who had immediately leapt out from under the banquette when he sensed I was getting up, we ran into the two Mustaches, who were talking with Macron at the front of the restaurant. When I went by, they averted their eyes. They were probably complaining about my behavior, or they were trying to get information, but I didn't care. The oysters, Pointel's presence, our conversation which promised to go on forever, it was all calming me. I had been right to leave my apartment. More had happened since my arrival at Bofinger's with Sabbat than had happened in the past five months. And the essential was yet to come. Great things, without a doubt, were going to happen that night, and my life would be changed. After all, wasn't I now fifty years old, wasn't I, starting with this night, going to enter into the second half of my existence? In my enthusiasm, I told Pointel it was my birthday. "How old?" he asked. "Fifty," I said. He shouted: "Champagne!" And Macron, who was standing right behind us in the frame of the large door that was open to the warmth of the evening, called over a waiter. "Two glasses of champagne for M. Pointel," he said.

We were smoking on the sidewalk, Pointel was looking at his texts, and I was contemplating the mountain of
ice on which crates of oysters were piled up, their shells,
when they opened, shining like diamonds. Mother-of-pearl
is another name for softness. It saves a life the moment it
appears. A life full of mother-of-pearl, that's what I desired.

"At first I thought Cimino was a woman," I told Pointel,
while emptying my champagne glass. "It was on the steps
in front of the Frick Collection, last spring, in April, the
seventeenth. The weather was gorgeous and New York City
was bathed in a pink light. Cimino had a Strand bag filled
with books, his face was smooth, absolutely without wrin-
kles, it was hairless, like the face of an adolescent. He was
wearing a baseball cap with the word FUCK on it, and with
his long, dark hair and his purple-tinted glasses he looked
like a diva. His movements were both graceful like those
of Gatsby, and hard, or distant, like those of a cowboy. He
was absolutely charming, his apparent insolence itself was
funny. An aristocrat—a character from Proust decked out
like a gaucho. Or Proust himself, wearing a denim shirt,
leather pants, and cowboy boots."

The first thing Michael Cimino asked me, I told Pointel,
while we were going back in to our table with Sabbat, and
after we ordered another bottle of pinot noir to finish our
Plateaux Prestige (I had eaten all the oysters, and as agreed,
left the rest of the shellfish for Pointel, who insisted that
I taste the crab), was if I ever slept. Not really, I had told

him. We had been walking through Central Park, a little breeze was blowing off the Hudson, the light sparkled through the leaves of the tall elm trees. Cimino had shaken my hand: "Fraternity," he had said solemnly.

According to him, it was unthinkable to sleep. He always slept with one eye open, because "we feel surrounded by things that can kill us," he had said. It was in the army, when he had joined up at the age of around twenty, that he had stopped sleeping. "I thought that sleep would distance me from the truth," he said, "so at night, in the barracks of the training camp of Fort Dix, so that I wouldn't sleep, I envisioned the United States flag. I made it flutter above my bed, and methodically, out of a desire to belong to nothing and no one, much less to a nation that had intentionally massacred the Apache, Cheyenne, Sioux, Comanche, and Mojave tribes, I killed off each star, until the flag was empty.

"You understand," Michael Cimino had told me, taking a bottle of vodka out of his pocket, which he had wrapped in a paper bag out of precaution, as they do in the United States, "so many have died in the name of America, and I'm not just talking about the soldiers sent to Iraq or Vietnam, I'm talking about all those whom America has killed and is continuing to kill. We should, for every death, for every hundred, for every thousand deaths, kill off a star from the flag of the United States of America."

Yes, right in the middle of Central Park, as dusk was quietly falling, and I was happy to drink the vodka after all those hours waiting for Cimino in front of Rembrandt's painting, he explained, relaxed, smiling, the importance of that act which in his opinion amounted to civil disobedience.

"In any event, the death of a galaxy is necessary for its rebirth," Cimino pointed out. "And that eddy of fifty stars no longer attaches anything to the sky of America but the eternally censured list of its dead. Furthermore, what else can the red stripes of the flag represent than spilled blood?"

In his opinion, the good old Stars and Stripes had throughout history consumed the blood of pariahs, it was the sacrificing consumer of America, the rag which successive governments have used to mop up the massacres. "They say that the stars represent the American states, but the truth," said Cimino, "is that they each represent one of the decimated Indian tribes."

While I was trying to give Pointel a precise rendition of what Michael Cimino had said, the two Mustaches sat back down at a table, right next to the entrance. Not only were they scowling at me, they were attempting to listen to our conversation.

I was about to tell Pointel what had happened with those two guys, but I was already unsure that what Cimino had said about America would interest him, so I spared him the labyrinthine and at the very least absurd details of my encounter with the Mustaches.

So, Cimino and I crossed the park toward the river. Once we were sitting in front of the Hudson, on a bench under a weeping willow, he said he was ready to read my screenplay. In the soft and light air of that late afternoon, while gulls were flying above the path, and sailboats were sailing between the skyscrapers, I took the bound manuscript of *The Great Melville*, which I had had printed in red, in homage to the publications of the Communist International, out of my bag.

Cimino immediately recognized the homage: "Like Marx!" he exclaimed. He had scarcely begun reading, holding a pencil he had taken instinctively from his pocket, when I understood that he intended to read my screenplay in its entirety. To read it there, on that bench, next to me.

Cimino turned the pages, he underlined lines, and of course I didn't say anything, I barely dared to look at him. I simply drank the vodka and from time to time passed the bottle to him. When I lit a cigarette, I offered him one, which he accepted without a word. And, while glancing at the script to see where he was, I tried to imagine what he would think of a certain scene, a certain line.

In the end, I expected nothing. I knew very well, I told Pointel, that the screenplay was nuts, and that Cimino, or any other filmmaker, would never film it. I even began to think that I hadn't written it for that. *The Great Melville* was above all a mystical poem on evil. The fact that it was being read by the director of *Heaven's Gate*, and precisely by him, already seemed incredibly lucky. More than lucky: it was a victory. And more than a victory—a consecration.

The mere fact that Cimino was reading my screenplay endowed it with that secret glory mentioned in the Scriptures, which is enough to change a little message into an ardent speech, a book of nothing into a breath of truth.

I thought that after such a declaration Pointel would stop listening to me. He had to have known for some time that he wouldn't get anything from me or my screenplay. I wasn't, nor ever would be, "bankable"; and even while admitting that he was curious about what Cimino had thought (and that he had vaguely wondered if that "brilliant fucked-up filmmaker," as he called him, might find my screenplay interesting), why would he continue to spend his time and his confidence on a guy who was happier living writing rather than turning it into business? A guy who had no ambition—or who put it in a place that society didn't recognize.

But I was wrong. Pointel was listening to me. He had put his phone away. He was really interested in what I was telling him. I don't think he cared as much as he used to about making profitable films. He was seeking to *see something else*, something that one rarely sees on screens, something that, perhaps, didn't exist, and of which some of us are the involuntary bearers. He explained all this to me when I apologized for my digressions. The deer had changed him.

I was at that point in my drunkenness when someone talks inside you. It was not just the names that were appearing from all sides in my head, but a euphoria that was opening up that limpid region where words discern a treasure. And that evening, it seemed to me that while talking I was joining that flow that makes up *The Great Melville*.

Macron came up to our table: would we care for some dessert? Pointel just wanted to keep drinking, and so did I. We ordered two glasses of Armagnac.

I needed to go to the toilet, but if I got up, Sabbat would again leap out from under the banquette to follow me through the restaurant, jumping for joy, and that I couldn't allow. I might be protected by Pointel, but Macron would not allow another infraction to go by unchecked. What to do? I couldn't very well ask the waitress to watch my dog while I took a piss. As for Pointel, with his crutches, he could scarcely stand. There was no way he would be able to hold Sabbat. I already imagined him falling down in the middle of the restaurant, the mauve tie in his hand, screaming in pain because of his leg, while the handsome, the great, the stormy Sabbat went from table to table looking for me, upsetting everything in his way.

I absolutely had to avoid such a catastrophe. So, as quietly as possible, I removed myself from the banquette in slow motion so Sabbat wouldn't perceive any change in weight. Then I went around the table on tiptoe, my finger on my lips to alert Pointel. I even avoided turning around. Just glancing at Sabbat might wake him up.

I went to the restroom. The two Mustaches had left. Walking in front of the restaurant entrance where Macron continued to greet new customers, I caught the eye of a woman standing on the sidewalk, smoking a cigarette and talking on the phone, crying. Her very white face contrasted shockingly with her black hair and her red lips. Her elegance clashed with the other diners, with the evening, with the venue. She wore an ermine jacket, a dark red skirt, and apple-green high-heeled sandals. I noted the details of what she was wearing because the colors dazzled me. I stood there, looking at her, like an idiot. She turned toward me, and our gazes met a second time, tighter than a hug. Her eyes were coppery green, her face, bathed in tears, was as regal as a royal kingdom.

All of a sudden I lost my balance and fell down, sprawling on the floor. It was Sabbat. He had leapt up on me, and now he was licking my cheeks. Now the lovely crier was smiling: she found my predicament funny.

Miraculously, no one came to scold us when I returned from the restroom with Sabbat. He immediately went back under the banquette, without anyone noticing him—and Pointel, who indeed seemed tipsy, was patiently awaiting the rest of my story while drinking his Armagnac.

18

CHARLES REZNIKOFF

Night was falling softly over New York, I told Pointel, and the sky was pink, orange, red. I was going to miss my flight, but I was happy. After all, it's not every day you have a meeting with the greatest filmmaker in the world.

Cimino read half of my screenplay, up to page 312, and he turned the corner down on the page, then, closing the manuscript, smiled at me. It was a smile as wide as it was enigmatic. Since Cimino was wearing his immutable dark glasses, I couldn't see his eyes. And no doubt, to understand the meaning of such a smile you had to see the eyes. But that smile reminded me of something, it reminded me of another smile, that of the Angel of Reims, that sculpture on the portal of the cathedral of Reims that is also called the Smiling Angel. I didn't have time that evening, since Cimino was getting up to throw out the empty vodka bottle, to explore the resemblance in more depth, but just as the Angel of Reims through his smile opens up to the infinite beauty of time, which he not only accepts like a child, but which he enlarges through his tenderness, it seemed to me that in smiling Michael Cimino was also carrying out the simplest of acts, that which goes beyond words: he was saying yes.

He would continue reading later. Could I leave him this copy? Night had fallen on the river, a streetlamp lighted the deserted walkway. We smoked a cigarette in silence, then Cimino suggested we go have dinner. There was a restaurant on Mulberry Street—the Paesano—according to him the last trattoria that had resisted the commercialization of Little Italy, where you could eat spaghetti *allo scoglio* as firm as that of Naples. But before that we had to: (1) find more vodka, and (2) take a ferry to Ellis Island, because that's where everything begins and everything ends, declared Cimino. And that evening, such a visit was even more important, it would be in homage to my screenplay, he said, because in fact, the main scenes of *The Great Melville* take place there. Cimino offered to be my guide— we would go down the river at night to the door of the New World, and in that journey he would be my Virgil.

A boat floated by through the colors of the dusk toward Ellis Island. The water reflected its movement, as if it were sending signals to those who hoped to set off for happier lands. Did they provide the name, or did they say that that land doesn't exist?

I thought of the last scene in *Heaven's Gate*, desperately sad, when, after the landowners have massacred the immigrants, Sheriff James Averill is standing on the deck of a yacht, in Newport harbor. The light is blue and orange, he is wearing an elegant jacket. Lost illusions open onto an endless sadness.

I took a gift for Cimino out of my Strand bag. I gave him the book by Jean-François Lyotard on Malraux which I had bought in Paris especially for him, a book that would perhaps help him in his research for the adaptation, announced a long time ago, of Malraux's *La condition humaine*.

And then he began to dig around in one of his Strand bags. He, too, had a gift for me, a book by a writer he had immediately thought of when I had called him and we had talked about suicide and revolution. Reading the first part of my screenplay had, he told me, only confirmed his hunch that I would like this writer. "Do you know Charles Reznikoff?" I didn't. "He's a sort of dry Faulkner," he said while looking for the book in his bag—"a Jewish Melville without a whale, if you see what I mean."

"A Jewish Melville without a whale," that intrigued me. Cimino really had a way with words, and that's exactly how I made the great Melville talk in my screenplay. Because after writing novels as fundamental as *Moby-Dick*, *Pierre, or the Ambiguities*, and *The Confidence Man*, without anyone taking the time to read them, Melville, completely broke—and having lost all hope—had to force himself to take a job in the customs office of the port of New York, where, for nineteen years, he led the existence of a spiritual bachelor, one of those men deprived of their god, as all of us are more or less today through our solitude, we who see only from afar, from very far, as in a former dream, as in a mirage invented through frustration and nostalgia, the foaming of an enormous mammal which, they say, would swim among the ocean waves with frightening grace, the purple and golden solemnity of a living basilica, and that the tales heard in our childhood invite us to consider as a treasure that would contain the universe as well as the abyss, like the immaculate name of a god who is gone, like the sparkling testimony of exile of the Shekhinah, in which the people of Israel see a divine presence.

There it was. While telling Pointel about my encounter with Cimino, I was exulting. Because that evening, in New York, I kept being fed by exhilarating things, things that didn't come simply from Cimino himself, which didn't belong to him, but which I had projected onto him, and which in some way had been illuminated through our encounter.

My good old name madness often tricked me. Sometimes it made me go astray, and since my arrival at Bofinger's, it's true: I was on the verge of exploding. But sometimes, too, that madness was propitious, and the names acted like keys. Then the walls fall, the labyrinth becomes an illuminated land, and I see behind faces, behind movements, behind every word, the sign of a truth going by.

By exercising my mind, the shape of that sign becomes clearer and clearer. It undulates like the crest of a mountain, and forms a land of triangles that, by adding one to the others, deliver you a message.

That happened to me one night at the Petits Oignons, and since then the occurrence has expanded. While talking to Pointel, I distinctly saw a new triangle appear:

ANGEL OF REIMS   ELLIS ISLAND

CIMINO

Then a second, shining with a mystical light:

MELVILLE   REZNIKOFF

SHEKHINAH

By adjusting those two triangles in my head, a story was written, flowing from a source—one that even launched me toward the source. Was I delirious? My mind was spinning around inside the names, that's all. That's when I was happy. It is there that experiences which flood your mind take place. You feel like you're bathing in a lake. The universe could not be more expansive.

I told Pointel that Cimino had then taken a few more books from his bag, works on the Indians, it seemed, and that he handed me *Testimony* by Charles Reznikoff, a compilation of lines taken from thousands of court proceedings, notes from trials, testimony that detailed the crimes committed in America between 1885 and 1915. Those lines, which Reznikoff worked into poetry, formed little scenes of blank verse, in which the violence of America was exposed. There were saloons, cotton plantations, the railroad, gallows—no heroism.

"The Goldhunters," "Machine Age," "Whites and Blacks," "Thefts—and Thieves," "Labor Troubles": those were the chapter titles—conflicts, more conflicts, thousands, millions of conflicts, and just as many deaths. We were in the criminal platitudes of origins, he told me, in the America of the ordinary massacre. It was the opposite of the Promised Land, and that opposite already foretold of our era of extermination.

Ever since Cimino had introduced me to Charles Reznikoff, I told Pointel, I read absolutely everything I could find of his in French translation, and in particular *Holocaust*, a small book written entirely from snippets of testimony by Nazi leaders during the Nuremberg Trials, and by Eichmann during his trial in Jerusalem. Reznikoff hadn't added a word, he simply put down on paper the words of the torturers as they were. And those words, because they were exclusively matter-of-fact, neutral—the words of engineers of death—made for the most horrifying Kaddish to the memory of the exterminated European Jews.

This summer, in between watching films, I would read *Holocaust* and *Testimony*, the two great books by Reznikoff, over and over. I would go from one to the other, forcing myself to read with Cimino's eyes in order to guess his favorite passages. And when I had read thirty pages of *Testimony*, in which the Indians, immigrants, blacks, and more generally the poor, kept getting killed, I went to *Holocaust*, in which the disappearance of the Jews was measured on each page: precise, incomprehensible, terrifying.

A strange book took shape in my head, arising out of that dual reading. A book in which crime assumed an autonomous shape and began to function all by itself, without any human, even the most infamous, playing a part. A hecatomb intended for the human species, as if History moved exclusively out of crime and *for it*—an avidness that nothing could satisfy would be rewarded in blood, in continual sacrifice intended for no god and which was performed without ritual. All those that the world had excluded—the Jews, the Indians, all the pariahs of Western society—were destined to feed that huge sacrificial bonfire. And from the depths of such a nightmare, help would never come, because it was impossible to save humans from an interminable, senseless crime.

And in fact, I said to Pointel, Charles Reznikoff's work, like that of Michael Cimino—and even more radically (without the melancholy that afflicts Cimino's films with a love of failure)—touches on a fundamental element that is related to taboo, and perhaps comes from something that hasn't been thought of.

I told Pointel that the works dealt with the *repressed Western absolute*, which made him wince. Reznikoff's book only marginally interested him.

"Because there is something no one wants to hear, because it seems excessive," I said, while drinking a final drop of Armagnac. "It's the link between the criminal history of Europe and the massacres on which America is founded. Of course, we do speak of the extermination of the Jews in Europe, and of the genocide of the Plains Indians, but who reveals the *link between them*? Who dares connect them? Who, through those two events, can fully realize how criminal the Western world truly is?"

Pointel interrupted me. He mainly wanted to know what Cimino and I had done—did we go to Ellis Island? He was really interested, he told me. No one had truly filmed that place. You saw it a little in Elia Kazan's *America America*, and in Coppola's *Godfather II*, but there is no film that focuses on it seriously. But Ellis Island was a place where they *selected* human beings, he said. There could be no more political or contemporary subject. All the security madness in which we are trapped today, that global obsession with control, and those quotas that prevent immigrants from escaping their plights, wasn't all of that born there, on Ellis Island, in the first decades of the twentieth century? What we call "Ellis Island," wasn't it a program whose most villainous principles are still being applied in Europe? It was a pity that Cimino wasn't making any more films, Pointel said, because only he would be able to show the madness of that human stockyard.

19

BLOOD FROM
THE BEGINNING

In fact, Cimino is still making films, I said. I realized it that evening when he began to talk about details. In the end, when the stories are done, he had said, when there is no more story, there are always details—only *they* survive. "The details," he had said to me, while looking far out over the Hudson, "are sparks of truth."

Then he stood up. "Listen to the details!" he told me. And then, with his frail silhouette and the quickness of a mime, in a few seconds he had metamorphosed the space we were in. The walkway had become a theater stage—a film set—and he began to tell a story of workers who labored in a cotton field.

"Let's call it *Blood from the Beginning*," he said, smiling.

He told—rather, he *acted out* —the story. As soon as he introduced a character by name, his hands sculpted a figure. Each character spoke through his voice, bringing to life the great fixed sky of Missouri, the dust on the verandas, the calloused hands of an old woman, the drops of blood on a leather apron.

Pivoting around, with a slight movement of his fingers or a simple rictus, Cimino revealed a character and launched him or her into the story. His arms moved, forming circles, spirals, his hands shaped the space, they cut into the matter of the world, and then, coming together at right angles, they created a frame.

Cimino *was directing*.

A crushing sun, he says. Late morning at the end of June, a harsh light. A dozen black women are stooped over in a cotton field. A few men are bent over, too. They are white, wearing uniforms of faded gray.

A tall, thin guy, his forehead covered by a dirty lock of blond hair, with a shirt of heavy fabric buttoned up to his neck, goes by on the road. Cimino says that softly, and you can see the blond guy, see the road. They both seem to come from very far away, from a drought that precedes them.

Cimino says that the guy is called Coleman and is pushing a cart with his load of furniture. Cimino is precise, he counts the items: a bed, a chest, a table, four chairs and a pile of clothes—all of that forms a pyramid, he says. You can see the pyramid. He says that a donkey is pulling the cart—you can see the donkey, as gray and dusty as the men bent over in the cotton field.

One of those men (Banks, a skinny young farmer) observes Coleman, who is climbing to the top of the cart, standing on the furniture, trying to untangle a telephone wire that is hanging above the road. The wire is caught in the furniture, it's going to be pulled down. With three movements, Cimino cuts a piece of space. He brings that wire, the road, the cart to life.

Banks advances, he wants to help the guy with the furniture. Woods, his foreman, shouts for him not to move. He points the rifle that was cradled in his arms. In fact, the white farmers are prisoners, they are harvesting for old Craig, a rancher who owns the entire county and whom the sheriff obeys. And Banks obeys, bending over the cotton again.

The black women are not prisoners, Woods leaves them alone, they are old Craig's slaves (and because they are slaves, they aren't watched). One of them—Gussy—sees Coleman lose his balance and fall off the cart.

The donkey is chewing a piece of cardboard, he doesn't move when Coleman's head hits a rock about three meters in front of the cart. Gussy wipes her hands on her apron and walks toward the body lying there.

The telephone wire that is barring the road continues to swing in the wind.

Gussy shouts, "He's dead!"

Woods, the foreman, turns around for a moment and looks at the road. Banks jumps on him from behind, cracks his skull with a rock, and takes the rifle. He runs to the cart, unhitches the donkey, and jumps on it, shouting. The donkey, frightened, takes off, while the other whites run to the cart, throwing the furniture on the ground, pulling open drawers and finding a watch and the framed photo of two children.

A shot is heard. It's Banks, farther away behind the field, who shoots the donkey, calling it a son of a bitch.

The sun has turned. Banks bursts into a house; a heavy woman with a long skirt and apron is sitting at a table in front of a bowl, the rifle doesn't frighten her. He says he's hungry, she answers this isn't a restaurant. Banks points his rifle: "Make me some eggs, quick!" A fat guy in his underwear, barefoot, with a mustache and a very hairy torso, comes into the room and hits Banks on the head with a hammer. It's Charlie Dade.

A group of scantily dressed young women come in, their breasts are heavy, indolent, some are entirely naked under their housecoats. They are terrified by the pool of blood that is expanding on the kitchen floor. "Get back to work," Charlie says.

The woman in the apron (she isn't named) pulls off Banks's shirt to mop up the blood, then makes some eggs for Charlie, who eats them while looking at the body. Egg yolk runs down his lips, he laughs to himself: "A real asshole, that one!" he says—and then he takes off Banks's boots while he continues to chew.

PROBLEMS

Charlie Dade puts on Banks's boots and walks around the kitchen proudly. Two kids walk around the body and sit at the table to eat some eggs. They are blond and dusty, like the donkey, Cimino says, and like the prisoners' shirts.

"You should go meet your daddy at the station," says the woman, "he must already be waiting for you."

They have caught a baby alligator in the river, and they are holding it with a rope and driving it with a stick. The tips of their fingers are bloody because the alligator bit them.

"Get rid of that nasty thing," says the woman to Charlie, pointing to the baby alligator, which is licking the pool of blood next to Banks's cracked skull.

"Lord! That's nasty!" cries the woman.

Charlie pounds the alligator with his hammer. The children run off crying with their little cadaver.

"Shit, the rifle," says the woman, "where'd it go?"

On the road, the two children find the dead donkey, then the overturned furniture, the scattered clothing. The sun is beating down, they are wearing broad-brimmed caps and one of them has the rifle slung over his shoulder, like a hunter. The alligator is limp in their arms, and they're going to give him a decent burial. The black women are working in the cotton field in the distance. A little girl who has been working among them approaches and strokes the already stiffening baby alligator. Policemen are standing around a body hidden under a cloth. One of them,

173

Craig's son, gestures to the kids to come over: "Is this your pa?" He raises the cover, the two children kneel in front of the body, the alligator falls into the sand. The cop sees the rifle. "Shit, that's Woods's rifle!"

Cimino stopped there, took a bow. I applauded. He burst out laughing: "There you have it—that's Reznikoff. It would make a great film, wouldn't it?"

I said to Cimino that he didn't need to film it: it had just taken place, I had just seen it, that evening, sitting on a bench, an unreleased film by Michael Cimino. I had attended a living projection of the film that needed neither screen, nor theater, nor any image. The images were the voice that produced them. That evening I understood, thanks to the last great living filmmaker, that film needed nothing other than words, and that in the end, the images that continued to be produced were superfluous, too much, they distracted us from what is being said when speech really speaks, when it really takes place, like that evening, on the banks of the Hudson. I understood that Cimino had never stopped making films. In truth, he made them all the time, he had just made one in front of me, he had found the means to *no longer stop making films.*

Instead of filming, a filmmaker spends his time looking for producers—setting up a budget. And Cimino, more than anyone else, had never stopped waiting and looking. But that evening, I understood that he was pretending to wait and to look, he was pretending to prepare his adaptation of Malraux's *La condition humaine*. Because in fact, he was no longer waiting or looking for anything. Not that he had given up on filmmaking, as some had lamented while secretly rejoicing that he was *finished*. On the contrary, he had begun to direct in his head all the films he dreamed about and he told them in detail from morning to night (to himself and to others). And the films that Cimino brought to life with simple movements and simple words, like a showman, like a magician, were connected to that original point—well before the invention of the magic lantern—where the image didn't exist. There has never been a need for the screen, and in the future there would still be no need. Words would be enough, they are what make us see.

In any case, the days of films projected on a screen would soon be over. Already, fewer and fewer people were going to movie theaters, and soon no one would leave their house. Cimino had anticipated this evolution of films, he knew that with the Internet images were born from anywhere without belonging to anyone. He knew that the images that jump around endlessly on the planet had not only aged film, but would soon cause film to die.

I then understood Cimino's smile. It confirmed his confidence in the names and the details. It seemed to say that it only took a dusty donkey, a baby alligator, and some fried eggs for a story to be created. And that making a film, like writing a book, consists of finding the story capable of saying the names and listing the details, that is, one that can make all the flesh there is in the world enter into our hearts in order to keep that story alive or to give it the life it no longer has. To save, for example, as Reznikoff did, the population of the dead in America between 1885 and 1915, or like David and Solomon to save the Hebrews in the time of the Alliance by offering them an existence in a land by way of a language that consecrated them. Cimino's smile said: "What joy to live in a story." And then he said: "Come on, let's go."

20

THE STATUE OF LIBERTY

And then we took a boat ride. Cimino slipped my screenplay into his Strand bag, we took a taxi to Battery Park, at the very bottom of Manhattan, and from there we got on the ferry.

It was the last one of the day. We hesitated to take it because it didn't stop at Ellis Island or Liberty Island, it just made a turn around the bay. But Cimino didn't want to give up. It seemed to him, given where we were, that it was absolutely necessary to see Ellis Island, even from a distance. It was the place, he said. That is where we had to go.

We had bought a bottle of vodka and some cigarettes. The sea air was intoxicating. I was euphoric. Cimino looked around the dock somberly. Did I know that there had been more than three thousand suicides on Ellis Island? When you entered the main hall, the one with the metal bars, he said, you were watched from a gangway by immigration doctors who were looking for trachoma. You climbed the stairs, full of hope, dragging your sorry belongings, you hadn't yet crossed the first barriers, and already one of the doctors decided that you wouldn't get through the door.

It was impossible to escape the Eye, Cimino told me. "My family went through there. All those who one day had been watched by that Eye continued to be pursued by it. It never left you. And myself, I never stopped feeling its weight. The Eye of America, watching you, judging your every action, evaluating each of your thoughts—and proclaiming, with the calm impunity of those who have a place at the top of the stairs: *he is not one of us.*"

Before boarding, we had to pass through a security check, as at the airport. The prospect of being searched was nerve-racking. I had thought that Cimino, with his indomitable nature, would be a problem, and that we would have difficulties, but no, he was wisely obedient, and even at ease, with the security procedures.

When he emptied the contents of his bag, an ebony box drew the attention of the security personnel. They asked him to open it, and in a bed of dark red velvet appeared a silver medal stamped with the face of John Wayne, whom Cimino admired (it was, moreover, John Wayne who had given him the Best Director Oscar in 1979 during a ceremony which, Cimino pointed out, proved to be the final public appearance of the favorite actor of the "great John Ford," whom he believed, he said to the customs officers, was the best American filmmaker of all time).

The medal made the agents laugh, and it was an opportunity for each of them to tell the others what his favorite western with the great actor was: Cimino praised *The Searchers*, in which, according to him, John Wayne had abandoned the baggage of a tired hero, which Clint Eastwood would soon continue to carry in his stead, and simply transported with him the emotion of mourning, and with that mourning the end of a certain America.

The wind was blowing on the sea, the cool air overwhelmed me. When we approached Ellis Island and the old red brick buildings appeared, I shivered with horror. That impeccable abandon, that perfect calm in the site's decommissioning, resembled those of the Nazi camps I had visited in Poland.

What was Cimino thinking about? He was standing at the stern of the ferry, his elbows leaning on the rail, his chin resting in the palms of his hands. With the lights of the night, his face seemed astonishingly young, feminine, melancholic. From time to time he brought the little bottle of vodka carefully wrapped in a paper bag up to his mouth. And his dark glasses, the cap that covered part of his face, the gloves he had put on since we had gotten on the boat, created a sort of carapace, as if he were trying, still and forever, to escape the Eye.

And it's true that at times, like that evening, he managed to extract himself from humanity. He then seemed closer to a jaguar than to any human being.

I said it before: my screenplay *The Great Melville* took place in large part on the tip of Manhattan and on Ellis Island. I had never been there, but I had imagined that this territory where Melville had worked toward the end of his life when he had become a customs inspector was cursed. In my screenplay, his ghost returned to haunt the place, he appeared in the stairways of the greeting center, in the hallways of the Federal Immigration Bureau, like an old Shakespearian king whom one constantly ignores, and who persists, after his death, to exert a sovereignty that no one ever recognized in him when he was alive.

In a scene that Cimino had read on the bench, Melville's ghost reshaped the crew of the whaler in *Moby-Dick*—the *Pequod*—which is made up entirely of pariahs. And all those damned of the earth pooled their energies together through an insurrectional crossing of all the oceans. From port to port, as refugees would come aboard, and mainly those from countries at war in Africa and the Middle East, the ship would assume the role of a new Ark.

Cimino contemplated the Statue of Liberty, which stood out in the night with the solemnity of a monument to the dead. Kafka was right: she wasn't holding a torch, but indeed a sword. That of Justice? The statue's disturbing look, rather, said that the sword was for cutting through lives.

I had joined Cimino at the railing and told him that the death of the stars that he saw stuck on the American flag was already inscribed here in the blind look of that big woman. "I hate this big false Lady Liberty!" he said to me.

He handed me the bottle of vodka and took the ebony box out of his bag. He handled it carefully, and when the box was open, opposite the medal, there appeared, nestled in the same red velvet fabric, a revolver.

It shone in the night, like a silver jewel. Cimino took it out and pointed it at the Statue of Liberty. I don't know if he intended to shoot, nor even if the revolver was loaded, but in the sky of New York Michael Cimino's gesture formed a perfect line, like an arrow flying through space. His arm outstretched in the sky mirrored Lucifer's action when he breaks his chains above the Place de la Bastille. It was a clear gesture, filled with meaning, whose significance seemed immemorial to me. And even if Cimino laughed, even if for him this gesture was primarily a joke—and also, he confided to me later when we were having dinner at Paesano, to celebrate my screenplay—he was performing a very ancient ritual act, that of a follower protesting against a false god, because in a certain way he was extinguishing the flame, like the sailor who off the coast of Piraeus had proclaimed, "The god Pan is dead!"

In every gesture there is the hope of an outcome, a sign that one has entered a world in which something is going to be offered. In Cimino's gesture—under the guise of the joke of a wild child—I saw the binding of the very ancient tie that unites the sky and the earth, a tie that is constantly undone and that we restore in the time of a flash, when we trace, even unwittingly, an invisible line between two fires. It is the gesture of the sacrificer: between the flashes of silver of the revolver and the flame of Liberty a path was lighted. And probably the one who passes between the two fires receives what is given only very rarely—he is connected to the gods.

That's what I had always liked about Cimino—he had fire. In him, everything was connected to the sacred. His words, his choices in life, were inscribed in the spiritual. Even when he drove his old Ford on the roads of Montana going to his ranch, even when he took the elevator in a European palace where he had been invited to present a retrospective of his films, even when he did shots of vodka on a bench on the Hudson River with a French writer, that man *was on fire to the tips of his fingers.* He lived according to his gods. And at every moment, he saluted them.

For men like him, every moment has two sides, one that turns toward the profane world, where dollars represent the kind of life we can live, and one that turns toward a stranger, most likely invisible, world where mystery, rather than calculation, dictates truth.

And when a cop came running over from the bow of the ferry yelling at Cimino to drop his gun, he got rid of it. It had fallen into the water in a little burst of silver, and now in its place, through an act of prestidigitation whose secret he alone knew, he was holding the John Wayne medal. The cop didn't understand, he had begun to throw Cimino up against the rail to put handcuffs on him, but you can't handcuff someone because he is holding a medal of John Wayne, much less because it was creating silver sparks in the night.

Cimino laughed. "What the fuck are you doing?" asked the cop. "I'm conjuring the evil Eye," Cimino replied, pointing at the statue whose head, lit up by projectors, was that of a monster.

Walking away, the customs officer shrugged his shoulders. Cimino couldn't stop laughing. The reflections on the water created stars. The stars were really there—not on the flag, not in the flame of Liberty, but on the water.

21

ARTEMIS

It was 11:00 p.m. The restaurant was emptying. Pointel and I were about to leave when a woman came up to our table, wearing a black cape, with long red hair and smoky glasses with Bordeaux rims. She was accompanied by the young woman I had admired earlier, the one who was crying on the phone.

It was amazing how the woman's ermine jacket looked like Dalmatian fur. I had the impression that someone had skinned Sabbat. I even leaned under the table to verify that he was indeed there. And in fact, he was sleeping curled up, with all his fur.

Pointel and the redheaded woman kissed each other warmly on the cheeks, they seemed to be close friends. Pointel invited her to sit down at our table with her friend. The redheaded woman said they were going to dine at a table reserved upstairs, but she would be delighted to sit with us a few minutes and have a drink. Pointel immediately ordered a bottle of champagne, which Macron poured for us, smiling obsequiously.

The young woman in ermine didn't say a word, she sat on the banquette next to me and began to tap out some texts very quickly.

The redheaded woman sat next to Pointel, and that's when I recognized Isabelle Huppert.

"He's just met with Michael," Pointel said to her.

"Michael?"

"Cimino."

Isabelle Huppert looked at me carefully. Pointel told her I was a writer.

"Have you published any books?"

"What about you, have you been in any films?"

While sipping my champagne I realized it was one glass too many. I was about to slide into a second round of inebriation, heavy and unpleasant, the one that puts emotions to sleep and leads you into darkness.

I was looking at Isabelle Huppert, and several scenes from *Heaven's Gate* came back to me—scenes in which her youth lit up the film with a tragic sweetness. She was quite simply extraordinary in that film. Childlike as an Amazon, professional as the owner of a brothel, both wise and intrepid. By herself she gave the film the color of lost love.

There's the scene where she and Kris Kristofferson have just made love. Isabelle Huppert is holding a sheet she has wrapped around her chest, and then, coming out of the stable, Kristofferson is holding the bridle of a magnificent black horse that he's giving her, and behind the horse, carefully hidden in the shadows, there's a gorgeous carriage coated in black varnish in which Isabelle Huppert's tears of joy are reflected.

Another scene, infused with a warm and golden light like a Renoir painting: she is bathing naked in the river and comes over to rest her head on her lover's shoulder while he is sleeping, his head leaning on the wheel of the carriage. When you've seen that scene, you know what peace looks like—it's a face sprinkled with freckles and drops of clear water.

There were moments, sitting in Bofinger's, when I passed out for a time. I no longer distinguished the outlines of the faces around me. Oblivion was beginning to swallow the smallest detail. In its place, there floated snippets of Cimino's film. Part of what I'm telling in this chapter and in the following ones, comes from what the young woman with the white face, whose name was Léna, Léna Schneider, later told me.

I wanted to talk to her, but I felt that I was going to start babbling. Her face had something severe and attractive in it, like a blank page, it made me want to dive into it. On the banquette, our bodies were almost touching, and my arm brushed against hers. It was good to be a bit ill at ease, I even felt joyful. Indeed, despite its having inevitably turned into a bender, this birthday evening was a success. I was meeting people, you could even go so far as to say I was alive.

Isabelle Huppert and Pointel were talking shop. I didn't really understand. She had just gotten back from a shoot in Tokyo where she had worked on a somewhat unusual film which would not be distributed in theaters, but seen only on the site of a private club specializing in depravity. She had had a great time, and now she was in rehearsals for a few performances of an odd version of *Phèdre*, which she had played onstage at the Odéon Theater, and which the director wanted to perform in Berlin.

There was also the question of the Carax film—apparently, she was a member of the cast. She asked Pointel if the film was going to happen. He explained how difficult it still was today to say the name Carax in the French film milieu. A bit like Cimino, Carax had really gotten into trouble during the filming of *Les Amants du Pont-Neuf*. The budget had been exceeded so enormously that no one wanted to work with him anymore, much less invest money in his new projects. Carax and Cimino, said Pointel, were the last poets of an era in which the current film industry was no longer interested. It was no longer interested at all in film, only in itself. One might have thought that their names could have been beneficial to the industry, since Gaumont had at one time financed Godard's films. But no, the industry no longer even pretended that it was interested in anything at all, especially not in art.

And so Pointel was looking elsewhere, far from the European networks. There were huge possibilities in Hong Kong and Shanghai, where Leos Carax was considered a hero. He was also looking in Qatar, where a lot of money was circulating in support of art, culture, and film.

Isabelle Huppert said that Carax was sending her kilos of books on finance, and audio files in which, in his dragging voice, he recorded his reflections on the world crisis and the way in which he saw her playing the role of the president of the International Monetary Fund. Those recordings, she said, were extraordinary. In them he described the life of the one he called "the president of the World of Finance" in the smallest detail. Her diet, her sex habits, the newspapers she read…everything was spelled out, with crazy minutiae, as in a novel.

Isabelle Huppert exuded a charm that could seem harsh, but when she smiled you saw on her face that troubled tenderness that belongs to solitary types, and which they are used to keeping to themselves. Those who live in a desert have acuities that guide them brutally. The rest of the time, they meditate. Because she expected nothing from others, she could be interested in them freely. And so, outside of filming, she lived in a weightlessness that made improvisation—and encounters—possible.

She and Pointel seemed to be laughing about all that craziness into which they had embarked. They had clearly already made movies together, international productions, which they remembered more or less fondly, but the prospect of the Carax film delighted them. They were like two adolescents who had found the perfect game.

Léna Schneider didn't participate in the conversation. Like me, she was happy to listen. I observed her furtively: her pretty white face was concentrating, and in spite of my intoxicated state, I was full of desire.

Sabbat suddenly appeared. His head came out from under the banquette, he put his paws on Léna's thighs, and she seemed delighted.

"Is this your dog?" she asked, caressing his head.

"No, he's not mine, it's a complicated story. What about you," I said, pointing to her fur jacket, "is that Dalmatian?"

"It's fake," she replied, smiling. "I didn't kill a dog to make a jacket. You know that Dalmatians are sacred animals? They are the dogs that Pan offered to Artemis. A Dalmatian never really belongs to its master, but always to the goddess of hunting."

"Are you the goddess?"

Léna's laugh was crystalline, childlike. I thought about her tears on the phone, about the obvious passion that animated this woman.

"Artemis," she said, "is the daughter to whom her father gives everything. He says yes to anything she wants, he spoils her. She wants to own all the mountains, she wants the bow and arrows, she wants several names, a torch to hunt wild beasts, and an escort of nymphs."

"Why several names?"

"To defy her brother."

I didn't understand.

"Apollo. Can you imagine having Apollo as a brother? When Artemis, still on Zeus's knee, asks him for several names, it's because she knows that true privilege resides less in knowledge—reserved for Apollo—than in multiplicity. Each name is a piece of that spark that lights up the sovereignty of the god."

I asked Léna what Artemis's names were.

She then smiled and put her finger on her lips to indicate silence. It's an ancient gesture, the gesture—precisely—of a goddess. I had advanced too quickly. One doesn't ask such a question. Either one knows the names or one discovers them oneself.

Those who have witnessed mysteries laugh and cry, like everyone (in a few minutes I had seen Léna do both); but they alone can explain the nature of their laughter and tears, because they live an autonomous life, a life that unfolds through signs exchanged behind the veil, a perfect life.

This woman had a mystical honeycombed head, I was sure of it. She knew that truth isn't exchanged like a cultural commodity on which one places a label and a price. And then I really liked that sharp—serious—way she had of talking. Through her voice, I sensed a landscape of fire and lunar woods. I saw her moving at night between the

leaves up to the slow waters shadowed by willows and pop-
lars. Very old lines came to me, ancient lines upon which
theophanies occurred: *she has gods in her blood*, I said to
myself, she is sheltering a solitude that renders her open to
the mysteries.

In short, Léna Schneider was having an effect on me.
Even if I was drunk, it was a good beginning.

She explained that she was the director of the Musée
de la Chasse et de la Nature. There was a new exhibition
opening at the museum, one devoted to an American
photographer—a certain George Shiras, who, almost a
century ago, had found a technique to photograph animals
at night—and she had invited Isabelle to see the exhibition.

That photographer, she said, was a hunter from Wiscon-
sin. It was pretty amazing and, at the same time, logical.
He had replaced his rifle with a camera. At the moment he
took the photo, he was still and forever a hunter, the way we
all are when we look for the perfect image. "You know," she
said to me, "that during the hunt, the hunter gives a name
to his prey, the name of a beloved person, which bestows
good luck on the hunt and makes it a successful sacrifice.
Well, I think it's the same thing with art."

22

THE FIRE EXISTS

In the end, the women decided to eat at our table. Isabelle Huppert ordered raw meat, a sort of steak tartar, without any preparation, which was served the way she asked for it—in a shallow bowl—and which she ate with stupefying gusto.

As for Léna Schneider, she ordered the Casting of oysters that I had wanted earlier in the evening. They brought another bottle of champagne, and all four of us toasted the hunt, goddesses, and strange film directors.

Pointel had started to droop a bit while I was telling him my stories, but Isabelle Huppert's arrival had given him a second wind, and even a sort of youthful vigor. When our two friends had finished eating, he suggested that we go have a drink somewhere else, but Isabelle Huppert thought it was very comfortable where we were.

"How is Michael?" she asked.

I told Isabelle Huppert that Cimino had become a sorcerer, a shaman—someone who makes film live in the invisible. I described his odd appearance, and the trick he had played on the officer on the ferry, but I couldn't say if that story of the Statue of Liberty that I told in detail amused her or upset her.

She had seen him again a few years ago on the occasion of the release of the extended version of *Heaven's Gate*. She had accompanied him to various cities in Europe and remembered that he would get up at dawn to read Tolstoy. "Two hours every day with *War and Peace* were better than any exercise," he said.

She also said that he had one of the most absurd diets, which considerably complicated his schedule. For example, since he drank mojitos in the morning, and in the hotels the bartenders didn't arrive before noon, they had to buy all the ingredients so Michael Cimino could make his drink himself and could drink as much as he wanted starting at 8:00 a.m.

I really liked the affectionate way Isabelle Huppert talked about him; and even when she mentioned his "bizarre way of dressing"—the brown leather pants, the cream-colored Stetson, and the gloves the color of fresh butter—it was always with tenderness: "He has this fabulous elegance," she said, "that something extra, difficult to define, that some great artists have, a sort of nobility. It's a pity he's not directing anymore," she added.

I said, on the contrary, Cimino was the only one still creating films. Thinking about film. Living film. He and Godard, let's say. Cimino no longer needed a screen to accomplish his work, and, in a sense, the screen had even become an obstacle to his visions. Because he was above all someone who had understood that the fire had disappeared, I said. The fire that animated people no longer existed, Cimino knew this. He was even one of the very few who knew it.

There was the fire, and that fire went through Robert De Niro, Christopher Walken, and Meryl Streep in *The Deer Hunter*; it wrapped in its immense flame the world of immigrants from Eastern Europe in *Heaven's Gate*, and carried them up to the final massacre. "It gave its will to live, its intensity, its innocence to Ella Watson, your character," I said to Isabelle Huppert, "but today, the fire has gone out, like a dried-up spring. Whereas all civilizations were founded on the idea of guarding the fire, our civilization is one of extinction. It is horrified that the fire burns and has seen to it that the fire dies—so we live among the ashes."

Isabelle Huppert didn't agree: "There will always be those who will manage to light that fire for us," she said. "The world, I don't know, maybe you're right, maybe it is dead. But there are incredible people, unique individuals who exist, and they are not necessarily the most spectacular. Some of them are discreet, they don't express themselves much, and sometimes they are even imperceptible.

With them, believe me, your fire, even if it is invisible, will never go out."

There was no one else in the restaurant. The waiters had cleared the tables and were setting them for the next day. The perfectly ironed white napkins in each plate sealed an absence that extended to the entire room, earlier so loud and now sad, as if the shadow that had fallen over us and wrapped our still lighted faces with little wavering rays had come to take refuge here, in the hollow of each plate, for the night. The glass dome, the aquarium, the lamps with yellowish shades had also taken on more serious tones, as if their colors *were falling*. They had gradually abandoned their brilliance to enter one after the other into sleep.

I already knew that I wasn't going home. The night called me, it seemed to me that it had been welcoming me for hours and wouldn't let me go. I was going to pass through this night, and too bad if I ultimately collapsed. Sometimes, weakness and euphoria coexist.

Macron came up to our table. We could stay as long as we liked, the restaurant was honored to host such a great actress, he said—and he offered to pay for our after-dinner drinks himself.

Isabelle Huppert graciously accepted the offer. She asked for a pear liqueur; Léna Schneider, a vodka; Pointel and I had another Armagnac.

Isabelle Huppert was about to propose a toast, raising her glass, in which sparkled the final glimmers of the evening, when she suddenly pointed her finger at the window: "Look!"

We turned our heads, even Sabbat, whose muzzle was resting, aligned perfectly, on Isabelle Huppert's outstretched arm: she was pointing at a figure outside, on the sidewalk, a guy who was decked out like a cowboy with a Stetson on his head. We burst out laughing, and Isabelle Huppert's finger continued to linger for a long time in the air after the figure had left, as if the shadow that had invaded the large dining room was also beginning to weigh down our already sleepy movements.

Sabbat had sensed that we were going to leave, and he was getting jumpy. I got up and went out with him for a few minutes. He was mad with joy and began to run up and down the sidewalk among the oyster shells.

I lit a cigarette. The wisteria, on the other side of the street, seemed fresh, welcoming, stuffed with that dark humidity into which it feels good to slip. Ultimately, it *was* possible to live. With stories, with all the stories contained inside stories, we advanced casually from one island to another, we made the beginning and the end join, and *we felt better.* In the worst case, I could always go into that greenery over there and gather my wits under that cascade of flowers. There wasn't just my room—there were other places where I could breathe. The movement of this evening gave me some hope.

Because, to be honest, I had left the restaurant primarily to look at Léna Schneider. Sitting next to her, I wasn't able to see her face very well, and now, through the Bofinger window, in spite of the darkness that surrounded her body as well as those of Pointel and Isabelle Huppert, the circle the three of them formed looked to me like an incandescent hearth, as if it were they who were lighting the night. The light that continued in spite of everything to shine in Paris came from those three people leaning toward each other. Isabelle Huppert was right, the fire exists, it was there, that night, on the other side of the window.

Léna straightened up on the banquette, smiling, started laughing, and the moment she raised up her hair to put it in a bun, I saw her neck. Her face, suddenly freed, offered itself to me, vertical and nervous like that of a white horse.

Her face was huge, as wide as a glacier. I really felt it would take me years to explore a territory whose whiteness seemed even more brilliant than when I saw it for the first time. A milky whiteness, like the snow whipped by the wind on the prairies of the Western Indians, which, like mother-of-pearl, took on bluish tones in which violent emotions sparkled.

I came closer to the window to see better. It was as if I were being sucked in by that face. I thought of the immaculate dress covering those who are saved in the Apocalypse of John, that vestment illuminated by white flames that shoot the chosen up to the throne on which the Very Holy is sitting, and which wraps them in a froth of glory. At the same time, while contemplating Léna Schneider's face, I developed the hard-on of a wild dog.

She turned toward me, we looked at each other for a long minute. It was as if she could see my erection. I was going to change into a deer, probably I was one already, and antlers were growing from my head, like a forest of phalluses on the verge of erupting, which would soon be cut off by the dogs.

She smiled at me, the others turned toward me, Isabelle Huppert gave me a little wave, and Sabbat and I went back in to them.

23

THE VISCONTI HORSE

Isabelle Huppert was telling us about the filming of *Heaven's Gate*. In April 1979, she had scarcely gotten out of the airplane when Cimino picked her up in a Jeep and drove her to a real brothel in Wyoming or Idaho, she couldn't remember which. Anna Thomson, the actress who later played in *Sue Lost in Manhattan*, who became a close friend, was with her. They drove for hours, the mountains stood out in the sky with their snowy peaks, and while driving, Cimino explained to Isabelle Huppert, sitting next to him, that he didn't want anything left to chance. Since she was supposed to play the madam in a brothel, she had to learn how to act like a true madam.

"Will I have to sleep with the men?" she had asked, to tease him. In the back, Anna held back her laughter, and Cimino's assistant was uncomfortable. As for Cimino, he didn't flinch, he was always serious—sweet and serious. He told Isabelle Huppert that it wouldn't be necessary, she just had to observe.

"Anna burst out laughing then and while the jeep was traveling over the sparkling landscape of the Rockies, I wondered," said Isabelle Huppert, "if I hadn't made a huge mistake in letting myself be dragged into the madness of this man who for weeks constantly called me at night on the phone without for a moment thinking of the time difference. I had accepted the part immediately, but he continued to call me. His idea was that a film does not start just on the first day of filming. It's a whole experience, 'The *Heaven's Gate* Experience,' as he called it. And when at three in the morning the phone rang, I knew it was him, and with an enthusiasm that made it impossible to scold him, he would tell me about an episode in the history of America that would clarify his project, or would explain to me in detail a fundamental scene whose psychological implications I could contemplate later, if I wanted. Except that after the call, it was impossible to go back to sleep. Cimino had really succeeded in getting me excited, I was overexcited, and when I arrived a few hours later on the set of Pialat's *Loulou* after not having slept, and Depardieu arrived looking terrible because he had spent the night bar crawling, Pialat yelled at us, saying with actors like us we shouldn't be surprised that French film was fucked, and Depardieu and I would run away to the makeup trailer to hide our laughter.

"At the time," said Isabelle Huppert, "Michael wasn't at all the man he is today. Of course, he was already a genius, *The Deer Hunter* had changed the history of film, and he was already obsessive, a complete fanatic, with a vision of his film that was as precise as a poem and demands that the producers saw as arrogance. But physically, he was another man. Roundish, with shapeless sweaters and a thick mop of black hair. And he spent his time eating. They said crazy things about the filming. They said, for example, that he had kilos of cocaine delivered to him by helicopter. But it wasn't drugs that interested Michael, it was food. All those stories were invented by producers because the studio was ruined. They passed the buck to Michael, it was in their interest that he be seen as a megalomaniacal tyrant, an uncontrollable junkie.

"From the window of my room, on the second floor of the little brothel, I could see the Rocky Mountains and the huge sky that was always blue. There was a big yard behind the house, very green, with fruit trees, cherries, I think, and a large apple tree standing alone in the middle of the grounds. And, in the neighboring field, a horse with a chestnut coat would stick its beautiful red head out over the fence.

"The 'girls' were very young, they were in their early twenties, like me. There were five of them: Abby, Kirsten, Jamie, Kay, and a fifth whose name I don't remember. They were very hard, both ultraviolent and vulnerable, completely messed up. One of them, Jamie, was already destroyed from drugs. She was gorgeous, but her teeth were rotting out.

"The one who was responsible for managing the brothel, and whom I was supposed to be inspired by for the film, was Emma. She was a bit older, around thirty, had distant origins in France. That's probably why Cimino had chosen her.

"Every girl had a horrible story, and I was ashamed of my very easy life. They spent their time in shorts and flip-flops in the yard, stretched out on ratty sofas, listening to the radio, leafing through magazines, and smoking cigarettes. Emma would burst into the yard when a customer asked for one of them. They then had to go get dressed quickly in a trailer, put on a dress, some makeup, get rid of that look of a lost girl of Wyoming, and race up to the second floor.

"In the beginning, they were pretty mean to Anna and me. The situation was intolerable. We were staying in a hotel, like tourists, and were very comfortably documenting their suffering. Anna and I felt terrible. We wanted to get out of there. We said to each other that our presence was a way of legitimizing slavery. So we kept apologizing, and that made it worse, because they thought we were pitying them.

"They never spoke about the customers. Once, the youngest one, Kirsten, a pretty black girl, very slender, whom I liked a lot, told me things I don't want to repeat.

"Anna and I spent our days roller-skating so we could get ready for the big dance scene in the film. There was an old record player, and in the evening, around the barbecue, we listened to entire operas of Verdi, or Fleetwood Mac, country songs, drinking sangria under the big apple tree. It's funny, I can't remember the girls' faces, not even Emma's, even though I talked to her a lot. The images I have, almost forty years later, are those of the horse and the apple tree.

"I remember a legend, I can't remember if it is Indian. A horse hides its head underground for a year and becomes a tree. If you bring your ear to the trunk, if you have enough song in you to listen to a tree, you can hear it galloping. I think that that apple tree had some amazing things to tell. It galloped underground, and its roots deepened the history of the prairie. And it's funny, you would have thought that the horse was trying to get close to the apple tree because it was always there, next to us, its head over the fence. Maybe it was listening to the inner galloping of the tree.

"The horse's name was Visconti. I thought it was Michael who named him that, because I knew that *The Leopard* was his film of reference, but no, the girls called him that, they had found that name for him. Anyway, they didn't know Michael, they had never met him. When we got there he just talked quickly with Emma, everything seemed to have been sorted out in advance by the studio.

"I spent hours on the phone. You couldn't hear a thing, the connection was terrible. What's more, the phone was mounted on the wall, it was in the entrance, right at the foot of the staircase that went up to the rooms, right where everyone went by. I would sit in the rocking chair, and I spilled out my distress to my friends in France, who told me to get out of there, return to Paris, what was that film, anyway? I got yelled at by Emma because I spent all my time on long-distance calls, so I gave her all the money I had on me, spending hundreds and hundreds of dollars just like that.

"And then, I remember, I called Godard. I was supposed to start work soon on *Sauve qui peut (la vie)*, and I was dismayed because I was perhaps going to stay locked up in this place for months, Michael hadn't told us anything. He was great and called us every evening, but it was always to make sure that Anna and I were indeed immersing ourselves in our roles. In any case, production had been so delayed that we wouldn't be shooting anytime soon.

"And so, I told Jean-Luc Godard where I was, I told him that I was living in a brothel, and that enthralled him. 'What luck!' he said. Luck my ass, there were girls there reduced to such misery, and he thought that was great because *Sauve qui peut (la vie)* was a film about prostitution, my role would be that of a prostitute, as in Michael's film, and Godard told me: 'Don't move, I'm coming to see you.' So he took a plane, and came to the set, not the brothel, but there, in the fake town that Cimino had had constructed, and that's how the two greatest filmmakers in the world met.

"On one of the last evenings, it was really hot, we had set out lanterns and made a ton of sangria that we drank with a ladle. We ended up getting really close to the girls. I say 'girls' because that's what they called themselves: 'Come on, girls!'

"With the heat and the sangria, I was dripping sweat, I went upstairs to change. I had put on a pair of jean shorts and a little red-and-white-checked shirt tied at my navel. I was on the stairs, barefoot, and a man walked up. I can still see the scene: the guy said something nasty to me, he blocked my passing and started rubbing up against me. I screamed. Emma arrived right away. She talked to the guy, who must have been around sixty, a sort of businessman, she told him I was her cousin, he blushed, as red as my shirt, then he mumbled, he was afraid of a scandal, and he apologized.

"I immediately told the girls about it, and they burst out laughing. That evening, Anna danced barefoot under the apple tree in a little black dress, like Marilyn Monroe in *The Misfits*, and then we joined her. And while we were dancing, the horses came up to the fence. There wasn't just Visconti and his wild mane, but a little herd that surrounded him: black, cream, champagne, six or seven horses that put their heads over the fence. Maybe they heard the galloping of the apple tree, as we heard it that evening through our drunkenness and our joy, and maybe they came to share in that drunkenness and joy. In any case, all of a sudden, without any coordination or discussion, we all bent down, one after the other, and slipped through the fence, we each jumped on a horse, and started galloping through the night, first through the field, then farther, much farther, to the mountains that went on forever."

Part Three

NAMES

24

DR. BACH'S ELIXIR

The light woke me up. My head was pounding and my mouth felt like it was filled with cotton. There was grass everywhere, I was wallowing in it, I was shivering. When I tried to get up, I heard a voice: "Stay where you are!"—an unpleasant, grating voice from behind me.

I couldn't turn my head. I felt heavy, and I needed to take a piss. The voice continued: "This is an apartment building, it's private property!"

Couldn't they just leave me the fuck alone? I just wanted to get my bearings. And my back hurt, I couldn't move, maybe I had broken something.

I made an effort. Everything was murky, damp, dirty, but the voice was getting closer: "Get out of here, now! I'm calling the police!"—then I recognized Mme Figo.

I got up quickly. The trees wavered in the pale colors and I saw the little yard turn around me, the acacia bushes, the trunks of the plane trees, the lamps on the grass that were still lit up like huge mushrooms. I was home, on rue de la Py.

Mme Figo's silhouette was moving in front of the glass doors, with her set of keys hanging around her neck, wearing her ever-present smock, hands on her hips, full of disgust for this drunken bum sleeping in the yard. I knew that was her obsession: she saw bums everywhere. According to her, they had gotten the entrance code for the building, and at night they slept in the stairs, dirtying the common areas with their cheap wine and their oily cans of food.

So, wavering, I tried to smile to reassure her, I even said, "It's me!"—and she cried out.

Since she was running toward me, I thought she was going to hit me. But she helped me sit down and wiped my face with a handkerchief. Her gestures were very gentle, caring, I didn't understand, I closed my eyes.

"Are you ill? What happened?"

I discovered my face was bloody. I also had blood on my hands and on my beautiful pearl-gray shirt, which was ruined. Or was it wine? I always manage to spill it on everything.

Mme Figo straightened up, suspicious. "Have you been drinking?"

I answered, timidly, "No, no."

She assured me it was blood, I had been mugged, was that it? This city is really not safe, with everything that's going on out there, you shouldn't stay out so late. She took me by the hand and led me into her *loge*.

In the bathroom mirror, I looked at myself. What the hell could I have done last night? I couldn't remember. While I was rinsing my face with water, Mme Figo answered the phone.

"I don't know," she said. "I don't know where he is, I don't keep track of my renters... Why don't you just call him... I don't know anything, I'm not his secretary..."

I thought she was talking about Tot—or maybe about me. I had a fleeting vision of the two Mustaches, and a shiver went through me, my clothes were wet, I was going to get sick. In the mirror my head looked huge. I didn't have any wounds, but a really ugly face, that of a morning spent in hell. My mouth was swollen, my eyes empty, my hair dead. My hands were black from the dirt, and the tips of my fingers hurt. I tried washing them with soap, but the dirt wouldn't wash off.

Leaning over the tap to drink some water, I raised the sleeves of my coat and, on my left arm, there was a name and a number written in black marker: Léna 06 67 87 41 59.

Out of reflex, I checked to see if I had my phone. Outside coat pockets: nothing. Inside pockets: nothing either. In the lining? No. And the pants pockets? Front, back: nothing at all. I was panicked. Not only had I lost my phone, but I didn't have my wallet, either. I looked again: coat, pants. Nothing. There was my notebook, still impeccably rolled up in the lining, there was my empty flask, a pack of crushed cigarettes, a lighter, but no telephone or wallet.

Mme Figo was waiting for me in her *loge* with a cup of tea and a slice of her husband's favorite cake, a specialty from Porto, with jam. I scarfed it down. Mme Figo's solicitude was disturbing. It seemed too easy, even seductive, to collapse there, in her *loge*, like a wet mop. But I wanted above all to go home, so I toughed it out.

She had me sit in her desk chair, asked me to check to be sure nothing was broken, suggested I go in any case to the emergency room of the Tenon hospital, the one right behind our building. I agreed (I already knew I wouldn't go). I felt completely drained, on the verge of collapse, the way you are when you've had too much to drink, tears in my eyes. I could have lain down on the ground, like a dog, and slept at Mme Figo's feet, nice and warm, all day long. But I thought that in spite of her change in attitude toward me, I shouldn't go overboard.

"What happened?" she asked.

I didn't dare tell her that nothing had happened. I had just drunk like the damned, and spent the night shouting with joy to the point of collapse. She really thought I had been mugged, I didn't want to disappoint her, I just said that I couldn't remember a thing.

"You're in shock," she concluded.

I took another slice of cake, which I swallowed with a big glass of water. When Mme Figo took my hand, I thought it was out of tenderness. I held her hand as if I was going to kiss it.

"Your keys," she said.

"Huh?"

"They're still in your apartment, right? Take the spare and bring it back right away, I'm counting on you, okay?"

Before I left her *loge*, she asked me if I had started making plans to move.

"What do you mean, move?" I asked.

At that, she became annoyed. I saw she was forcing herself to hold back her anger, given the circumstances, but I was, in fact, impossible, irresponsible. On October 1, I had to vacate my apartment, and it's true, I had forgotten. Probably Mme Figo thought I didn't give a damn, which is wrong. I was just distracted. Aside from what related to my research—my *great research*, I said to myself, laughing inside—things flew right out of my head. In any case, I wasn't going to start thinking about moving. I wanted just one thing: to sleep.

As soon as I walked into my apartment I ran into the kitchen to take some aspirin. The clock read 6:20, and even if I was staggering, even if this day turned out to be difficult, it was a pleasure to come home. I was going to stay in bed. Too bad about the phone, too bad about the wallet. In any case, there wasn't much in it, just a ten-euro bill and my credit card. But since the card was completely maxed out, it was pointless to get upset. I could take care of all that later.

It was dark: the bulb at the entrance and the one in the kitchen were out, I had never bothered to replace them. I cursed my negligence once again, but the darkness didn't bother me, and it was pleasant to move around in my place as in a cave: nothing divided the shadows, solitude filled the corners; it is possible that an apartment without light suits the mind better: the night lives there as the mind does.

That morning my room smelled like rain and wet soil, but maybe I was the one who smelled like that. I got undressed quickly, threw my clothes on the floor—coat, shirt, pants, socks, and underwear—forming a little pile in the entryway.

The fridge was empty, I had absolutely nothing to eat or drink, not even a bottle of water. I drank directly from the tap. It was really absurd, this mania I had of living day to day, without planning for anything, allowing myself out of negligence to slip into the void. This morning, that void jumped out at me, and I was no longer sure it was so adventurous, even so spiritual, as I had liked to believe. It sometimes seems to me that I deliberately cast a spell on myself, just to see if I would be able to break it. It's my way of living this novel.

I sat down completely naked on the kitchen stool to watch the Efferalgan tablet dissolve in a glass of water. In general, the freshness of the fizzing did me good. I just needed to put my head over the glass to feel the benefits of the paracetamol. But that morning, I didn't feel anything at all. My headache was so powerful that it wasn't going to go away for a day or two. I had really drunk too much with Pointel. I didn't have the strength to list all the alcohol that we had mixed—and hadn't I continued drinking with Léna? Having arrived at a certain point, desire takes the shape of an enigma: what burns without being consumed? I ran after that fire. Even if it couldn't be found, it nevertheless seemed to me that every night brings me closer to it and that a truth shimmers around it. Excess doesn't lead just to disorder: I like how it also scorns misfortune. A momentum travels through tormented shapes; I recognize my needs in it.

There was a little bottle on the table that belonged to Anouk, Dr. Bach's elixir. It was a potion made in the mountains of Auvergne that helps overcome the most diverse emotional states. She had told me about it somewhat skeptically, had left it here the night she had slept over, and for weeks the little bottle had sat here and I hadn't noticed it.

Dr. Edward Bach categorized emotional states into seven large groups, each of them giving rise to a variety of elixirs whose essences were adjusted to the specificity of the imbalance of the soul. Anouk had listed each of those groups carefully, and while the Efferalgan tablet was dissolving, I found the list on the back of the bottle. There was disappointment, sadness, fear, doubts, indecision, lack of confidence, and lack of interest in life.

It was undeniable that Dr. Bach had put his finger precisely on the most salient ills that affect the human species. In that regard, he promised that his elixirs "would act in depth through their subtle nature to help reharmonize your psychic and energy balance."

Personally, I was all for it—especially this morning.

This particular little bottle was intended specifically to fight against disappointment and despair. It was written right there. Dr. Bach had even added: "For the fatigue of the brave who never give up, but who don't recognize their limits."

That was exactly what I needed. I'm the guy who doesn't recognize his limits. But really thinking about it—and God knows that that morning, reflecting was difficult—in my case, it was less a matter of courage than of intemperance: I simply couldn't stop.

Dr. Bach promised "release and regeneration" to the one who chose to take this elixir. I didn't hesitate, I needed that new balance. I was in such a state that I could have drunk any potion at all, even the least effective. And what particularly pleased me with Dr. Bach's elixir was that there was cognac in it. A very small dose, alas: twenty milliliters, or just about nothing, but it was still something. I opened the bottle, and while hoping "to relax," while praying to be "regenerated," and for my "psychic equilibrium" to be "reharmonized," I drank down the entire bottle. Mixed with the Efferalgan, one never knew, Dr. Bach's elixir might perhaps perform a miracle.

25

THE WORLD IS FULL
OF TEETH

I looked around my room. I was overjoyed to see the swallow and the manuscript, my pile of books, papers, my wonderful sofa bed. Even if I had been away only one night, it seemed I had been separated from them for too long, I had abandoned the only place where I could truly breathe, had deserted my solitude, the point I consider a north star.

I was still drunk and felt heavy, my head ached, but it was a pleasure to be alive, to have the night in my blood and to have lived while laughing. Yes, I had so much night in me that I felt like Don Juan, whose immense thirst both tormented and protected him. People are almost all fossilized—not him.

There are some who ask for signs, others seek wisdom. As for me, I let myself be led by a movement that is unconnected to reason. Is that madness? I don't think so. Even in the throes of intoxication, when everything is blurred—when my mind is erased—I can see a ray of light. It is a discreet ray, but it shines enough to light a path.

So it doesn't matter that it's impossible to receive what is given in that way, it doesn't matter that this chance is only expressed through a light that hides away. By staying in bed in my room, it always seemed to me that I was opening myself to that truth which can only be expressed through silence. Does this tale bear a trace of that? I hope so.

I was warm, I got up and opened the glass doors. Immediately, with the cool of the outside air, my blood began to move. Seeing the sky grow lighter when you've spent the night partying makes you feel like you might disappear. You could evaporate like the mist. The oblivion of the night is heady, but that of the morning hopes for deliverance. I stared up at the sky, whose layers of gray looked like they would never dissipate. In such thickness, I recognized my head in the grips of the migraine. A few windows were lighted in the building across from me, the morning was trembling in an indecisive light, the leaves of the plane trees awaited their share of the light, and for the time being, nuances were sleeping. I was waiting for the Efferalgan to take effect. Maybe I should take another? Every time I bought some the pharmacist insisted I should take only one tablet every six hours. But I didn't give a shit. He wasn't the one whose head was exploding. If it didn't start improving, I would take another Efferalgan, then I'd make some coffee, and when my nausea had calmed a bit, in the afternoon, I would go to McDonald's at the Porte de Bagnolet and have a Big Mac, as I usually do when I'm suffering the effects of a hangover.

Taking advantage of the open glass doors, my forearms resting on the balcony rail, I breathed in the air of the yard and imagined my face plunging into the freshness of the acacias. From my third-floor balcony, I noticed Mme Figo talking with a neighbor below. Mme Figo's face was turned toward me, and she was calmly looking at my cock.

It looked like she was signaling to me. The inner court-yard was silent. You could hear the faint chirping of a bird that had come out of its thicket. Hardly raising her voice, Mme Figo said, "The keys!" I went to get them in the entrance, and, still naked (I was aware, but in slow motion, paralyzed by the drunkenness), I threw them out the window. I had aimed for the grass, so they wouldn't hit her on the head. They landed at the exact spot where Mme Figo had found me earlier. She picked them up and added them to the ring of keys she wore around her neck. The woman she was talking to, an old woman with a shopping cart, looked up at me, her mouth open.

I lowered the shades and lay down. The TV screen was empty, but in the darkness it diffused an opaque ray that gave a lunar relief to the shapes in the room. Even if the TV wasn't on, there was always an image—an *empty image*—a surface where absence was concentrated. The most pro-found darkness can be pierced without the help of any light, or only the one that animates the blackened sky—even the shadows glimmer. But can one kill an empty image? I once dreamed that the sky had disappeared, that it had been absorbed into a point and then erased. That the sky was only a point, nothing seemed more unbearable. That is, however, what you experience in front of an empty screen. You melt like black paint into the image that absorbs you.

My head hurt too much to watch a film, so I watched the empty screen. Rather, it watched me. Its presence filled the room, it threw reflections on the minuscule space I had managed to create between the wall, against which my head was resting, and the TV. It is in that position, immobile, lying on my bed like a dead body, protected by the row of papyri and the swallow and the box with the manuscript, that I usually entered the vertiginous state into which the names placed me.

I hesitate to write this, since I have been so vigilant in keeping such a confession secret. However, I must: why did I undertake this chronicle of a period of my life if not to share mysteries with you? For several years I have been living in different dimensions at the same time. If the life of an intoxicated obsessive might possibly turn me into a character in a comic novel, another life is superimposed on that one, which is just as solitary, but more mystical, in which the search that animates me requires less picturesque figures. At night, when I achieve calm, I begin to meditate.

Primed by intensive film watching, at any moment of the day or night, my thoughts, all of a sudden, are readjusted. A suppleness is freed in them. And then an orchard emerges, first in my head, then in the entire space of my room, where names begin to float around, one after the other, names that I've written behind me, above my head, on the wall hidden by the pillow. Two names rise up in the air, you might think they were dancing. They meet, a third joins them, a triangle is formed—I'm rapt.

That's what happens. Whether it's noon, 9 p.m., or four in the morning, I say names, they come together, time opens up.

With my hangover, the names would probably not show up. I waited for the Efferalgan to take effect, closed my eyes, but I already knew that I wouldn't fall asleep. The images of the night were coming back to me.

I smiled when I thought about my encounter with Léna, and despite my headache, I savored it. It was good to have met a woman like her. How long had it been since that had happened? When I closed my eyes I could see her imposing body, I heard her voice, and, becoming excited again, I felt the softness of her hips, her lips, her first name that carried with it an entire distant world, that of the East and of sparkling autumns, also one of wild animals, hunting, and sacrifice.

It had been a crazy night, and as usual, because of the alcohol, I had forgotten entire chunks of it. But some moments rose up with ardent precision, and now, with my eyes open, I relived them. I saw Isabelle Huppert tell us goodbye and get into a car whose door was held open by a chauffeur. I also saw Macron shake Pointel's hand, and Pointel walk away on his crutches, his phone stuck to his ear. I saw us, Léna and me, smoking a cigarette. There was Sabbat, who was sniffing in the gutter shaking his tail. There was a mountain of empty oyster shells on the sidewalk. Léna's telephone had begun to ring and she told me, "I don't ever want to talk to this guy," and she gave me the phone.

It was a man's voice. "Who are you?" he asked. I answered, "Michael Cimino." "What?" "Cimino." He got mad: "Who the hell are you? Give me Léna." "That's not possible." "Why not?" "Sometimes, things are no longer possible, you used to talk, and now you don't." "Did she tell you that?" "She didn't tell me anything, but I understood." He shouted, "Let me talk to her, asshole!"

I closed the phone and gave it back to Léna: "It's done." The phone rang again, but Léna turned it off. We ran to the Place de la Bastille, Léna stopped a taxi, Sabbat jumped into it, the driver protested: no dogs. But Léna promised more money. I can still hear her saying a name: "Chez Orphée," then she read the address from her phone: "seven, rue Fontaine, near Pigalle," and we set off.

The name of Orpheus slipped into my head like a portent. It seemed that I, too, was penetrating underground, that night we were going to visit the dead. And now that name was turning above my sofa bed. It contained everything and lit up the others, which began to sparkle in the dark like little lights.

What happened down there? I remember a little—flashbacks. At the entrance to the nightclub, there's a crowd: guys, girls, really noisy, with beers, spilling out onto the sidewalk. I think I see the two Mustaches in the crowd, but Léna leads me to a hidden door. A bouncer is sitting on a bar stool. This is Chez Orphée.

There's a line to get in, I'm reeling, a guy comes up to me saying he knows me, he says he is the "Mayor of the Night," and that I had autographed one of my novels for him during a signing in a bookstore a few years earlier. We get in, thanks to him. The bar is very long, I order vodka-gingers, we drink, we dance, I can't remember if we kiss—I think so. It's spinning between the bar and the smoking room, the dance floor is tiny, Léna's body undulates like a wave of laughter, we drink more and more, it doesn't stop.

There is a blank—a hole of several hours—then I see myself in the street, with Léna, arm in arm, I'm looking at my phone: it's 2:20 (I can still see the time exactly). We arrive at the Musée de la Chasse et de la Nature, we cross a paved inner courtyard, there is a glass door, Léna turns the key in the lock, we go in.

Everything is dark. Shadows run along the walls, as in a cave. A winged shape moves, it seems to be flying above our heads; the semidarkness cuts reliefs where the wings grow. I think it's a bat, stiffen, and lower my head, trip on a step and fall to the ground in the entrance where a mirror throws back a grotesque image.

The fall does me good. I sober up a bit. With the light from my phone, I can see steps, a ramp. I stand up, and on the steps, through a little skylight, stars spin around in their blue-black shine. I regain my wits, but I have trouble climbing the stairs. The reflections vacillate, I have to hold on to the railing.

In this bluish halo deer heads are floating, the head of a boar whose yellow eyes are staring at me, and there are gaping mouths filled with teeth hanging all along the walls.

Léna is ahead, at the end of the gallery, she signals for me to follow her, and again I lose sight of her. A polar bear looks at me, standing on his hind legs, huge, his mouth open, his claws reaching out toward me, and everywhere there are heads of does on the walls, victims of massacres, their fixed stares shining in the darkness like pearls.

I take a corridor on the right, and stagger in a darkness in which green slips in with the black with the beating of wings. An odor of ivy, fresh, mossy, lightens the darkness. I advance, my arms out in front of me, like a sleepwalker.

And suddenly there are peacocks, foxes, wolves, lynxes, a multitude of beasts that are running in the corridors. I speed up, and now, with the reflections from the glass cases,

I discover, hiding in the corner of a room, ready to tear me apart, a snow leopard, a panther, a rhinoceros, crocodiles.

I had lost my bearings. Drunkenness runs in front of you, and while laughing you run to catch it. The darkness gallops through forests. Since that night, I've been existing in the company of wild beasts, and my vertigo is so enormous that while hunting on the edge of a cliff, drool on my lips, I get ready to leap off onto my prey. I jump off the cliff along with the prey and fall into the void, as in a conscious dream.

Léna had disappeared. She had told me about the apartment at her work where she lived. It was on the top floor, under the roof. I thought it was crazy that she lived here, in the midst of these animals. At Chez Orphée, she had told me that she would sometimes walk around at night with a candle in the corridors of the museum. I could imagine her traveling through the museum slowly, as in a dream, with the pallor of the Gradiva.

Since that night with Léna, every moment for me has become an awakening, or a falling asleep. It's night, it's day, any time. But I should probably go back even farther, to the very beginning of this story. I don't know if my eyes are open or closed. Did I dream of Cimino, New York, the Statue of Liberty? Did I really see those films where the deer were offering me their heads? And Tot, Anouk, Pointel, Isabelle Huppert—do they really exist?

I'm lying on my sofa bed, near the Porte de Bagnolet, surrounded by my fetishes, and at the same time I'm with Léna, moving in slow motion around the rooms of the Musée de la Chasse. At the same time, I am deepening an age-old experience and am advancing through a labyrinth. I approach a wall, I go away, I want to pierce that veil where images cover my name. Something will always escape humans, and will never stop burning without us— our desires come from a distant night.

I try to understand. While going deeper into the Musée de la Chasse et de la Nature with Léna, a thought came to me. If today I try to clarify it, I discover the degree to which it protected me. How can that thought be named? Does it even have a name? I can only formulate it by the term "miracle." I believe that if you don't hope for a miracle, nothing will ever happen. If you don't seek a miracle you become servile.

Yes, from the beginning, I've believed in my star. Throughout this journey, during which my solitude has only deepened, in spite of mistakes, in spite of bad choices, I have at every moment been that star (I imagined myself to be), I, who have never stopped believing in the existence of a spark, a divine dust in madness, even if madness doesn't know the word for terror, and recognizes neither joy nor pity.

Léna appeared in a doorframe, then immediately disappeared. Going into a dark red room where a boar was looking at me, his tusks pointing violently toward me, I found her ermine jacket lying on the ground. Then, between two doors, her skirt. Farther still, her blouse.

Was she going to lure me to the ultimate source, to that lake located in the heart of the woods where, uncovering her breasts, revealing her thighs, her pubis, the goddess, with her fingers slipping into her vulva, sprinkles the voyeur hiding behind an oak tree, and with that gesture puts him to death?

Too bad if I was going to get whacked. I had an enormous hard-on, as in a dream. I had to catch Léna.

I kept going through rooms, losing myself in the corridors of that museum where the animals just kept on coming: the polar bear, the deer heads, the boar, every time I went by, opened their jaws. Advancing in the darkness, seized with anguish, drunk, staggering, I thought of a line written in my special notebook, a line that I had on me, rolled inside my coat, that came from Bernard Lamarche-Vadel, a writer friend who had killed himself a dozen years before, whose name accompanied me since the beginning of this adventure and in whom, because he was clear, because he had guessed a pyre at the heart of the human species, I saw a great priest, maybe even a sorcerer: "The world is full of teeth" was the line.

I began to repeat it, probably to conjure away the anxiety the night and the shadows had induced: "The world is full of teeth," I said, and I began to laugh—"The world is full of teeth," isn't that an incontestable truth?

The lines you repeat are like prayers thrown against a wall. You think they'll break, but it turns out they break through the wall, it turns out the visible reaches the invisible—and they coincide.

And then I heard Léna's voice. Was she beckoning me? I had the impression she was humming, it was dissipating, I couldn't hear very well, but it sounded like the melody from *Don Giovanni*: "È aperto a tutti quanti, viva la libertà!" (It's open to all—long live freedom!).

I finally ended up in a sitting room where the smell of a storm was floating in. The space was big, walls paneled in wood, a bit of light came in from an open window in front of which a curtain was moving.

A large stag with a red coat was staring at me silently. Its antlers were rising above its head, a huge crown whose points were entwined. It looked like it was wearing roots on its head. And between its branches, its palms, and its antlers, there unfolded a sephirotic tree similar to the one whose branches drawn in red marker shine on the wall of my room, right behind my head.

Léna's voice invited me to enter. In the darkness, I could first make out her eyes, then her hips, her brown hair, the whiteness of her curves; little blue rays of light shone above her breasts. She was lying down, naked, on a leather couch.

She was still wearing her apple-green high-heeled shoes. I knelt down between her thighs. She laughed. I slipped my fingers into her mouth, into every orifice. I heard her heart beating everywhere, and while she was sucking on my index finger, a flame rolled in my belly, alive, on fire, and clear.

Opening my mouth between her legs, I rediscovered that forgotten emotion that bathes embraces. I had on my tongue some of that dew, that powdery rose that is mixed with your saliva when you're in love.

Léna took me in her mouth with a very sweet smile. We didn't talk. I had begun to tell her stupid little things, but she put a finger on my lips. She was right: making love interrupts the flow of words that society inflicts upon us.

In just a few seconds I came. When I was in her mouth, I wanted to be inside every part of her; it would have taken several of me to quench my huge desire for Léna.

The deer was watching me, and a new triangle formed in my head, composed of Léna's face, her cunt, and the antlers of the big stag. Between the three there flowed a breath that transmitted a new ardor; and even though I had drunk liters of alcohol, my desire was alive, with a violence that the presence of the animals had fueled. If a new god settled down somewhere on earth, and if he sent letters in his name to be disseminated among humans, they would be found between the legs of a woman and the antlers of a deer. And it seems to me today that those letters are turning around in my head while I'm writing these lines. I can still taste Léna, and can also see the antlers. The one who can decipher the whispering between a woman and a deer will hear the name of a god.

Léna led me into a little room whose walls were covered in black silk. The ceiling was full of owl heads; their blue eyes stared into the dark as if the moon had become ferocious. What was opening up between this woman and me? What had just been murmured between our lips? What is that raw song that ripples with so much clarity? Léna stuck her finger in my anus while looking me in the eyes, she got on her knees to suck me, then turned around, her arms leaning against the wall, holding her ass tightly. She was laughing, her polished nails shining in the night, I slid into her from behind. Through our pleasure *the animals flooded in*, they cried out in our throats.

26

THE THREE YUCCAS

"Holy shit, the dog!"

I leapt out of bed. Where was Sabbat? I ran into the kitchen, into the bathroom, I opened the door to the toilet, I even looked in the closet and under the bed, but I knew Sabbat *couldn't* be here. Yesterday I had gone out with him, and this morning I had returned without him.

It was obvious, it was logical, it was clear: I had lost the dog.

I must have gotten up too quickly. With the hangover burning my head, I lost my balance and fell down. My head hit the little stand in the entryway, and I blacked out. The TV started up by itself. Tot had explained that the neighbor below me had the same remote as mine, so when he turned on his TV he also turned on mine. And it happened that I was sometimes awakened in the middle of the night by a film that, flooding me with its light, exhorted me, as images do, to join it.

That morning, it was Marlon Brando's face that rose up out of the darkness of the room, and I was immediately caught up in my passion. I had left the DVD reader on, and it was the end of *Apocalypse Now*, the moment when the shaved head of Colonel Kurtz invaded all the darkness into which the film slowly introduces you—when the head alone takes the place of the war.

It's a terrifying moment that takes your breath away, that punctures the simplicity of our presence and turns us invisible, in that darkness where, without even knowing it, our movements unfold. We have gone up the river, it's the end of the river, we arrive in the land of the dead. Bodies are piled up around a temple, bodies are swinging from the branches of the palm trees, bodies are rotting in the moss. The voice of Colonel Kurtz rises up from the depths of the temple: "I have seen horrors," he says. Lying on his pallet, in the shadows, he pours water on his head while reciting verses by T. S. Eliot:

> *We are the hollow men*
> *We are the stuffed men*
> *Leaning together*
> *Headpiece filled with straw. Alas!*
> *Our dried voices, when*
> *We whisper together*
> *Are quiet and meaningless*

As wind in dry grass
Or rats' feet over broken glass
In our dry cellar

We're in a monk's cell, in the chapel of a pagan warrior, in the inner sanctum of a god who kills. There are books on the table: the Bible and *The Golden Bough* by James Frazer; there is a typewriter, a sheaf of paper on which he writes down his curses against America, against politicians, against the army.

"It smelled like slow death in there," says the voice-over: it's the slowness of the sacred, a dampness of darkness where ritual and killing are the same.

One day—and it doesn't matter if it's the day after a drinking binge, in the pathetic and teasing vapors of a hangover—you understand that the ritual is endless. You understand that even if no one is attending it, even if the vases are empty, even if the officiant is missing, *it is taking place.* You have the revelation that the gods are dead, but the ritual continues. You sense that a watermark is being created in silence over the history of men.

What is holding the world together? I've read that it is the breath of children reciting the alphabet. And so if the children stopped reciting letters, our heads would explode, like that of Colonel Kurtz.

At the moment when Captain Willard raises the machete to cut off Kurtz's head, a buffalo is sacrificed, the curtain is torn, the blood of the buffalo and that of Kurtz flow at the same time. Captain Willard goes down the steps of the temple, the machete in his hand, holding Kurtz's manuscript, the people bow down: the one who kills the king becomes king.

It was at that moment that I shook myself. What the hell was I doing watching *Apocalypse Now* again when Sabbat had disappeared? There wasn't a minute to lose, I had to find him, otherwise Tot would kill me. Wasn't I Sabbat's guardian—wasn't I supposed to watch out for him?

In the shower, I asked myself how it was possible to lose a dog. It was absurd, you *can't* lose a dog, he had to be somewhere, someone was playing a joke on me. I was beginning to sober up. I made some coffee, and I pulled on a white dress shirt. Could the dog be at Tot's by chance? Maybe I had quite simply taken him there, without remembering. But that was unlikely: when Mme Figo had awakened me in the yard, the dog was already not with me. Could he have gotten into Tot's by himself, could he have taken the elevator and opened the door? Unless Tot had in fact returned during the night and let him in, in which case all was well.

I knocked on Tot's door. No response. I turned the key, there was no one—not Sabbat or Tot. It smelled closed up in there. I hadn't been in for some time. Instead of taking Sabbat to Tot's after each of his walks in the yard, out of pity for the poor Dalmatian, I had started to keep him with me. In the end, I hadn't really realized that we were living together. It was natural. There was Sabbat and me, Tot had flown completely out of my mind, and suddenly I realized I had completely forgotten to water his plants. That was the smell: dead plants.

I ran into the room where Tot had constructed a sort of altar to his three yucca plants. You couldn't see anything. I couldn't find the light switch; I walked gingerly to the window to raise the blinds.

How could I have forgotten the plants? Tot was fonder of them than anything else. He had asked me not to water, but to *hydrate* his three plants. He had gone so far as to show me—now I remember—how to dust their leaves by passing a damp sponge over them. He had suggested, with a surprising delicacy for such a hard man, to spray a bit of filtered water on each stem three times a week. A device to filter the water was next to the sink in the kitchen, next to the watering can and the sprayer, and of course I hadn't used them.

I could see Tot in his combat boots and fatigues explaining these subtleties to me with the serious, slightly wacky voice of a gardener. And so I wouldn't forget anything, he had written instructions for me on a sheet of paper that he put on the edge of the little table where the three plants were sitting.

Once I raised the blinds, the light spilled in over the yuccas. It was a catastrophe. The three plants, which Tot had placed at different heights in a spacious gradation, and whose lush leaves blended together forming a single, vast foliage whose range of colors went from sage to emerald, passing through nuances of lichen and almond, were gone. Those three plants had shriveled and the foliage was now nothing but a fan of skeletal stems, the leaves dried out and gray. It looked like a pile of ashes. There were even spiderwebs between the leaves.

I put a finger in the pot, but instead of the damp, very black soil, which three weeks earlier still nurtured each of Tot's plants, there was only a dry crust, hard and cracked.

It's true that Tot had said there was no need to water his plants a great deal—I only had to *mist* them (I can still remember that word). And since he guessed that I was perhaps not going to water them at all, he sought to reassure me about the dangers of daily watering, pointing out that those types of plants required only minimal hydration, let's say twice a week. And I have to admit that I had taken Tot's unexpected easygoingness as authorization not to worry about it too much. If Tot himself thought it was unnecessary to water his plants every day, then I would be able to think about it at leisure, and even, stretching the envelope, not to think of it at all.

I told myself that when I took Sabbat out in the evening, from time to time I would fill the watering can, and *basta*, it wasn't a problem, that simple act would do the trick. But now, I hadn't been in Tot's apartment for some time, and even today it was because of an inexplicable, aberrant event that I had gone into the place.

I sat down in the club chair that was opposite the gun locker. I felt terrible. Not only had I lost Tot's dog, but I had let his plants die. If he returned, right then, he would probably kill me. Sliding down a bit in the club chair, whose softness deliciously hugged my exhausted body, I wondered if Tot would kill me for having lost his dog or for having allowed his plants to die. Not that Tot didn't love his dog, but he was more attentive, more delicate, and to be frank, more affectionate toward his yuccas than toward his dog. He always had that brutal attitude of the lord toward Sabbat which, personally, disgusted me.

In general, Tot's behavior was violent. He moved around in the darkness from which we are spared, and came out only with that anger that one gets when in contact with evil. While I was contemplating his dead plants, and the rifle barrels were reflected through the case, the head of Colonel Kurtz—rather, that of Marlon Brando—kept appearing to me. That morning it blended with that of Tot. A head floating in the apartment, murmuring in a voice that was addressed to me, a threat, the last word the colonel uttered in *Apocalypse Now*: "*the horror!*"

To be frank, I found a certain beauty in those three dried-out yuccas. They could have been a sculpture made of coral, a stone bush, as if the desert had started to grow in the middle of Tot's apartment. Wasn't that desert his truth? Wasn't it the very truth of that world into which I was plunging? The darkness, swallowing our thoughts, fossilized them. If you abandoned your mind to it, if you offered it entirely to the biting teeth of evil, it would take only a few days for it to dry out and assume the look of those poor, calcified stalks.

Yes, it was Tot's soul that I saw, and I feared seeing mine, as well.

The morning light was still gray, a gray-white that, while rubbing against the misty leaves of the tall plane trees, came through the glass doors of each apartment in the building, diffusing a dirty transparency. I remembered the first times I took care of Sabbat, those times when, as I sat in this club chair contemplating the nuances of the sky, he would come stretch out on top of me, his paws curled around my neck, and would sleep, sighing. I had thus spent moments that at the time I didn't know were marvelous. And that morning, while my destiny was playing a dirty trick on me—or rather was revealing just how extreme, how indefensible, my negligence was—I felt nostalgia.

While contemplating the yuccas, I remembered that Kafka saw negligence as a capital sin. The word "sin" might have made me smile, but no word seemed more accurate at that moment. Losing Sabbat couldn't be the result of simple and vulgar negligence. It came from a spiritual deficiency. There was a problem with my life. Even when I wanted it to be free, open, empty enough to be fully accessible to truth,

I realized, that morning, that instead of going toward that truth, instead of devoting my solitude to the rigor of its call, I had deviated from my path, I had distanced myself. Kafka wrote: if impatience banishes humans from paradise, negligence prevents them from returning.

In spite of my bizarre way of life, in spite of my deviance and my guesswork, I had long believed that I was *living in the true*. I had believed this because I had the names. Those names offered me a reserve of light that I thought was enough. But that morning, in Tot's chair, I realized that the light was limited, and that it probably wasn't enough to get me out of this. I could save myself, but not entirely. A *half-grace*, does that exist? Grace is everything, or there is none. It was obvious that I had just lost something more than a dog.

So it was that morning, sitting in Tot's club chair, with a headache that I thought would never leave, that for the first time I wanted to flee. I had to give up the apartment in a week: why not leave right away? I had put myself in such an absurd situation that it would be impossible for me to justify it to Tot. Such a methodical man could not understand how someone could lose a dog and let plants die. Anyway, was it really understandable? The longer I stared at Tot's gun cabinet—and in particular at the Haenel rifle, the most fearsome of all, he had told me—the more it seemed obvious to me that it would be impossible to explain things to him. And what would I tell him, anyway? I thought, almost out loud: *I refuse the duel.* It's true, there was no way I could face down a monster like Tot. That guy was roasting in hell, that much was obvious, he was seething in rage in its darkness, he had entered my life only to lead me in turn into his black fire. The proof: his dog and his fucking plants. I hadn't asked him for anything. He had left and hadn't sent any news, and I found myself living in his world, in his place, with torment that wasn't mine, a guilt that crushed me because of him. He had quite simply entrapped me, I had allowed myself to be captured in his desert universe, and now I was at his mercy: I had committed the sin that allowed him to reign over my mind.

While looking at the Haenel rifle, I stood up. Maybe all was not lost. There had to be a meaning in all of this. I just needed to think clearly and everything would work out. First, save the plants. Start watering them a lot. Soak each pot in a basin of water. Can yuccas be brought back to life? I didn't really know much about the theology of plants. Maybe it would be better simply to buy three new plants. With some patience, I could find some yuccas that resembled Tot's, and if he noticed the substitution (because you can't trick the eye of a fanatic), I would explain that during his absence a heat wave had stricken all Paris flora, and he would probably be grateful for my having given him the most beautiful, the youngest, the most vibrant of all yuccas.

But I was out of money. Not only had I lost my credit card, but it was maxed out. So unless I found someone

to loan me the cash necessary to buy them, which I figured would be a lot, falling even within the realm of luxury
(because those fucking plants, in Paris, cost an arm and a
leg), that solution wasn't practical.

Maybe Pointel. I could tell Pointel about this misad-
venture—with some luck he would think it was funny and
would give me the money. Anyway, I should have asked
him for some last night. Once again, I had been negligent,
because Pointel had indeed intimated, when I had met with
him last spring, that there was always a screenplay to edit,
a letter of intent that needed finishing touches, all sorts
of writing work which he couldn't handle by himself, and
that a writer like me would be able to do very handily. But
instead of telling him about my difficulties, and offering
him my services, I had gone into a detailed account of my
meeting with Cimino, and so the evening was lost, through
a thousand and one tales, and I no longer remembered how
Pointel and I had parted. Had we foreseen getting together
again, had we decided on something that my drunkenness
had made me forget?

That was it: call Pointel. Settle the problem of the
plants. Settle the problem of money.

As for the dog, he had to be with Léna, that was obvious. I was thinking a bit more clearly now. Yesterday evening Sabbat had gotten into the taxi with Léna and me,
he had been with us all night, and, given my condition,
at the moment I had decided to return home, very late,

maybe even as the sun was coming up, Léna had probably preferred to keep Sabbat with her, and she had been
right. How, dead drunk, could I have taken care of a dog?
I don't even know how I got home. That had to be it,
Sabbat had spent the night in the Musée de la Chasse, I
could breathe easy.

I checked to make sure Léna's number was still on
my arm. Good—I would call her. I looked for my phone:
where was it now? And then I remembered with dismay
that I had lost it.

Find some money. Find the dog. Find a phone. Again, I
didn't know where to start.

Maybe Tot had a landline. I stood up all of a sudden
and looked in the entryway, the living room, the bedroom
(because unlike me, Tot had a bedroom, a real caphar-
naum, a frightening hole filled with random things); and I
vaguely realized that people don't have landlines anymore
(and furthermore, Tot didn't have a cell, either).

In the kitchen, I opened the fridge. Something big,
plump, suspicious, was sitting in a plate, wrapped in alu-
minum foil that allowed a bone to stick out. There was
also, I recognized it happily, a family-size box of Kiri cheese
(twelve portions), which immediately comforted me. And
on the upper shelf, a bottle of white wine on its side. I didn't
hesitate, I found the bottle opener and opened the wine,
which was delicious. I ate one of the Kiris. It had to be
cocktail hour. I drank down several glasses. I had to wake

up now. So I said out loud, bursting out laughing, that line that was the incipit of one of my old novels, and which, today, seems funny to me: "Now you have to get back to life." And it was true, it was time—I had to get back to life, I had to find Léna.

27

THE ABSOLUTE

My faith was renewed. I ran down the stairs making my to-do list: (1) find a phone (for example, at Phone Call, down the street); (2) call Léna; (3) get some money—rather, get some money first, because without money how was I going to be able to pay for my phone call? But where would I get some money? Borrow from whom? In the area there was only Guy the Cobra, or Walter at the Petits Oignons. Maybe Anouk, she lived nearby, on rue Orfila, but I had forgotten her address.

I couldn't really see any of them lending me money, but I absolutely couldn't be hindered by details, or get discouraged. It was essential that I move forward, otherwise I would end up dying, too, like Tot's yuccas. I could already see myself, half-asleep in his club chair, with the bottle of white wine empty beside me, spending my days contemplating the sky while waiting for Tot's vengeance.

Crossing the little yard, I thought of Mme Figo. Now that she seemed to like me, she would certainly agree to lend me her phone. I walked faster, but there was no one in the *loge*; and since Phone Call was closed, I went to the Petits Oignons.

The cool air did me good. There was a light softness in the streets, the gray sky of a Parisian summer, with children playing exuberantly in the parks, and that happy agitation of 4:00 p.m. I had thought, because of the hangover, that it was still morning. The leaves of the chestnut trees on avenue Gambetta formed a canopy above me. I was wobbling a bit, but I just had to follow the rows of trees to get to the Petits Oignons, where, I hoped, Walter would let me use the phone. I could have taken another Efferalgan and eaten something. Tot's Kiri didn't really count as breakfast. Usually, in the aftermath of excessive drinking, a Big Mac was just the thing to complete the hangover sequence, but today I had to choose action instead.

The red front of the Petits Oignons appeared in the distance, like a familiar haven, and my heart was full of joy. Scarcely had I arrived when someone bumped into me, and I fell and hit my head on the bar, a little dazed.

It was the Baron, eyes bugging out, dressed like a soldier of Malcolm X, a beret, belt, military boots. He had punched me—a friendly punch, he claimed. He burst out laughing while holding on to my arm.

"*Compañero*, I've been looking for you everywhere!"

He was terribly drunk and was flailing, making big gestures that exasperated Walter. I didn't have time to open my mouth, the Baron was already railing against our blindness, he had foreseen it, he said, he knew there would be death, he was against extremisms and against killing, he was horrified by this bloodbath, but he had told us, no one in France had prepared themselves spiritually for battle, no one had understood that through those mindless terrorists it was the powers that were expressing themselves, not states, not lobbies, but minds. A battle of archangels that were confronting each other through cycles of revelation. And last night, the sanctuary of the martyrs who participated in the mental word of Allah had grown, and even if personally he condemned those acts, he could only deplore how we continue not to hear what is playing out in the sky and on the earth between Islam and Christianity, not even to have the intuition that spirits were running wild, because we knew it. The more spirits run wild in the sky, the more massacres increase on earth. And if the terrorists blow themselves up with their belts of explosives, it's because the sacrifice is carried out to strike terror into all those who are not capable of the absolute, said the Baron, and he repeated that line almost in a shout: *"If the terrorists blow themselves up with their explosive belts, it's because the sacrifice is carried out to strike terror in all those who are not capable of the absolute."*

Walter, who was washing cups in the sink, asked him to be quiet now, but the Baron didn't even see him.

"You consume, you enjoy, but where is God in your life? Where is the absolute, that's the question they ask you…"

A guy protested: "Right, the absolute, it's massacring innocents, is that your absolute?"

"My absolute is elsewhere, I'm talking about the killers; that's what they say, they say it to me as much as to you, they say to us: *look at yourselves, your soul is dead.* They say: you are the disorder of the world and we are upsetting that disorder."

And he began to shout again: "*The transcendent is punishing you!*"

A soft voice spoke up: "A bit of compassion for the victims, please."

It was Gloriot, he was returning from the toilet.

"I do feel sorry, comrade," the Baron replied, staring at him, "but I'm talking about up high, I'm talking about the crossing of absolutes."

Walter rapped on the bar. "That's enough! Stop this crazy talk now, or you can leave!"

The Baron narrowed his eyes and calmed down. He began to stare at me and grabbed me by my coat: "The archangels have decided, it's taking place out of the dark mist, they want to make us bleed. Don't you understand that Allah and the Virgin Mary are fighting over heaven…?"

"Holy shit, I don't want to hear any more," said Walter.

The Baron looked at him. "You know what the sacred is? *The sacred is when everything dies.* Anyway *he* knows," he said, pointing at me.

Walter looked at me suspiciously, I was uncomfortable; I was waiting to be able to mention the telephone, the money, the dog.

"What are you talking about?" I asked.

"You don't know? There was an attack. Where've you been?"

"An attack, here in Paris?"

"More than a hundred dead."

He handed me a copy of *Libération*. On the front page, lying on the sidewalk in front of the terrace of a café, bodies were covered with white cloths. It looked like it might have happened right here, in front of us, in front of the Petits Oignons. The headline—"Carnage in Paris"—woke me up. Where had I been at that time? Walter was right: I was living on another planet.

Walter gave me a coffee and a glass of water, I didn't have time to tell him I had no money, because the Baron had resumed his logorrhea. He claimed that he and I had a mission, and only we could accomplish it, because I possessed the right path and he the left. Together we could rebalance the world.

The Baron's ravings had brought my headache back. I wanted to vomit. I needed an Efferalgan, I needed something to eat, I needed ten thousand things, it wasn't possible anymore, I was suffocating, get out of here, quickly, but it was impossible, I was paralyzed.

I said I was sorry to the Baron, I saw what he meant, even if it seemed presumptuous to still discern even a bit of spark in my behavior. My path—if I still had one—was perhaps also related to the left hand, it was increasingly dark, the light had abandoned me, I was soon going to burn in hell like him, I sensed that hell wanted me.

The Baron listened to me with a serious air, but disagreed: "Your soul is safe. There is a path that goes through hell, but which is unharmed. You are on that path, you see the infernal, you're disturbed by it, but you're not involved—you are intact."

Walter stopped washing cups, he was looking at us, dumbfounded. "Tell me, guys, are you serious?"

I tried to interrupt and asked, loud enough so that everyone standing at the bar could hear me, if anyone had seen a dog, I had lost my dog the night before, a Dalmatian called Sabbat, he had disappeared, I was looking for him everywhere.

"Isn't that Tot's dog?"

It was Guy the Cobra's voice, he was sitting at a table with a beer. I was saved. I went up to him, he offered me a beer which I gratefully accepted. I could tell him everything.

He was doing very well. He had just received an enormous shipment of Bergman, Tarkovski, Renais, it was a welcome change from stupid French comedies which he sold by the caseful. Had I had time to watch *Fitzcarraldo*? Absolutely, I'd seen it, I had loved it, it was one of those psychotic-operatic films that I loved, and he was right, it was like *Apocalypse Now*, and perhaps even better (but *Apocalypse Now* spoke to me spiritually). It was an ecstatic film. Not only did what it says come out of an altered state, but it was filmed *from* an altered state, and in a sense it was itself that altered state. And what interested me, even if, in my opinion, it didn't have the metaphysical strength of Coppola or the political power of Cimino, is that it radically raised the question—as unintentional as it was outdated— of heroism. Lacan, I said to Guy the Cobra, defined the hero as both the one who does not give in to his desire and the one to whom wrong has been done: doesn't that sum up *Fitzcarraldo*?

Guy the Cobra agreed. To carry a boat up a mountain, construct an opera in the Amazon, what could be more beautiful? In his opinion, if the guy was considered a madman, it was above all because he did it *for nothing*.

It's true, I said. In the eye of the Lord, one sees no madness. And what isn't reflected in the Lord's pupil doesn't exist. Those who are called madmen, I said to Guy the Cobra, are only the witnesses of the insanity of the world.

We burst out laughing, and someone put a hand on my shoulder. It was the Baron. He had to leave, but we could pick up this conversation another day, when circumstances would be more favorable. He grimaced and squinted in Walter's direction—then, after a military salute, he left.

I explained everything to Guy: my hangover, the dog, the phone, money. He took two twenty-euro bills out of his pocket and handed them to me with his phone.

I then raised the sleeve of my shirt to read Léna's number, and Guy started to laugh, that sort of absurdity pleased him.

I went out to make my call. Léna didn't answer. There was a voice message recording, but I hung up right away. What would I say? I hadn't prepared myself, and what number was I going to leave for her to reply to? Good God, everything was so complicated. And it was even a bit delicate. After all, we had spent the night making love, and what had we agreed upon *after*? Did we make plans to get together again?

I tapped in her number again while forcing myself to assume a relaxed but preoccupied air. Yes, that was good, "preoccupied." She had to sense that, while being a serious guy, I saw things with amusement, that I wasn't a drag, not the type to fill her voice mailbox with a sob story. If I called her it wasn't to croon vaguely post-sex, but because I had a reason, granted a bit absurd, but real, to talk to her. Nonchalance, detachment, details. I would ask her if by chance she hadn't come across a Dalmatian, which I might have unintentionally left at her place. The story of Tot's dog was going to help me see her again, we already had a story.

Her voice answered: "You have reached the voice mail of Léna Schneider."

But whether it was an excess of wine or an unexpected bout of timidity, my heart started to beat very quickly, my mouth was dry, in fact I wasn't ready at all, but it was too late: I launched into an interminable sentence punctuated with forced laughter. I was delighted with our encounter, I said, truly delighted, the night was marvelous, really marvelous, and I hoped she was okay. As for me, I was in Olympian shape, I said, stupidly bursting out laughing. But now, during that very beautiful night, I had lost three things: my phone, my wallet, and my dog. Yes, I know it's crazy to lose a dog, I said, again laughing stupidly, and anyway, it isn't really my dog, maybe she remembered my telling her that at the restaurant, it's my neighbor's dog, and suddenly its loss was not only problematic in itself, even terrible, because the poor dog, if he wasn't with her, was then out on his own, somewhere in Paris, but in addition that loss put me in incommensurable difficulties because its owner was an extremely irascible man, and—

A beep cut off the recording. My message was a catastrophe: not only had I just left a babbling voice message on the phone of a woman the day after a night of making love to her, but in addition, I told her a ton of stupidities while cackling like a demented moron.

I was at my wits' end. Maybe I could record another message, making up for the previous mistake? No, it was better to give it up, I risked digging myself in deeper. Anyway, I now had only one desire: buy a pack of beer, go back to bed, and drink it in bed to forget all this insanity.

Guy the Cobra joined me on the sidewalk. I gave him back his phone and we smoked a cigarette together. He asked me if I knew anyone among the victims. "I don't know," I responded, "since last night I'm not sure of anything anymore."

What about him? He was going to get out of Paris for a while. In any case, with what had happened last night, he wouldn't be able to sleep or think about anything else. He had to leave and he was leaving today, now, right away, with his van, to go to a little house he had restored in Auvergne, in Mont-Dore, in the middle of lakes and volcanoes. He didn't have any electricity for the time being, but he just had to drive a few hours from Paris while thinking of the lake of Guéry, and climb the side of the Croix-Morand, for the blue of the sky and the clarity of the rocks to immediately ease the weight, and he could finally find silence again.

We went across the rue de la Chine. I told Guy that a few years ago I had lived here in a car, parked exactly at number 27. It was when I was participating in the insurrection of the *Renards pâles*. We were masked, we had no identity, because identity was only a trap, an agreement to be controlled. Only the absence of identity was revolutionary, and to us the future could open up only in that way, through the immensity of a letting go where each person, by freeing himself from his attachments, would make *time return*. It had been a final chance, a final collective joy before a general flatness. Today, Paris was asleep, like all of France, like all of Europe. And everything was controlled by interests that saw to it that we kept sleeping, that we would continue to consume our anesthetic, and that politics and the future would take place without us.

Guy the Cobra had also taken part in events. And then solitude had ultimately seemed more important to him. In the end, he told me, the only true politics consists in keeping one's soul, and even more simply, in *having a soul*.

"Do you know anyone who has a soul?" Guy asked. "And do we really have one? How can you know?"

An open and free life demands silence, he added, while we were going down rue Orfila in the direction of the rue des Pyrénées where his van was parked. It seemed to him that they never stopped stealing silence from us, and that night it had been stolen once again, it had been totally destroyed. By massacring a hundred innocents, they had made it impossible for us to be at peace, we were being drowned in the noise and the furor to prevent us from thinking. Each crime, he said, brought us closer to that chaos from which, one day, we would no longer be able to escape, because we will have so much noise in our ears that we will no longer recognize hell.

We had arrived in front of his store. Guy continued to speak with a gravity that surprised me. Mountains and silence are the same, he said, shaking my hand, mountains rise up from universe to universe, they are never immobile; and silence itself moves around, it seeks air through the calm of the heights and obtains an intoxication that no human life can give it.

Guy got into his van and drove away. I lit a cigarette. The bench, the chestnut tree, the edge of the sidewalk formed a perfect triangle. What if I stayed here? It's possible at any moment to restart completely. It takes only a propitious figure, and geometry saves us. Yes, that triangle pleased me: bench-leaves-sidewalk, it was ideal—what happens under a tree is always in the realm of the sacred. But I didn't need to jump on it. There were other triangles, thousands of others, they constantly adjusted themselves between walls and the bodies of passersby, between cars and the movement of words, they ran around the streets of the city, hurtling down boulevards and sneaking around public parks, where they blinked like stars.

I saw them now, I saw only them. They offered themselves to me like a promise, like a smile. I had my solitude, I had names, I had triangles. It was good to enter that lightness, to be there entirely for the clarity, to receive its affirmation. It was new, it was obvious: the outside is lighted through bursts that attract truth. I would never go home again.

28

A LAKE RIGHT IN THE MIDDLE OF PARIS

At the ticket window in the Musée de la Chasse, I asked for Léna. A young woman with a sunburnt face told me she was in a meeting all day. She couldn't be disturbed, but she had left an envelope for me.

I tore open the envelope. There was my wallet and my phone. And this note: "Meet tonight at Le Fumoir, 8 p.m.? Hugs, Léna."

I was crazy with joy, I raised my arms to the sky. The young girl seemed amused.

"Where is the dog?" I asked.

The girl sat up in her chair, I apologized, said goodbye, and left.

Léna didn't mention the dog. If he were with her, she would have said so in her note, right?

I had several messages on my phone, which never happened. One from Pointel, who had really enjoyed the evening, and proposed we get together again; one from Anouk, who wondered if I had any news from Tot; and a third from Léna, a simple missed call. She probably wanted to tell me she had my wallet, and then, when she heard the phone ringing, realized that she had my phone.

Even if Sabbat was still outside, and I was truly concerned about him (because how can a dog used to being fed manage to survive on the street?), I felt better, not because I didn't care anymore, but because things were improving.

I left a message for Anouk, telling her I didn't have any news from Tot, but that I had lost his dog. Had she by any chance seen him, was he by miracle with her?

Then I called the pound. They told me they hadn't found a Dalmatian. Anyway, they never found Dalmatians, no one ever abandoned a Dalmatian.

"Mine wasn't abandoned, he's lost."

"What do you mean, lost? You can't lose a dog!"

"Yes you can, he's the proof."

"Well, be more careful next time."

I had been given two numbers, and I tried the other one. It was the pound in Gennevilliers, which brings in animals lost in Paris and throughout the *département*. Could they have already brought him back there? I got an answering machine. The pound's hours were 9:30–12:00 and 1:30 to 5:00 p.m. It was 5:30, I would call tomorrow. I would also call veterinarians, as the girl had advised me to do when I called information. When I asked her for the number for the pound, I pointed out that I had lost my dog and she had admitted that she had also just lost her cat, and that I should call not just the pounds whose numbers she would give me, but also the national canine database. In her opinion, it would also be good to put up signs with a photo of my dog everywhere, and maybe even go to the bakeries in the neighborhood, because the people who take in stray animals—old people, in general, she said—talk about it when they buy their bread. I could also report the loss of my dog at the police station. Finally, there was an Internet site, soschiensperdus.com, something like that, I could also try.

The pound. The canine database. Veterinarians. The police station. Signs. Soschiensperdus.com. Of course, I would do everything. I had to act quickly. It was the twenty-fourth. In a week I had to leave the apartment. Everything was moving quickly, and in spite of my distress at Sabbat's disappearance, this acceleration was perhaps the presage of a new life, of a life finally lived, in which I would move at my own speed, at my own slowness, in which nothing would ever come to interrupt my thoughts, not even a television screen, not even films.

That acceleration had gotten me out of my bed, it had opened me up to the labyrinth of encounters, to the density of activity, to all those details in time that are scattered randomly in the streets. But above all, it had transmitted to me a truth even more secret than the one that animated my solitude, a truth to which, even while writing *The Great Melville*, I hadn't had access. It was a truth so close to silence that nothing shone in it anymore. Or it was drawn nearer to another truth, itself bundled up in its own secret, it, too, discreet, tenacious, exhausted by isolation, seeking to know that which exists beyond solitude.

Police vans were lined up along the boulevards, there were armed men on the sidewalks and, on the faces of the passersby, a new fear, a fear that would take time to erase, a fear that perhaps would never be erased, but would profoundly mark every face, would imprint its indelible marks, darker than fatigue, those marks that you see under the eyes of men in countries where freedom no longer exists.

I ran to Le Fumoir, an elegant café across from the rue de Rivoli and the Louvre, but I was an hour early. The chandeliers, the calm, the chic wood paneling made me ill at ease; my presence seemed displaced, as if the whirlwind that was agitating my mind since last night was unable to enjoy it. I, who had just spent months stretched out watching films, couldn't stay still any longer.

I left quickly. On the other side of the street, the Colonnade de Perrault beckoned me. With the night that was beginning to fall, the majestic whiteness of its stones sparkled like the hide of a whale. I smiled, happy that Moby Dick had returned. Every time my life expands, the white whale appears, with the faithfulness of a goddess. While walking toward the Cour Carrée, I was carried by the scent of the fresh cinnamon that embalms the green cliffs on the coasts of Java. The sidewalk I was on was the ocean of a whaler—the great Melville was with me again.

I walked through the Cour Carrée, which was deserted. Silence turned around in it as in an open-air cave. The coolness of the basin rose up along the pavilions, and along the walls I saw a cavalcade of does, gazelles, and ibexes running to the stars, their elongated mouths open to the red-and-black sky, as if thirst, more ancient even than origins, indicated a source beyond the roofs, in the clouds.

If fifteen thousand years ago I had been able to lick the walls of Lascaux where those does, those gazelles, those ibexes were flying above a hole, I would have obtained absolute clarity, become as clear as one is when one makes love, and that clarity would have traveled through time to the present, to the Italian lake where I'm writing this book.

I passed through another entrance and found myself opposite the Pyramid, delivered suddenly unto this large space full of breaths where before me the Arc du Carrousel and the Tuileries were sliding. The sky was red, the evening wind raised my chest. There were still a few groups of visitors who were taking photos, but already the walls of the Louvre were returning to their solitude, to that nobility of the stone that addresses only itself.

That is where it happened. Usually, I need to be lying down, I have to be in a state of concentration, fluidity, with the swallow, papyri, and red box placed perfectly around my body. But for the first time, it happened outside, in one of the most touristy places in the world. I was fully there, I had never been *better there*—and at the same time, I was no longer anywhere.

The animals continued to snort around me. They swarmed to a spot that seemed to annihilate them. Exaggeration is an effect of love. Owls, bears, buffaloes, were invading the space. Bulls traced wild lines on the walls; a herd of bison made the walls tremble. They were all consumed by that passion that pushes us into the abyss, by the thirst that is never slaked, by the desire to extinguish the horror.

I was like them, I was that frightened camel that was galloping toward the exit, that auroch blinded by battle, that antelope looking for water. I have been alone for too long. I began to run with the herd.

How can I describe what happened? In a blink of an eye the Louvre courtyard emptied. The Pyramid was gone. The tourists, gone. Even the equestrian statue of Louis XIV was gone. In their place: a lake.

With all the alcohol I drink, I'm used to visions. Everything is slightly changed, colors are freed. But here, it was something else, it was as if I was suddenly reaching that which exists under the crust. A lake, its immense calm, a lake right in the middle of Paris.

I began to laugh, I said to myself, like Rimbaud: I saw a lake where the Louvre once stood. And why not, as long as we're here, *a school of drums made by the angels, or carriages on the road to heaven?* Why not monsters, mysteries? But what happened that evening was not simply the hallucinations of a poet. Granted, there was a lake, but above all *there was nothing.* All shapes had been shattered, the lake was clearly empty.

I was already telling myself, reassuring myself: *I've encountered a lake, and it is empty.* I even savored the line. And now, all of a sudden, the lake was filled. It took only a few seconds for the surface to begin to sparkle, and for the huge space that goes to the Place de la Concorde, over there, after the Tuileries, and goes up the Champs-Élysées to the Arc de Triomphe, to be entirely filled with blood.

A lake of blood instead of Paris. It was probably my own way of incorporating what had happened the night before, of being part of the pain. Because now, I could sense it, there would no longer be any limits to the killing. Death had entered this city, which always thought it was impervious, which had even intimidated the Nazis. And not only had it been a victim—a hundred innocent people whose names we would soon know, men, women, children—but those deaths also splashed onto the living, who, I understood this evening, would never be the same, because no one, not even the survivors, escapes the logic of sacrifice. When a sacrifice takes place, the world is disturbed until a circle is drawn. But it's an illusion to believe that one dies only inside the circle. The circle says: now, we die—it says nothing else. It doesn't say if we can protect ourselves. Nor does it say where it begins or ends. The circle of sacrifice is limitless, and so death, when it befalls some, touches us all. And so we in turn become sacrificial bodies, bodies that may be sacrificed at any moment.

Thoughts were knocking together in my head. That chasm toward which the beasts hunted by the hunter were rushing was there, open in front of me like a bloody mouth. At first I was afraid of falling into the hole—of drowning in the blood of the beasts. I stood at the edge of the chasm, hanging on to a balustrade of the Pavilion Sully. But now I didn't fear anything anymore, not the blood or death. A strange calm invaded me, as if that was what was needed for that pool of blood to appear so clearly. I abandoned myself to the madness. Looked straight at the abyss. Anyway, hadn't I been crazy for a long time? Isn't madness the truest means to see a pool of blood as big as a city appear—and to take part in the tragedy? I thought that perhaps I needed to become crazy to become wise. Yes, *become crazy to become wise:* what a plan. Advice from Saint Paul, I think.

Yes, holes occur in life; we try to avoid them, but that's not a good idea because holes always point to the huge hole that enables the world to breathe. We imagine we are separated from all things by a hollow space whose edge we aren't even in a hurry to reach, and then one day the hollow space opens at our feet, and the hole grows to the dimensions of the world: we are inside it.

But I was lucky. I wasn't yet inside it. I was on the edge. Because, all around the Cour Napoléon, on the balustrades of the first floor, there are a hundred statues representing illustrious figures. Their names are inscribed in stone: Rabelais, Saint-Simon, Bossuet, Pascal, Rousseau, La Fontaine, Poussin, Froissart, Philippe de Champaigne, Molière. They are perfect names that exist absolutely. They are filled with time and are signs of memory. They are what prevented me from falling into the void, from giving in to the vertigo, from allowing myself to be fascinated by the slaughterhouse. The names drew me in, I loved them. I said each of them out loud, and instantly the danger disappeared. I even added names that weren't there, my own names, those that are in my head and form a tree on the wall of my room. With that recitation the lake disappeared. The Pyramid reappeared, the Carrousel and Tuileries, too, and even the tourists, those who hang around in the evening to be photographed before going back to their hotels.

That exorcism was impressive, and I was afraid. Because while playing with names, with the murmuring and the silence, one moves within the sacred: one begins to slide from shape to shape, up to that red-and-black interval where the world is no longer the world, but just a blinking ray of light.

I looked at the time on my phone. Now I was late. I started to run in the rain, and arrived out of breath at Le Fumoir.

29

THE DROPS

Léna was sitting next to a window, pale and silent, her eyes lowered, reading a book. Her face was whiter, milkier than the night before. She was wearing a low-cut black dress, with aquamarine earrings and a necklace of small blue stones carved into petals, which she had been wearing the night before.

In a second, my desire for her swept through me with the violence of an earthquake. Seeing her lighted in that way, with a pensive face, I understood that she attracted me because she was unaware of the light that passed over her. In her, discretion was confused with indifference. She was perhaps that way with others, but was above all like that with herself.

And there seemed to be something in her that her softness protected, something she even perhaps prevented from being defined. There was a form of absence in her in which

I saw the irreducible, a secret, more intense than love, which society would never manage to reach. Such a thing was not the result of distancing herself, as it was in me, but came out of that constancy of reason that grants authority to its own clarity. Léna never called for help, I don't believe she ever experienced aimless wandering.

I walked up to her table, she raised her eyes to me, I asked her what she was reading. She showed me the book's cover and, smiling, answered: "Ovid's *Metamorphoses.*"

She reminded me that, the night before, I had told her of my passion for the story of Actaeon, the hunter who turns away from his usual prey to follow the goddess he had seen in the woods. It's a well-known story. Actaeon surprises Diana bathing, surrounded by her nymphs. Diana's nakedness is taboo. When she realizes that she has been seen, she looks for her quiver, her bow, her arrows, but being in the water, she is disarmed, and so she splashes the voyeur, and when the drops of water fall on Actaeon, he is turned into a deer, which his dogs then attack and devour.

In my opinion, it was revolting that Actaeon was condemned to death for having seen a goddess naked. It shouldn't be forbidden to look at a naked woman, even if she is Diana, the most chaste of goddesses. I had said to Léna (at least she told me I did, because I had forgotten almost everything) that my entire life was founded on the idea of seeing goddesses naked and not dying from it. She found that funny. She had picked up a copy of Ovid, in which the death of Actaeon is told, so she could discuss it with me.

"By the way," she said, "I haven't found your dog."

"I thought goddesses were infallible."

"Goddesses have great weaknesses, that's why they are dangerous."

It was that evening, even more than during our love-making in the Musée de la Chasse, that I became aware of the mystical honeycombed interior of Léna's head. Nothing suggested she had partied for half the previous night. She did have some darkness under her eyes, but it was hardly noticeable, and only accentuated the mother-of-pearl pallor of her skin. Nor did anything indicate that we had made love a few hours earlier. We were carrying on a conversation, with a naturalness that calmed me. The pile of shit I was carrying around with me, those aberrant visions that fell onto me in full daylight, that delirium that the names brought forth in my head, that almost permanent hang-over—all of that was spared her. She was there, wholly available, nothing seemed to undermine her. Her presence came from a sort of gift, and it was enough to be at her side to feel touched by grace.

I continued to see the lake of blood, the dead yuccas, I heard the Baron shouting. I was *invaded*. I wanted to destroy that torment. I asked Léna if she had managed to work today. Yes, she had slept an hour or two, but that had been enough. She was happy because Isabelle Huppert came by to see her at the museum. They had visited it together, and after seeing the photos of George Shiras, Isabelle had enthusiastically agreed to do a reading of the text that Jean-Christophe Bailly had written for the exhibition. Two images in particular had attracted her attention: one, which she found magnificent, of a doe that is bathing in a lake, and whose neck rends the water with a softness that, to her, is no longer seen in any human; the other, of a stag whose antlers, reflecting in the water, are transformed into tree roots.

Isabelle Huppert, said Léna, had sensed perfectly that what is fugitive is desirable, and how the charm of what escapes us here slips into a miraculous light, that of the underbrush and the banks of a lake in the night that belongs to no one.

Because through that exhibition, Léna wanted viewers to live what isn't seen—wanted the invisible life of wild animals to be revealed, as if it were displayed for the first time in the visible world.

One day, said Léna, there will no longer be any animals. Humans will have taken all their pelts. There will no longer be a furtive figure, no more trembling gazes in the leaves or underbrush; nothing will be fugitive anymore. Forests, mountains, plains will slowly slide into our dementia, and it will be we who tremble, delivered to the ferocity of our own teeth.

What Léna said struck me to the point that I still recite it today, while walking in the forest, while I replay the details of that adventure in which the figures I attempt to assemble are passionately blended.

While eating dinner (she had a risotto with asparagus, I a steak tartare), we talked about the previous night. She had also drunk a lot, but while I had ended up losing consciousness, she had *passed through her drunkenness*. And returning to the details of our encounter, it seemed that we were already beginning to tell our story, the way lovers do.

As we went over the chronology of our evening, it was impossible to figure out the exact moment when Sabbat had escaped us. Had he been attracted by another dog, been lost in the crowd in front of Chez Orphée, had we parted company before the Tendre Voyou? Because at some point during the night, Léna told me, we went to that bar whose name she adored: Tendre Voyou—Tender Scoundrel—a nightclub one of her friends owned, where we had eaten something and continued to drink. Our drunkenness was joyful, endless like a fit of laughter, she said. The bar closed at 2:00, and we took a taxi. "I asked you for your address, but you were completely gone, you didn't hear anything, so we went to my place, do you remember?"

I remembered everything that happened at the Musée de la Chasse, I told her, and in particular our compatibility, which seemed as precise as the disquiet that it inspired in me. That night, I had broken the curse of Actaeon: I wasn't dead.

"That's because you looked at me with righteousness," said Léna. "The problem with Actaeon is that he is watching Diana the way he watches all his prey, with the eye of someone who wants to kill. So she sends his look back to him. She kills him."

According to Léna, the virginity of the goddess was only a ruse, she hadn't found anything better to set herself apart, that's all. If she hid herself from the gaze of others, it was not to remain untouchable, but because no mortal knew how to look at her. To really look at someone goes beyond desire, she said, and Actaeon had indeed looked at her badly. He had looked at her with the eye of a predator—he had looked at her *like a dog*. And so she, quite logically, set his dogs on him.

Léna read and reread that page of Ovid to me, and she noticed that between Diana and Actaeon—unseen, and as if in reserve—there was what she called an "esoteric hymen." In other words, a mirror.

The true object of the mirror is not to reflect, said Léna, but to give an image. That image is interposed—and so it gets closer to the veil, which the goddess wraps around her to distance those who think they've grasped her.

Well, in Ovid's tale, there were drops. Those which Diana sprinkles on Actaeon. And in those drops, the entire world is condensed through the perfection of an iridescent miniature. What Diana sprinkled on the voyeur was the entire scene he had just witnessed: the grotto surrounded by pine and cypress trees, the little spring where the goddess is immersing her virginal body, the nymphs around the huge body of Diana, and the reddening which the inopportune gaze of Actaeon caused.

The sprinkling of water was what Léna found most beautiful in that story. And she even believed that there was an unknown truth in those drops, as well as in dew, in tears, in the sweat of lovers. Drops are perfect, said Léna, they convey sensuality. If Actaeon had watched differently, it would have been there, in the mother-of-pearl iris of a molecule of water, that he could have joined Diana.

Had I ever seen *The Garden of Earthly Delights* by Hieronymus Bosch, she asked me, in which there is a transparent bubble inside of which two naked lovers caress each other?

I asked Léna what, in her opinion, Actaeon should have done to look at the goddess appropriately, and thereby escape her anger.

"It's very simple," she said. "It's called love. All he had to do was stop ogling and jump into the water."

In the street, in front of the Saint-Germain-l'Auxerrois church, we kissed. I finally felt light. Deliverance removes the weight of concerns, it grants us the clarity we are lacking. That night had the clarity of snow. I sensed the presence of a river, as if it were flowing inside my stomach.

Melville wrote that we are a piece of broken bread from the Last Supper. Léna's cheeks were a bit red. She wanted to walk barefoot in the grass. "I'll feel better," she said. I knelt before her and took her foot in the hollow of my hand. It was an amazingly pleasurable sensation, like stroking a doe. I undid the strap of her shoes, took them off, slipped off her stockings, and she plunged her feet into the grass.

30

THE HUNT

I spent three days looking for Sabbat. I took the RER commuter train to the Gennevilliers pound twice. I went to a dozen kennels. I looked at hundreds of abandoned dogs. I called all the veterinarians in Paris. I asked the garbage collectors if they might have picked up a dead dog. And I walked around for hours, at night, during the day, thinking that it would take a miracle to find Sabbat, but that I owed it to him, and that walking to the point of exhaustion was a way of paying him back, of expiating this sin, perhaps of redeeming myself.

For those three days, I didn't go home.

I was afraid of Tot, that's true. I thought about what he had told me about hunting: that death was its only goal, and that he liked to kill, that the moment when the prey is in your sights is the ultimate satisfaction. I thought of the Haenel rifle, with which he would track me down.

I thought of the specific form of killing he would inflict on me.

That night, after traversing the entire city once again, from the Porte de Champerret to the Porte de Bagnolet, completely exhausted and worn out by the absurdity of such a mission, I finally returned home, opened my door, thinking: if Tot is there, let him kill me, and I collapsed on my bed in my clothes.

Three hours later, I woke up with a start and ran to the TV. I unplugged it immediately, put it into its box, and took it outside to the landing. I put my ear to Tot's door. Had he maybe come home? With Tot, you never knew. He lived as if he was in a tomb. I turned the key in the lock and readied myself for a confrontation. Without even turning on the light in the entryway, I walked in. There was no one. I returned to the landing and carried the TV box into his living room. The three yuccas were still there, utterly dead. I looked at the gun cabinet, and without really knowing what I was doing or what hand was guiding me, I opened a drawer where I found a little key that fit perfectly into the lock of the gun cabinet. I took out the Haenel rifle, a box of cartridges, and a carrier in which I put everything. Then I took the big screen out of the box and put it in front of the gun cabinet. I scribbled a few words on a piece of paper and taped it onto the screen.

From the entryway table I took the keys to the Jeep, as if I were Tot. I took the elevator to the underground garage and walked to the Jeep.

What was I doing, exactly? I was cold and empty. I could have died as easily as saved the world. I don't know if when I drove off I still thought I was going to find Sabbat or do away with myself—if by fleeing I thought I was putting an end to this story or was going to pick up speed and drive the car off a cliff.

As I was driving out of the garage, after the automatic door had shut behind me, the scene returned to me.

It was an afternoon at Tot's. We were drinking beer and Sabbat was sleeping peacefully at our feet. Tot suddenly proposed that I take a ride with him. He stuffed some blankets into a sack, picked out several boxes of cartridges, put two rifles into leather carriers, and went into the kitchen, where he put a large slab of bacon, a few sausages, and some slices of bread into a bag. And with several packs of beer and the bottle of vodka that I had gotten from my place, we went down to the underground garage where Tot parked his Jeep, into which Sabbat jumped with obvious joy.

We drove in the direction of Fontainebleau, at least that's where Tot said we were going. I was already so drunk that the billboards on the highway at night were blurry and it was impossible for me to make out anything in the names of cities other than traces of light where crazy stars were zooming past. I didn't understand how it was possible to hunt in a forest where the kings of France had ritually pursued stags and boars. I asked Tot: didn't we need a permit, and was it actually hunting season?

I reminded him that in that forest, intended for Louis XI and his pack of dogs, they had released a prisoner wearing the skin of a stag, so that his pitiful existence would be confused with that of the animal prey. Tot, impassive, just shrugged his shoulders. The dog stuck his head in between us, he knew where we were going—and trembled in anticipation.

Soon the woods appeared around us, and Tot stopped to open a gate. The sky was black, green, gray. The road wound amongst thick vegetation that filled the night.

Tot was carrying our two rifles across his back. I was trudging behind him. The moon slid between the fir trees. I let myself be led like a child. I was cursing. Rather than follow Tot, I wanted to lie down at the foot of a tree and go to sleep.

We emerged, coming out of the trees, into a field lighted by the moon. I staggered several times in the mud before climbing the wooden ladder up to a raised cabin where Tot had sat down with Sabbat. It was one of those shelters where hunters spend nights watching for a fox, partridges, or larger game.

I had completely lost my bearings and thought I was in a sailboat. Around us, the expanse of leaves formed a black mass, an ocean of foam in which I wanted to dive. Tot held me back several times by my collar. He was drunk, too, but was chuckling, unchangeable. I collapsed at the back of the shelter, enveloped in a stupor out of which I continued to babble: we had to keep an eye out, I said, because the whale was going to appear, and then we would see, emerging from the depths of the night, that explosion crowned by gulls announcing the breaching of the whale. At that moment I would cry out—loud enough so that the whole crew would hear, and so the captain would immediately order the harpooners to get ready—"Thar she blows!"

When I woke up, the forest was dripping in blood. I began to tremble. Was it the underbrush or the antlers of the great stags? At a moment in your life, you understand that blood must flow in order for you to stay alive, just as sighs must cease and light burn. So you advance, hoping the darkness won't cover your soul. And to realize that hope, you consume everything in the darkness that seems the opposite of hope.

That night, I wanted to set that forest of blood on fire, change that scarlet ocean into a pyre. And then in my madness I shouted that we had to spare the whale. Tot had one knee on the ground, his eye on his sight, he didn't hear me. At his side, Sabbat, looking in the same direction, waited for the shot to run off. It was a nightmare. Tot had turned his dog into a killer, they both were going to massacre my whale. I thought I shouted, but the words were stuck in my mouth. In my head, everything was confused: the moon and the rounded back of Moby Dick, the leaves and the waves, the night and the ocean. All around me there was only an indistinct body, glimmeringly white, where the signs of the hunt and the truth were confused, where the Dalmatian was only the sleeping mask of the deer, where the deer concealed the lamb, where the lamb was dying, like the whale that is sacrificed in all the oceans, like human beings that are exterminated on every continent.

"We've killed the white whale!" I screamed. "We have scorched the earth, decimated herds, cut off buds, destroyed relationships, emptied springs. We are the assassins of the world, and more than the world, of God, and more than of God, we have killed so much that that is all that remains: crime, crime everywhere, and only crime."

Tot turned around: "Shut up!" His face was so frightening, so close to the death he was about to inflict that my heart froze up, and I fainted.

A shot woke me up. There wasn't anyone in the cabin. I looked at my phone: it was 3 a.m. I went down the ladder, horrified, my head pounding. In the distance I heard Tot's voice giving orders to his dog. That a Dalmatian would attack a prey like a hunting dog seemed horrible to me.

Sabbat emerged out of the underbrush barking, jumping around Tot, who was carrying a doe on his shoulders. A long trail of blood was dripping on his fatigues. Sabbat's mouth was also dripping with blood.

We got back on the road to Paris. Tot was speeding on the highway, I dozed. The sight of the doe's body spread out in the back made me sick. Sabbat, awake in the night, watched over the dead deer. Tot suddenly stopped on a bridge, just before Paris, to answer his phone (it was Anouk, she was worried, and Tot liked nothing more than those moments when he made her suffer, he took great pleasure in it).

We were on the Asnières bridge. Tot put on his warning lights. There was very little traffic, but, since it was still night, I thought it was dangerous to be stopped in the breakdown lane. I got out of the car, found the warning triangle in the trunk, and put it a few meters behind us.

Returning to the car, I got close to the edge of the bridge. The lights of Paris sparkled in the night. I noticed a female shape that was standing up on the edge, close to the void. I ran to her. It was a woman. She had seen me, her eyes shone in the night. And when I was only a dozen meters from her, I suddenly went down. I had been thrown to the ground. I tried to get up, but the guy was stronger than me. He was crushing my head with his boot. I barely had time to see the woman throw herself into the void, when I cried out, "No!"

A car passed by, I wanted to call for help, but the headlights blinded me. The guy behind me had released the pressure on my head. I stood up, turned around: it was Tot.

He was incredibly angry. His eyes blazed, he was clenching his fists. I ran to the place where the woman had jumped. I climbed onto the parapet: below, the water was black, you couldn't see a thing.

"Quick, we have to call for help!"

"Too late," said Tot.

I screamed and threw myself at him.

The fight between Tot and me, as mismatched as it was, was an experience I couldn't escape. The essential does not always reside in that which enlightens us, but sometimes in a path, often necessary, leading into darkness.

So, had I dreamed that bridge scene? I don't think so. If I had forgotten it, it's because it was the prelude to a series of nightmares that glued me to my bed with a fever for several days, and which I preferred to forget. To have abandoned that woman to death seemed like a crime to me—a "crime of iniquity," as the Scriptures call it.

Her image haunted me. I kept seeing her jumping off the bridge, her eyes shining from the bottom of the water. Then the vision was confused in my head with that of the deer, whose body, cut up in pieces, was in Tot's freezer.

I was delirious for three days. I took no medicine and didn't see a doctor. During those few days when the fever almost carried me off, I was absolutely alone. The walls spun around me, I couldn't stand up. My body was drenched in sweat and I took in whatever was lying around my bed: water, wine, even whiskey. The ground seemed like a pool of nothingness where the stars came to be crushed. In my delirium, I summoned a universe from which humans were excluded, a universe where the gaze of animals would alone bring the light of day. But while climbing through the insides of a cave that dripped with blood, I realized that the blood was mine, and that the animals painted their frescoes on the walls with it.

I was constantly screaming in my sleep: the woman on the bridge was running in the woods, where Tot killed her with a bullet to the heart; then she was lying, her stomach naked, bloody, in the back of the car where Sabbat, his mouth dripping blood, was eating her arm. Or I would see pieces of her body frozen in little bags, and among them her eye, surrounded by ice cubes, which continued to watch me.

I think it was my anger at Tot that saved me. I wanted to throw my fever onto the entire globe and make it roil in the firmament. I wanted to spit the fever out of my mouth and set cities and flawed human relationships on fire.

Perhaps it is out of such abysses that marvels like those told of in the Apocalypse of John emerge. The visible world is an imperceptible trace in the infinite revealed through suffering. Between the prey and the gunshot a horizon trembles. All hunters have seen it at least once. They know the tiny, fragile, inconceivable difference between what disappears and what remains intact.

Because of Tot—and also thanks to him—I had thus come back from the brink. Can the world come to its own end? And can evil be everywhere in it? That was an experience I think about over and over with disgust, but also with fear. It must be impossible that the part that reasons in us be anything but spiritual.

Maybe you think I should have gotten away from someone like Tot, or at least have avoided him. But rather than always protecting yourself from or avoiding the devil, it is sometimes wise to feed him. Too much distance is in his favor. At the time, I was very close to him—I breathed in his breath.

Since those nights of fever, I didn't see Tot again. He went away, as he often did, leaving Sabbat to me. A note under my door, scrawled in haste, saying, "I have to leave. Don't forget the dog." And in a sense, it was during that demented night when a woman committed suicide that this story really began. Rather, that it turned around and found the point that made it go in another direction.

31

PLACE DE LA RÉPUBLIQUE

So I was at the wheel of Tot's car. Something was breaking loose in my head, and it was probably best not to know what that thing was. I had to leave my room in three days, and not only did I not know where I was going, but I hadn't even thought about it. Was I confident? That moment, when clarity tears away the veil, I felt it getting closer. What did Tot and our demented rivalry, his dog, his dead plants, matter to me? What did that apartment, those films that I had watched like a demon, matter to me? I had finally finished with that period, and now I was going to live.

That afternoon, when the Paris sky was dark and rainy, I still hoped to find Sabbat, but my search had taken a rather irrational turn. I was driving around randomly. If Sabbat was to come back to me, I thought, it would take a miracle. I had abandoned any logical plan and was driving around aimlessly.

Going through different neighborhoods, I thought back on various times in my life. Each time, there had been the idea of a new beginning—of a *new life*, and each time it was like I was living in a novel, in particular during that period I had told Guy the Cobra about, when I had lived for several months in a car on rue de la Chine, at the time of the *Renards pâles*.

Driving around, I listened to the radio and its bad news: more attacks in Brussels, Istanbul, Berlin, hundreds more refugees drowned off the coast of Lampedusa, more heads cut off in the desert, more massacres.

After driving for hours, I stopped at the edge of the Place de la République. For several days, thousands of people had been gathering around the statue. Everyone left a note, lit a candle, reflected, remembering the victims of the attack. I got out of the car and leaned against the hood to smoke a cigarette. I was waiting for Anouk, who had asked me to meet her here, around 8:00 p.m.

Earlier, on the radio I had heard the name of each dead person, and it seemed that those names were spinning in the sky, above the Place de la République. They moved around the leaves of the plane trees like fireflies.

If you say the name of a dead person, it is metamorphosed into sparks and joins the sparkling others that populate the world. Because in saying the name of someone who has just died, you're celebrating *all the dead*. It was my Dogon friends who had taught me that, at the time of the insurrection of the *Renards pâles.* They had taught me that in dying, a Dogon of Mali is one with all those who preceded him in existence.

So I thought there was no reason that such a marvel should not take place this evening, on Place de la République. Hadn't we, at the time, transformed the statue of Marianne into a baobab? Hadn't this place secretly become an extension of the Bandiagara Cliffs?

While smoking my cigarette I started to recite the names of the victims of the attack. Earlier, I hadn't paid a lot of attention to the names when they were read over the radio, but now, however, I remembered each one of them. I felt like I knew them: *they were coming back to me.*

A soft chant came out of my mouth, and a strange tongue was invented through it, a language traversed by spirits, which made the border between the living and the dead tremble.

At the same moment, a cloud of doves rose up above the square. Did they have names? With a simple rustling of wings, they wrapped the square in a pink clarity.

Anouk arrived, wrapped in her aviator jacket. She raised her head to the cloud of doves, her pretty gray eyes full of tears.

I opened the door for her. We stayed parked in front of Le Temple d'Or without moving. Her perfume was soft, amber, I think. When she took off her jacket, I saw she was wearing a little black velvet ribbon around her neck, like

Manet's Olympia. She turned the rearview mirror toward her, put on some lipstick, and asked me for a cigarette, which she started smoking nervously. Her breathing was rapid and made her chest rise. I also lit a cigarette; neither of us spoke.

All of a sudden, she asked, as if scolding me, what I was doing with Tot's car. I responded that I couldn't continue to look for Sabbat on foot. She calmed down, then confided that she had lost a friend in the massacre, the other night. She was devastated, didn't know what to do. So she spent her days here sharing her grief with people who had also lost someone close to them.

I asked her the name of her friend, and when she said it, I told her I had said it out loud a few minutes earlier, it was good to say names, it was a form of prayer: to say a name out loud was to keep it in the world of the living.

She looked at me without saying anything, then played nervously with the glove box. When you push the button, the door opens slowly, and a small blue light comes on automatically. I sensed that Anouk was familiar with the glove box, and that she liked that blue light. Her fingers slid along the dashboard, as if she wanted to assure herself of the consistency of a moment whose fragility rendered the two of us vulnerable. She seemed as likely to take out a gun as to burst into tears. She turned the dial of the radio, searching for a station, and we listened to a song by David Bowie, who had recently died, about resurrection.

The little blue light vibrated between Anouk's fingers. That evening, the world seemed clouded with sighs. Was she hungry? Did she want to go have dinner somewhere? She just wanted to drive, listen to songs while driving on the boulevards, going from one street to another, all night long. So I started off. First we drove around the square, where the light had gotten bigger, and it wasn't just the candles of mourning that lit up the night that way, but the effect of the doves, the fireflies, the names that went from one mouth to another and which were written on little bits of paper. While we were driving away, Anouk continued to look at the cloud of lights that, in the rearview mirror, rose up to the shoulders of the statue, like the breath of fire.

We began to roll through the night. There were slow scents, a few voices in the trees, and little groups that drunkenly animated the café terraces of the rue Oberkampf. I stopped to buy some beer, which we drank in the car while smoking cigarettes. The night recovered a bit of its softness, and between Ménilmontant and Belleville, in the chestnut trees on the large sidewalks along the boulevard, there were even a few chirping birds.

Anouk noticed the rifle bag sitting on the back seat. "Are you hunting, now?" It turns out Tot had called her from Canada, where he was being detained for some debt that he owed. He had lost a colossal sum while gambling, the law had gotten involved, and until the trial he couldn't leave the country.

Had she had anything to do with two strange guys, two guys with mustaches who were looking for Tot everywhere? No, she didn't know what I was talking about. Since we were going over everything, I asked her if she remembered the woman who had jumped from the Asnières bridge whom Tot had prevented me from saving. Yes, Tot had told her about our confrontation, and she was on his side. You don't prevent someone from killing themselves. Suicide is an inalienable right. It is unacceptable to deprive anyone of that ultimate freedom.

At Stalingrad, as we were beginning to drive along the elevated Métro toward Barbès, we were stopped by the national police. They were getting rid of undocumented squatters, the boulevard was closed, we had to go another way.

While I was cursing, one of the policemen came up to the car. Anouk had just enough time to hide the rifle bag. Had the cop seen the beer cans that were lying on the back seat? He asked for my papers.

What the hell is it in France with ID papers? I didn't have them—it had been a long time since I had had them. One day, out of love for a woman who had destroyed hers, I destroyed mine, too.

But I didn't say anything to the policeman, and pretended to look for them in my coat pockets.

Anouk held out her teacher ID card. The cop noticed that she worked at Deuil-la-Barre, they began to talk, and it turned out he had been a student in the high school where she taught, which he found amusing.

The cop was summoned on his walkie-talkie, he ran off, and I quickly drove away. While going around the refugee camp, I noticed bodies under tarps.

That vision was really disturbing. I hadn't seen very well, we had gone by too fast, but I was sure that feet were sticking out from under the tarps, and that the bodies were covered up to their faces, as is done with corpses.

I asked Anouk, "Did you see that?"

But she was busy watching how the cops, behind the girders of the elevated Métro, were knocking down the tents and ripping apart the sleeping bags.

I had stopped, and a cop was yelling at us, "Get out of here!" Two people appeared, running on the sidewalk, with huge plastic bags and their faces covered with hoods. The cops were screaming now: "Stop! Stop!"

Just when the two runners were about to go by us, I opened the car door behind me. They got in without hesitation, and as the cops began to run in the street shouting for us to stop, I took off fast, laughing out loud.

Anouk burst out laughing, too.

I was elated. Seeing the thwarted cops in the rearview mirror, I said, "Look at their faces!"

Anouk and the two passengers turned around to see the defeated cops: they weren't going to shoot us, were they?

I rolled down the window and shouted at them, "*Assholes!*"

I sped off toward Barbès, taking the little streets that wind around the Ninth Arrondissement, and aimed for the Grands Boulevards, toward the Opéra. Our two passengers, leaning against each other, didn't say anything.

At one point there was a traffic jam. We were stuck, and I was afraid we would be caught. The cops had our description, they must have taken down the car's license plate number. Streets were blocked, police vans were everywhere. For a few seconds, I wondered if this deployment was for us, if maybe our passengers were fugitives. And then I laughed at such absurdity. We were stuck in front of the Grand Rex. They both looked at the facade lit up with red-and-gold neon, their eyes wide open. They had taken off their hoods to see better. They were almost kids, they must have been sixteen, seventeen at most.

The young man's name was David, the young girl, Arwa. They were Libyan. She spoke a bit of French, he, none. Their camp in Calais had been torn down, they were wandering in Paris, and above all didn't want to be taken to an immigrant center, because they would certainly be sent to Italy where they had initially landed, and everything would begin again. They were not very reassured, but thanked us for our help.

We stopped in front of a grocery store and Anouk bought them sandwiches, cookies, two little bottles of water, and a bag of cherries, which we all shared. Our two guests started spitting the pits out the window, so we did the same, and we began to laugh.

"So, where are we going?"

Anouk didn't really know. Arwa and David didn't answer. How about we go swimming, go to the sea? After all, we just had to leave Paris, drive an hour or two to Normandy, and there would be wonderful beaches where we could go swimming at midnight.

Since no one reacted, I said to Anouk that we were going to put them up. She agreed. At her place or mine? She lived in a little room, so I said we could all go to my place. I lived in a small apartment, there was only one bed, but we could figure it out. The only problem was that I had to surrender the keys in three days.

That made them laugh. Arwa said to me, "You're getting kicked out, too?"

She added that they didn't want to cause problems for us. In any event, they had been given an address in case they ran out of options, someone trustworthy, a friend of the family who would take care of them. They'd like to be taken there. She gave me a piece of paper with an address on it: 21, rue du Père-Corentin.

I knew just where it was. It was in the Fourteenth Arrondissement, next to the Parc Montsouris, at the bottom of Paris, near the Porte d'Orléans. We'd be there in twenty minutes or so. Since the main roads were blocked,

I took the small streets. We went slowly. Anouk offered cigarettes, and we all began to smoke. She turned on the radio and a song by Joy Division started playing: "Love Will Tear Us Apart."

I turned up the volume. Suddenly I started to cry. What is that place in us where emotions flare up without warning? The hour, drunkenness, a yearning for endless love? I had heard that song by Joy Division hundreds of times in my adolescence, but even this night it made me shiver. It's the most heart-wrenching song in the world. It might seem cold, but it burns; its fire is desperate, and yet it is consoling. It might seem that you're going to die, and yet you're reborn—it's my adolescence, and it's everything else. The dying world, the world being reborn, the approach of deliverance.

Were David and Arwa wrapped in this song, too? It looked like their eyes were closed, they were exhausted.

What could we offer them? Arwa said that they were happy to ride in a car in the most beautiful city in the world, and their only wish was that it would never stop, that this escape would be transformed into a voyage, and that the voyage would last as long as possible.

The darkness was teeming with movement wherever we looked. In the streets we took, there were dozens of homeless tents and sleeping bags lying on heating vents.

I asked them if there was something they wanted to see in Paris.

Arwa said, "The Wheel, the Big Wheel."

Anouk and I looked at each other: what was that wheel?

"In a garden," said Arwa, "next to a big square. They showed us a picture in school, they told us that it was the most beautiful square in the world."

Anouk said, "It's the Place de la Concorde."

It was on the way, so we went. Arwa asked us what we did in life.

Anouk said she taught philosophy in a high school, and was working on a thesis. Arwa wanted to do that, too, later on, philosophy, lengthy studies, never stop studying.

"What about you?"

"I look for a dog."

Even David burst out laughing, and his laugh was the crystalline laugh of a child; I thought, completely ludicrously, that that September evening, in Tot's Jeep, Anouk and I were transporting two divine children, two little prophets, a king and a queen, a brother and a sister who had come to save the world.

"What kind of dog is it?" asked David.

"A Dalmatian."

They didn't understand.

Anouk said, "Walt Disney... You know, the white dogs with black spots: *One Hundred and One Dalmatians.*"

David was ecstatic, now he couldn't stop laughing. And I explained, trying to be funny, that I couldn't understand at all how I could have lost that dog. Wasn't losing a dog

HOLD FAST YOUR CROWN

absurd, wasn't it inconceivable? I added that I spent my
days in Paris looking for him, because I knew he was somewhere, I knew he was alive, and that maybe he was even
looking for me—and David and Arwa stopped laughing.

We drove around La Madeleine. They were delighted,
because in these rich neighborhoods everything was lit up.
But in fact, there was no life in the center of Paris, there
were only dead zones, banks whose walls absorbed any
pulse there may have been.

While listening to the Joy Division song that night, by
letting myself be taken in by its coldness, I understood for
the first time how truly prophetic it was. The entire world
had become cold, there was no more "entire world," there
was no more world, there was now only cold, everywhere,
ice that covers the tragedy, that takes away the tearing, the
icy laugh of the predators who govern the planet.

Then the Big Wheel emerged in the night. It was turning with the silvery glittering of stars. David and Arwa
smiled, their eyes shining. Anouk was smiling, too, and we
began to drive once, twice, three times around the Obé-
lisque, whose golden leaves were sparkling. We went around
counterclockwise, we didn't stop turning. The night would
henceforth be round and silvery, the night would continue
to turn with us, it would salute the sky and the stars, forever.

32

THE ISENHEIM ALTARPIECE

On the evening of the twenty-seventh, Léna called me in tears. Her sister had just died. She didn't have the strength to go to the funeral alone. She asked if I would go with her. I met her the next day, on the platform of the Gare de l'Est, for the 11:05 train to Strasbourg.

So it was September 28, I still hadn't found Sabbat, I had only two days before being kicked out of the apartment: things couldn't be worse. But did I really think I would still be able to find Sabbat? I preferred not to think about it.

As for my moving, it would take hardly an hour. Over the years I had sold almost everything I owned. Of the thousands of books that had ended up covering the walls of my apartment up to the ceiling, that were piled up in the WC, in the bathroom, and even in the kitchen, I now had only enough to fill two or three boxes.

I just needed two other boxes, one for the DVDs, the other for clothes. Then there was the papyri, the swallow, and the manuscript—that was it. I had arranged for Mme Figo to take the fridge and the other furniture: the sofa bed, the bookshelves, the kitchen table.

So I was free to go with Léna. I was surprised, moreover, at how quickly she had invited me. After all, I didn't really know anything about her. We had seen each other twice—what did she expect from life, what did she expect from me, what was I doing going to a funeral?

Léna was smoking a cigarette at the end of the platform, talking on the phone. She was pale, very agitated, her dark blue dress cut through the grayness. She was wearing a light bottle-green coat and red high-heeled shoes, which gave her mourning a sort of arrogance. I took her in my arms. She explained that her sister had died from a stroke, alone, at night, in front of the Isenheim Altarpiece, of which she was the conservator. She had MS, she said, and went around in a wheelchair. She knew since the beginning of her illness that one day her body would be entirely paralyzed. There was no cure for the illness, she knew that, everyone knew it. And furthermore, the fact that her limbs would become stiff seemed a grace from God, for then she would share both the stiffness of Christ on the cross, and the cross itself.

While we were boarding the train and finding a place in the bar car, Léna never stopped talking. I knew that that torrential flow wouldn't end until the moment we arrived at our destination. She ordered a little bottle of whiskey, which she drank in one gulp, then ordered another. I did the same.

Anna (her sister) lived in Colmar in the family house, so she never got far from the object of her adoration, because the Unterlinden Museum, which housed the Isenheim Altarpiece, was a few streets from where she lived. She had always lived there, along with their mother, who had taken care of her since she had fallen ill and who had always pushed them both so they would become conservators, like her (she herself had worked at the Unterlinden Museum, then directed the Musée des Beaux-Arts in Strasbourg).

The two sisters had studied together at the school of the Louvre, then she, Léna, after several assignments in museums in Paris, including Orsay and the Louvre, was picked to direct the little Musée de la Chasse et de la Nature. Her sister Anna returned to Colmar, and for three years did absolutely nothing but study the Isenheim Altarpiece, which she had spent eight hours a day contemplating, and about which she had written the most complete treatise ever published. It was an absolutely insane book, Léna told me, not only scientifically irreproachable, providing analysis of every square centimeter of Grünewald's work, without stooping to offer any platitudes, but was above all a book that was traversed and even inhabited by a radical light, which no other art book had ever succeeded in exhibiting.

It was a light that came out of both philosophical reflection and a mystical act, a light that ultimately was another name for the love for and absolute faith one could have in art, a love and faith that had taken the place of the belief one might have in God, and perhaps coexisted with it.

That book, that opus, that madness, was greeted with stunned admiration by the art world, she told me, and when the position of conservator of the Unterlinden Museum opened up, it was obvious to everyone, and indisputable, that the only person who could occupy it was Anna. No sooner had she been named when she fell ill, and her limbs began to stiffen, "like those of Christ on the cross," she said. And very soon she could no longer walk, and had to go around in a wheelchair.

All the inhabitants of Colmar had met Anna one day or another in her chair, cursing the paving stones of the historical center, because morning and evening she took the same route. And she insisted on doing it by herself. First, there was the Place de l'Ancienne-Douane, then the bridge to cross, then the entire length of rue des Marchands that she had to climb, because it was sloping and full of obstacles, and finally the rue des Têtes which runs along the canal and ends at the museum. And if any of the inhabitants of Colmar offered to help her—there had to have been some—they undoubtedly remember having been scolded by a crazy woman who preferred to suffer, because in her opinion, if Christ's suffering had any meaning, it was up to us to lead our lives in that way.

After changing trains in Strasbourg, we arrived in Colmar in the middle of the afternoon. The city was stifling. The blue of the sky, the streets saturated with geraniums, the good mood of the passersby: all of it exasperated me. I had listened to Léna talk about a saint, and now we had landed in a festival. Loudspeakers blared out accordion music, and the entire city was decorated in honor of a wine festival that was whipping the crowd into a frenzy. A festival, I learned, was taking place in the Ancienne-Douane, exactly where Léna's family home was located.

Léna walked quickly, paying no attention to the noise or the crowd. As for me, I was far behind her, feeling like I was going to throw up. The whiskey had made me sick. I would have preferred to stop and drink a coffee or some water, but Léna was running, unstoppable, through a maze of little streets filled with tourists, where countless houses with flowered gables seemed to be the stars in a promotional film for the Alsace region.

On the Place de l'Ancienne-Douane, tables of drinkers, with yellow and red parasols, were grouped around a fountain upon which there was a bronze statue of a military-looking guy who was brandishing a grapevine. I immediately recognized the style of Bartholdi, the sculptor of the Statue of Liberty in New York. Incredible—even in the heart of a fiesta of Alsatian winemakers, Cimino was there. And the memory of his performance cheered me up a bit.

Léna headed toward a long, half-timbered house nestled in the shadows, which a row of firs protected from passersby. A large piece of black crepe was hanging over the front door.

I met her mother, a tall, energetic woman, very beautiful, who immediately invited me to have dinner with the family. But I refused, out of respect, and because I was uncomfortable. It was probably better to let the family be together, and respect their mourning.

I didn't know what to do with myself. I was stuck in the vestibule of this dark, low house where shadows passed in silence. I had lost sight of Léna. She had introduced me to two or three people, then had disappeared into a hall that led, I imagine, to the room where her sister was lying.

I waited for her while nibbling on some crackers, standing in the entryway, then I wandered into the kitchen where I was offered coffee. Léna's mother was receiving condolences there, and groups had formed and were talking softly about Léna's sister. Some were wondering about the future of the museum without her, others wondered if the ceremony would take place, as was whispered, in front of the Isenheim Altarpiece.

In the train, Léna had confided that she had written the text of a sort of eulogy, and that she would read it according to her sister's wishes, that is, in fact, in front of the Isenheim Altarpiece, with an open casket. The text wasn't a standard eulogy, it wasn't just an adieu. If she read that text, she told me, "nothing would be as it was before."

I sat for a half hour on a stool, near the large porcelain kitchen stove, whose green and white tiles represented the passing of the seasons. I closed my eyes. The light entered through a skylight, and a heavy torpor fell over me. All the tension of the last few days was relaxed. I saw the black-and-white figure of Sabbat running in the Alsatian countryside; I saw Tot locked in a room with barred windows in Montreal; I saw Anouk sleeping sadly in an RER train heading for Deuil-la-Barre; I saw Pointel suffocating under the weight of a deer; I saw Michael Cimino, boots, Stetson, and dark glasses, riding through a green field in Wyoming on Visconti, and giving us the finger while smiling like the Angel of Reims; I saw Isabelle Huppert in red shorts eating raw meat and talking to me about fire, laughing; I heard her words, "Fire exists"; and now they were all laughing, Tot, Pointel, Anouk, Cimino, and the loonies of the Petits Oignons, and also David and Arwa, and even Léna, whose crying I thought I heard, over there, in a bedroom where silence wrapped each emotion. And finally I saw, crackling through the flames of a bonfire, the image of the Place de la République filled with the dead bodies of the undocumented which had been piled up, layers of bodies superimposed on a pyre, at night, and now the statue of the République, itself, rose up and set the bodies on fire.

I decided to go out. Once I was out the door, the sun stunned me. The noise on the square was vile. The loud-speakers now played German pop songs. Couples were dancing around the fountain where Bartholdi's bronze statue sparkled in the autumn light.

I didn't know if it was a good idea to send a text to Léna. I wanted to say something comforting, tell her that she could count on me, tell her that I was nearby on the square, and that she could call me if she needed anything. But telling her where I was surely was unnecessary. She had other things to think about. And above all, I imagined the beep of an incoming text in the bedroom where she was reflecting at her sister's bedside, and I decided not to do it.

And so I took part in the drinking. At the table where I tasted the new wines of the Saint-Hippolyte and Bergheim winemakers, an old man, also a winemaker, told me that the sculptor Bartholdi was from Colmar, and that the plant the statue was holding (a general whose name I forget) was a grapevine from Tokaji.

The chaos got worse over the course of the evening, increasing the din. I was worried about Léna's family, and mentioned it to a woman who also lived on the square. She assured me that inside the houses you couldn't hear a thing. I sampled the local meats and cheeses, drank liters of "late vintages," and offered glasses to a plump young woman who wrote poetry, studied literature, and kept me company for part of the evening (walking away to take a piss on too-high heels, she fell on the paving stones, violently scraping her knees, and we had to call an ambulance).

Finally, around 11:00 p.m., I received a text from Léna wondering where I was. She joined me on the Jupiter café terrace where I was sitting alone drinking a beer. And, when she arrived, she immediately fell into my arms—she needed, she told me, love and alcohol.

I burst out laughing. I was drunk, but Léna didn't care. She was grateful I was there, she appreciated having a friend she could confide in on a night like this, a friend who had come with her to listen—someone, she told me mysteriously, who *understands the dead*.

She had fought for hours with her family to make sure the ceremony the next day would be what her sister had wanted. Her mother was on her side, she thought it was fine to display Anna's body in front of the altarpiece, but it seemed indecent that her face would be seen. The dead, in her opinion, had a right to privacy. To exhibit Anna's face in a place that would be open to the public bothered her. It was as if they were showing her body naked.

Léna had insisted: her sister had planned her funeral with great precision, which was entirely in line with the rituals that ran through her life. If they loved her, they had to honor her wishes, even in death.

––––––

I slept in the living room. I had taken a ton of Efferalgan, so that in the morning, despite the amount of wine I had drunk the night before, my head was more or less clear.

The undertaker arrived around nine; there was shouting, followed by a violent altercation between Léna's mother and a town employee who said it was scandalous. I got dressed quickly, ran to the kitchen to gulp down some coffee, and through the window, behind the hearse parked along the pine trees, saw some thirty people waiting.

It was 9:30. The sun was already beating down. I joined the group, lit a cigarette, and smoked leaning against a pine tree. At 9:35, four funeral home employees carried the casket out of the house. It barely made it through the door, and had to be tipped. And when one of the bearers lifted the cover to facilitate the operation, we saw it was empty.

The hearse departed, carrying the empty casket, and a few minutes later, Léna appeared, her face even more pale than usual. She was carrying, wrapped in white cloth that seemed to be on fire, the body of her sister.

There was a low murmur around me. Some people were stunned, as if Lazarus was emerging from the tomb, or as if the Virgin, sent especially this morning to Colmar, was enacting a pietà.

That vision was indeed extraordinary. But even more amazing than the appearance of the dead woman, taken out of her coffin to go through the streets of the city to join the Isenheim Altarpiece, was Léna's face, which stunned me, because it was of a whiteness that came from else-where, as if she had gone to look for her sister among the dead to bring her back here, among the living, carrying her in her arms.

Léna came out of the house and walked through the group of people, flanked by her mother and another woman I had seen the day before, who looked like them. Léna advanced slowly, straight ahead, and the morning light lit up Anna's shroud which in Léna's arms glittered in the sun like a cloth of gold.

I followed the procession, my eyes fixed on Léna's brown hair. The city opened up. On the square, and in each of the streets we crossed, passersby were immobilized, some made the sign of the cross, some cried, and others kneeled.

I hadn't seen her sister's face very well, it was hidden by the cloth, but her body seemed tiny in Léna's arms.

At the corner of the rue des Têtes, the procession came to a halt. People pressed around Léna, who perhaps was no longer able to carry Anna. Then we arrived at the museum, where the casket was waiting, its cover open in front of the altarpiece. Léna placed her sister's body in it, waited for us all to be seated, and walked up to a lectern placed at the foot of the coffin.

The scene depicted on the altarpiece was that of the Crucifixion. I don't know any more horrible one, and no doubt Christ's death has never been represented in such an unbearable way. He is hanging like a piece of meat, his flesh shredded, his bones broken, his body abandoned to the horror.

The casket was slightly raised, so that Anna's face could look at that of Christ. Between their two faces, there was Léna's, which now was looking at us. She took out a sheaf of papers that she slowly unfolded. She was wearing a black dress and a necklace of red stones. Her face, as I said, was of a whiteness of the abyss. Christ was upright behind her. It was an extraordinary tableau.

While looking at her sister's face in front of her in the casket, Léna began to read a text which she later gave me in the train when we returned, and which I recopied, with its title crossed out:

~~SPIT~~

I don't know whom I am addressing while talking in front of you today. Is it my sister? Is it the altar-piece, itself, or Christ on the cross, the Lord, who, you know, occupied all the space in my sister's life? Is it you, her friends, those close to her, her family? Or am I talking to myself—to my pain, my rage at having lost the one who was not only my sister, but the one who made me believe in life.

If I address the "Lord," as he has always been
called in my family, I'll be unkind: because I don't
believe in you, Lord, but I'm talking to you today
because I'm waiting for a miracle. I want you to
bring my sister back to life. Right now. I want you
to awaken her from death and make her rise up from
this casket. I want you to do for her what you did for
Lazarus. I expect that from you: a miracle. Bring her
back to life and I'll believe in you.

My sister always told me that having faith was
believing in miracles. So I'm waiting on you. It's
time, Lord. I'm going to talk to honor my beloved
sister; I'm going to talk so that you, her friends, her
relatives and her family, can testify that we tried
everything.

I can't be consoled. I'm going to talk, Lord, to
give you time to bring Anna back to life. You have
ten minutes. If my sister isn't resuscitated at the end
of my speech, I will spit in Your Face.

My sister was a saint, that is, a woman who
believed in silent things. For her, nothing existed
but the hidden sign in the darkness. And so she was
enthralled very early on with the Isenheim Altarpiece, which she had seen for the first time when
she was twelve, with our father, and his friend, the
painter Francis Bacon, who is probably the only

person in the world to have admired the altarpiece
as much as she did.

The path that leads to the heart of the Passion,
we all discover it from life; we aren't given the path.
Most of us are lost, and the voyage is infernal. But
since the path is opened for whoever can see a ray
of light, there is perhaps escape, perhaps a recom-
pense. Those are our lives. That of Anna, mine,
perhaps yours.

But Anna's had something more, something
you, alone, Lord in whom I don't believe, are aware
of. And that something more is before you. It's the
Crucifixion. She, too, was nailed to the cross; her
dangling legs were also dead.

I apologize for the harshness of my words, and for
my impudence. I don't wish to create a scandal, but
you know that no one ever says things—we avoid
saying them out of discretion and laziness. And our
spirit is stuck in a mutism we know nothing about.
We think we are talking because we are opening our
mouths, but our speech is always *something else*, and
today we must be able to talk, we must say things
that one cannot say.

If we really say things, we won't die—that's what
Anna believed. If we knew how to talk, if we lis-
tened to speech, death wouldn't exist. That's why
I'm talking to you today. I don't have the truth any

more than you do, but I want Anna to live again. And if we talk—if through speech we make live that which has lived ever since people have talked—she will rise up, I'm sure of it.

In the beginning there is darkness, we try not to fall. Our eyes open, we don't see anything. Then there are shapes. I see a quality in my sister that you have no doubt admired, as I do: she *endured*. She didn't like to suffer, believe me, on some nights we accompanied her in her crying, but when her life was finally connected to the altarpiece, when there was no longer any difference between that great piece of wood and that which hardened in her limbs, she began to be happy.

I dare say it. Some of you know, my mother knows, but I'll say it again: Anna was a saint. For she who devoted her life to studying this cross, from that torment, from that resurrection, nothing existed, perhaps, that wasn't represented in a few square meters of her altarpiece. Inside that piece was integrated the history of salvation, recapitulating suffering and transmitting its enigma.

She's the one who was nailed, as are we, even if we don't know it. Come close, and look: my sister, on that panel of wood in which her life is summed up, continued to appear by turns in the image of Mary Magdalene on her knees at the foot of the

cross, in that of the fainted Virgin in the arms of
Saint John, and finally, in Christ's suffering.

Fainted, on her knees, her arms spread apart,
nailed: that's my sister's life. From the wheelchair
that served as her throne, because my sister, and all
of those who have ever approached her knew, my
sister was a queen, and as a joke she compared herself to Anne of Gonzague. From her chair, where,
strapped in, her limbs like wood, she was held hos-
tage by their dead weight; my sister, whom some
among you loved, whom others feared, whom most
admired, my sister deepened grace.

The world exists inside the spread arms of Christ.
She told me that. I repeat word for word what Anna
told me: the world never exists better than inside the
arms that offer it shelter; it is the spreading arms of
Christ nailed to the cross that portray the existence
of the world. And if Leonardo da Vinci measured the
circle of the world by the circumference of the legs
and arms of a man, the Isenheim Altarpiece conveys
what cannot be measured, and that is called mercy.

I've often heard my sister say that word, "mercy";
so I say it to you so you can understand exactly where
she lived: on the Tree of Life, hanging between Wisdom and Victory.

One more word that the Christians among you
will understand, a line that she joyfully recited

when I watched her at the altarpiece: "Adam having stretched out his hand with intemperance to the forbidden fruit, it was befitting that the second Adam stretched out his immaculate hands on the cross."

My sister's body was racked with pain. All of Christ's suffering, she lived it. Christ's nakedness was hers: the shriveled arms, poor thighs, empty chest, belly stuck with thorns, the desolation that strikes the bones, the rib cage that retracts. I don't want to upset you, but it must be said, that's all. I never knew Anna to be light; the horror always tormented her—and I believe that she would have considered it useless, frivolous, perhaps even unfair, to be delivered from it.

She asked me to ask you a question: Is your heart intact? Is there anything whole left in you—a piece, a seed? Anna was entirely intact. A virgin. You didn't know? You might think we shouldn't say things like that here. I think it's debauchery that shouldn't be said, virginity alone should be proclaimed; my sister liked women.

What does it mean to be a virgin? One day, on the phone, because you know that Anna spent her life on the phone, she spent her evenings *telephoning*, as she said, citing Proust, she spent her nights calling us, so we could keep her company, and because the night terrified her—even when she was a child, she talked to me at night, she didn't want me to sleep, and I admit that I slept nonetheless, in spite of her monologues, as I fell asleep more than once on the phone while she continued to talk for hours. So, one day on the phone, a few weeks ago, she brought up the question of her death, and while I protested, not wanting to imagine her dead, she forced me to be her witness. She made me swear to carry out absolutely everything that she had decided on, including this reading in front of the altarpiece.

She planned everything, as you can imagine. She wanted her body to be placed there, with her head facing south to see Christ's body—*two dead face-to-face*, those were her words. The open casket, that was her idea. The procession in my arms, her idea, too. And those lines, which I am only repeating to you, because she dictated them to me.

So one evening, on the phone, after detailing how the ceremony of her death was to unfold, she mentioned her loves and asked me to talk about them. "Talk about what?" I asked. "Talk about my virginity," she answered. "I have never been penetrated by the penis of a man, that's the definition of virginity, isn't it?" She laughed when she said that. She said to me: "You tell them that when you read your text—you'll tell them that I was a virgin, that I didn't sin. Sin exists, but it wasn't for me, tell them.

Add that I'm an immaculate madwoman, tell them that: *I am an immaculate madwoman.* Tell them that I love to be stroked; that I am a woman. Tell them, in God's name." So I'm telling you.

In talking to you, I'm happy to make her voice return. Don't you recognize her clarity, her insolence? It is our dead who transmit life to us. It is because those whom we love die and we recognize in losing them a truth that mourning alone grants us: we are granted the gift of being alive. In dying, those whom we love awaken us: when we think of them, not only do we live better, but we have a heart. And if we never knew it, we finally know why we have a heart: to hear the voices of the dead whom we love. To open the passage so that the dead don't die and so the living stay alive.

The last time I saw my sister's eyes light up and her hand rise, it was here. She wanted to see the altarpiece she adored. I came with her, she was in her chair, she wasn't moving anymore, it was the summer, a month ago. We were in front of the crucifix, at the exact place where Anna is today; in silence, we contemplated it.

At a certain point, even when paralysis had completely taken over, and she was living in the prison of her body, which soon closed up on her completely, suffocating her, she raised a finger, then another:

the index and the middle finger, then her hand, inexplicably, rose up; her arm followed, and it rose up to Christ.

By fighting the stone that was taking over her muscles, Anna thus imitated the gesture that John the Baptist made, which we see to the right of the crucifix, and which is the last possible gesture: the gesture of pointing to that which is living—our gesture. The tip of my sister's finger, which rises while trembling, is what I have left of her.

In finishing, I must tell you why we are here. Some of you know the story: one night, when she was sixteen and still in perfect health, Anna woke up. She got up in a flash, it must have been three or four in the morning. It was in the house where she died, where you came to say goodbye. Anna jumped out of bed, and then she started dancing, she jumped around, like a deer. She put a coat over her shoulders and opened the front door and went across the city barefoot to the museum, whose keys she had since our mother already worked there.

Having arrived in front of the altarpiece, she turned on her flashlight, pointed it at Christ's body, and collapsed.

She couldn't get up; she never got up again. She was diagnosed with MS, but Anna would have nothing of it. Her illness, of which she was proud, her illness, which she delighted in, was faith.

By falling at the feet of Christ, by losing all her strength in front of him, she had converted. I've always thought that in front of a representation of Christ as terrifying as that of the Isenheim Altarpiece, one could only lose faith. But that's how my sister was: not only did she find faith in front of that large piece of wood, but she incorporated it, she became that wood to the point of dying from it.

And just as one day my sister collapsed in front of Christ, stricken by her vocation, we know, in front of him, that the bonds that tied him to the cross fell off. We know that at any moment, if we only devote our spirit to it, it is possible to hope for the untying of the bonds. It is possible to see Christ release himself from the weight of time and enter a new life.

That secret action that raises Christ up on the cross and keeps him from death, it is to that that I am now talking. I am waiting for Anna to be resurrected. I beg for the resurrection to come for my sister and bring her back to life.

After Léna had uttered the last words of her oration, she turned to the altarpiece and stared at it silently. The silence lasted several minutes. I also stared at the altarpiece, and it seemed that everyone did: we all did exactly what Léna did.

I remember thinking that each line of her speech had been embedded in me like those thorns that were stuck in the body of Christ. Or perhaps, on the contrary, that we were removing them all.

She walked to the casket, leaned over her sister's face and kissed her lips. We held our breaths, each of us hanging over Léna's lips, guessing, tasting those of her sister— hoping, sensing the return to life through the dampness of these two mouths that, in coming together, accomplished a verse from the Song of Songs: "Let him kiss me with a kiss from his mouth."

I repeated the verse several times and said to myself, crazily: this kiss is a door. If we enter through it, we will be saved. We will enter and we will leave—life and death will return. I thought a thousand things in a second. I saw the sparkling river where spirits drank. I saw the names that are written on my wall pass in front of me, as if they had been summoned. I heard each of them and I traveled fast through the leaves that they composed around my head.

It was a fire: between death and speech, a light was shining. Something must speak. The promise had been made. But where could that speech be found? Where does it speak? At every moment the fire speaks to us, and Léna had just answered it with her own fire. When she straightened up, I smiled at her.

33

THE WORLD OR NOTHING

And now I'm writing this book. It's 5 a.m. The candle on my table is burning slowly. The night is locked in a calm in which the birds are shivering. I close my eyes, and the whole story that this book tells begins to shimmer in a fairyland of details. I look out the window: the lake and the woods are quivering. All is still dark, but the first rays of light will arrive, and when it is really day I will go swimming.

Since I arrived here, on the banks of Lake Nemi, that's what happens: I settle down at the beginning of the evening at the desk in the little house I'm renting, and I write all night. I've arranged around me my papyri, the swallow, and a leather-covered box where I put my manuscript. Shortly before six o'clock, I go into the yard and, on a pebbly path, walk to the banks of the lake. I then sit in one of the chairs placed near the rose bushes. I put a blanket on my shoulders and light a cigarette while watching the colors of the sky. There is red, a bit of blue, and some gray that runs between them like lava. It looks like a fire, with ashes that become red, and which soon become purple, almost pink. A little yellow ribbon, as thin as a thread, runs above the village of Aricia, up there, where the pine trees stand out on the top of the mountains. Then the sky, all of a sudden, finds its blue.

In those moments I find limitless joy. There seems to exist in every day a moment to which the devil is denied access. If I could slide entirely inside that moment, life would be ecstasy.

Since I arrived in Nemi, I seem to evolve inside that moment. The sky is reflected in the lake, as in a mirror; and I swim there. Is it possible that life can be so clear, as fluid as a light wine that quenches your thirst and makes you tipsy? Is it possible that time erupts while opening up, and that you spend your life the way you swim in purple water? That tender silence that absorbs the breathing of the gods expands among the orange and lemon trees, in a silky blue light. The profusion is serene. I can't get over it.

A few days after I arrived, I went to see the ruins of the temple of Diana. I followed a path bordered by cypress, the sun was harsh. After the large openings dug out of the mountain, where a series of grottoes and tunnels begin, you end up in the sacred enclosure. The site has been abandoned: there are a few columns protected by torn tarps and a votive altar, where offerings are still brought to Diana.

That day, a bowl of figs was rotting in the sun, surrounded by red candles.

I headed toward one of the grottoes, the one that was framed by cross-hatched markings. Inside, the soil was damp, I dug a hole with the shovel that was in the jeep, then buried my red cookie box, the one containing the manuscript of *The Great Melville*. There, I was offering it to Diana. I was going to write another book, and that book needed all my thoughts, it needed to be the only one. And it was an act of devotion to Nemi: I intended to live here, so I needed to honor the site by offering a sacrifice.

On September 30, after I had cleaned the apartment and Mme Figo, following a brief inspection, had thanked me for the fridge and the furniture, I went to the *loge* to give her the keys. Just as I was about to start the Jeep whose trunk was filled with boxes, bending over to open the glove box, I found a book: *The Golden Bough* by James Frazer.

I remembered that Anouk was working on it for her thesis: she must have forgotten it the night we had picked up the two Libyans. I opened the book, and, instead of driving off, I began to read it. It was around 2 p.m., I was parked on the rue de la Py, right in front of my building. The afternoon was clear, promising. I rolled down the window and settled down to read more comfortably, with the book resting flat on the steering wheel. The air was full of softness; and since it was a Sunday, there wasn't much noise in the street.

Was my life emerging? Was I telling myself once again the story of a new life, a new departure, a renaissance? I don't think so. This time, I wasn't leaving anything or anyone; I just needed some light—I was ready to live. The expression might seem ridiculous: "ready to live," what does that mean? One is never ready, and at the same time, one doesn't stop living. But that afternoon, for the first time in weeks, months, years, I felt strong. I had confidence. Someone was making my heart beat. I smiled to myself at the wheel of the Jeep while repeating that line: "Someone is making my heart beat."

Ultimately, that's the only question: What do you hold dear? What do you *truly* hold dear?

I lit a cigarette. Through the open window, I breathed in the scent of the honeysuckle, whose large yellow-and-red flowers were opening like trumpets.

Having returned from Colmar the day before, Léna had slept at my place. She had laughed when she saw my lair: was I a wolf? And then *she had seen the names*. In that constellation scratched in red felt pen that unfolded over the entire wall of my room, she had immediately recognized the shape of a tree, and she had understood the tree it represented.

I was standing in the middle of the room, my arms stretched toward the wall, the palms of my hands open, and I showed Léna how I moved through the names. How a memory is invented by making the names dance. How it is possible to be traversed by a rain of sparks that transmit you in time, in memory. How the kingdom exists.

I told her I was going to leave Paris and look for a place to live, finally, according to the truth. The life of solitude I had led with films was certainly a way of advancing toward its brilliance—that truth, I was *seeking it*—but the disorder of my mind constantly took me off course. I needed a violent clarity in order to break with my own diversions.

Léna, sitting on a box in the empty apartment, listened to me attentively and said this wonderful thing: "The truth doesn't leave kings who love it and who seek it." It's a line that has illuminated everything. By receiving it that Sunday in September, I knew that my disorder, my madness, was only an already old vestment, a cloak in tatters that I was going to get rid of.

Since the beginning of this adventure—since that day in March when I went into Pointel's office and he gave me Michael Cimino's phone number—it seems I had penetrated into a land where the truth is constantly asking me a question, always the same: are you able to hear me?

I'd like to ask you the question, too: are you capable of *living in truth*? Who can claim to be at the height of such enormity? Do we even know what it means?

I thought a thousand times that I was going crazy, but never as much as at the moment when Léna put her lips to those of her sister, and when all of us were waiting for the impossible, when we had seen it within arm's reach—when we knew it was going to happen. I don't know what happened at that moment, and I haven't talked about it again with Léna: such a thing renders understanding useless. In writing this book, I think of it as I write each line; I wonder if I've seen what I've seen, if I've thought what I've thought, if I was really there.

And in kissing Léna in turn, it had seemed that I was entering into a story that was no longer only mine, nor that of two people, but that the Song of Songs continued to live through the bodies of those who knew how to listen to its miracles, and it was written anew each time lovers believed in it.

And so, that Sunday when once again I was beginning everything again, I thought: *I believe.*

I opened *The Golden Bough.* The first chapter is called "The King of the Wood." Léna was right: the truth doesn't abandon the kings who love it and seek it. On the contrary, it has signs everywhere, one need only open one's eyes, read books, listen to what time tells you.

It begins like this: "Who does not know Turner's picture of the Golden Bough? The scene, suffused with the golden glow of imagination in which the divine mind of Turner steeped and transfigured even the fairest natural landscape, is a dreamlike vision of the little woodland lake of Nemi—'Diana's Mirror,' as it was called by the ancients. No one who has seen that calm water, lapped in a green hollow of the Alban hills, can ever forget it."

Frazer continues, explaining that Lake Nemi is still surrounded as it once was by a wood of oaks. And at the bottom of steep slopes that go down to the banks of the lake, the goddess Diana had a sanctuary, known by the name of the Sacred Grove, whose arches were bathed by the water. The goddess was called Diana of the Woodland Glade. And if, like her Greek incarnation, she reigned over the hunt, she was above all the figure of a cult, because she protected refugees who kept coming into Latium, hiding to escape the Roman law in this wild forest where a strange sovereignty was granted them.

Indeed, a priest watched over the cult of Diana, and that priest was one of the outlaws. Some called him Dianus, because he was the mystical lover of the goddess. And everyone considered him a king because to obtain his power he had picked a bough whose legend later enthralled Virgil, who made it the attribute of Aeneas when he descended to Hades.

But, writes Frazer, it wasn't enough. To become King of the Wood, to break a branch of the sacred bush of Diana, you had to kill the presiding king. Thus royalty fell to the one who caused blood to flow, and who then risked losing his own life at any moment. It took only a vagabond, an outlaw, an escaped slave, to enter the sanctuary and pierce the heart of the king with a sword, for sovereignty to change hands.

This story fascinated me. It harshly unveiled the violence that is at the heart of the sacred. It blew the whistle on sacrifice and putting to death that—I have felt this forever—secretly orders the history of the world. No need to be nuts like the Baron to know such a thing, no need to pontificate on a spiritual war. The very course of time was putting people to death. Every act secretly concealed a murder.

I felt I knew that story intimately, as if I was constantly living it, as if, in it, something was pointing at me: the name of Nemi had been calling me forever.

And then there was Diana. There was the sensuality promised by those Italian places, a sensuality that in reading Frazer I imagined to be bitter, dark, full of danger, but burning like an embrace. There was the splendor of a lake where the delights of a life of swimming were reflected. Finally, there was the idea of a spring, and that's exactly what I needed: to find a spring, abandon my spirit to it, release my body there.

I didn't hesitate: I decided to go to Nemi.

From that point, things went very quickly. I had been driving for ten minutes when my phone rang, it was Pointel. I couldn't answer, but I stopped at the bottom of Père-Lachaise to listen to his message. He asked me to call him back. He said he had something important to tell me.

I called him back right away, and he asked if I had heard. Heard what?

"Cimino is dead."

I met Pointel at his office, on rue Notre-Dame-de-Nazareth, the same office where I had gone to see him in the spring with *The Great Melville*. Walking up the little wooden staircase I had the feeling I was retracing my steps, as if this story was necessarily going to come together, as if Cimino had to die so I could finally leave that circle.

Pointel was really upset, he took me in his arms; and when I told him I was surprised, because I thought Cimino was immortal, I saw his eyes fill with tears. And it's true: I couldn't understand how someone like Cimino could die. Hadn't he passed some time ago to the other side, to that world where art breathes all by itself?

We started to talk about scenes from his films. Pointel loved the huge wedding scene at the beginning of *The Deer Hunter*, with the glances the shy lover played by Robert De Niro gives Meryl Streep from the opposite side of the room, also with the Russian Orthodox service during which the couple drinks together from a cup of wine while trying not to spill any, at the risk of incurring misfortune. "And you remember," Pointel said, "it's heart-wrenching as you the viewer see, when no one during the ceremony sees anything, that a tiny drop is spilled, like a tear of blood, on the tie of the young guy who is leaving for Vietnam, and we know then that he won't return alive."

There were also all those unforgettable scenes of Russian roulette that Pointel especially liked, and the red headband Christopher Walken wore on his forehead like a misguided Christ in the sacrificial madness of the war, and the hunt for the deer in the mountains, and Robert De Niro who, sighting the deer, doesn't kill it.

As for me, the first scene that came back to me was at the beginning of *Heaven's Gate*, when one of the immigrants from Eastern Europe begins to cut up the cow he has stolen to feed his family. On a wire, strung all around his wooden cabin, out of which escapes thin smoke, he has hung white sheets that hide the operation. The young man is very agitated, we see that he doesn't know what he's doing. He leans over the cow trembling, with the immemorial knife of the sacrificer that he holds as if it were a writing pen, and then he cuts as well as he can pieces of meat right off the animal whose flayed flanks sag, gaping, against the facade of the cabin, as in the painting by Rembrandt. We hear the galloping of an approaching horse, the shadow on the sheet gets bigger; and while the terrified young man turns his face toward that shadow that now darkens the entire scene, we hear an explosion, the sheet tears, and the young sacrificer, a huge hole in his stomach from which blood is spurting, collapses on the cow and dies on the exact place where he was cutting off the flesh. It is then he who is sacrificed—he is the animal. We hear the cries of his wife who runs out of the house, and through the large white sheet that is now in flames, a hole shows us the face of the killer.

It's extraordinary, I said to Pointel, how that scene condenses all the violence of Cimino's films, to the point of being the ideal representation of his oeuvre. And we agreed that through the metaphor of that pierced sheet, one could read the gesture that Cimino would have made to crush the screen, to seek through film to raise the veil, to burn it if necessary, to seize something that perhaps existed neither on one side of the screen nor the other, but only in the act itself, tragic and endless, of passing through it.

And then I recounted the final hours I had spent with Michael Cimino. It was after our little boat ride in the bay around Ellis Island. The trick he had played in front of the Statue of Liberty had overjoyed him, he seemed very young that evening. A spark sometimes lights up in the eyes of lions. Its reflection travels through nights, and glimmers like a victory. In the taxi that was taking us to Little Italy, Cimino had the spark.

The driver was a large, noble-looking black man, whose headgear was similar to the one the jazz pianist Thelonious Monk wore. Looking at Cimino in his rearview mirror, he said to him, "You look like a prince, man!" Cimino smiled. He had my manuscript on his lap. And while we drove through New York, he followed its lines with the tip of his pencil.

With their dark glasses, Cimino and Monk dialogued in silence. I was also silent, and like them I smiled: it was a starry night.

We arrived at Paesano, the trattoria which Cimino claimed was the last to offer true Italian cuisine, where the owner greeted him with hugs. In the little restaurant where they served us a magnificent chianti and where we devoured mozzarella *di bufala* and spaghetti *allo scoglio* whose praises he had sung, Cimino began to speak Italian wildly, like an eternal immigrant.

All evening he talked only about literature, and above all about Proust, whom he admired, and whose *Le temps retrouvé* he was rereading. "Melville and Proust are the greatest," he said.

At the end of the dinner, he ordered almond cookies that we dipped in little glasses of vin santo. They were the cookies of his childhood, perfumed and crunchy, the famous *cantuccini di Prato di Mattonella* which the owner gave me as a gift for my trip back, so happy was he that someone would eat them in France.

The act of eating such a cookie made it seem like we were performing a sacrament. And since Cimino was eating with dark-blue silk gloves on, the movements he made to dip his *cantuccini* in the sweet wine were like those of a magician who, plunging his hand into a hat, pulled out flowers, satin ribbons, a top, jacks, a torrent of sparks. But during that evening, it was the entire world, with all its insanity, that came out of our glasses, the world with its jokes and its old dreams, with its illusions, its drunkenness, its pain. And when we had finally eaten all the cookies, Michael Cimino ordered two glasses of asti spumante. He took off his dark glasses for the first time, looked me right in the eyes, raised his glass high and, citing the last verse of Dante's *Divine Comedy*, proposed a toast to "l'amor che move il sole e l'altre stelle" (the love that moves the sun and the other stars).

It is thanks to Pointel that I am writing this book. Because that day—the day of Michael Cimino's death—he had the idea for a book in which I would tell in detail what I had told him, that is, my encounter with Cimino in New York. He told me that I absolutely had to write that book, and it would be called *The Great Cimino*.

At the beginning, the idea made me laugh, but Pointel was very serious. When I told him I was leaving France, and that I was leaving that day for Italy, to live on the banks of Lake Nemi, he immediately opened a desk drawer, took out his checkbook, and wrote me a check: "This is an advance," he told me, and he added, "Finally, you see, it wasn't Melville, it was Cimino." He accompanied me to the door, and while I was going down the stairs, he said, "We'll make a film out of it!"

Was I really going to write a book about Michael Cimino? In starting the car, I laughed to myself. About Cimino, maybe not, but a book, yes. Up until today, I hadn't thought about it. And now I really wanted to. That hadn't happened to me for some time. I could thank Pointel for that. And I was going to deposit his check as quickly as possible.

I drove to the Porte d'Orléans on my way out of Paris. A novel, I said: I'm going to write a novel. After all, hadn't I lived through true fiction these past few months? Pointel was right: Cimino's death made that idea necessary; but in meeting him, I had also encountered a thousand other things that had started to burn in my life. I had to tell about that, that flaming.

I first took the highway to the hills of Auvergne. I wanted to see Lascaux. I won't tell about my visit to the cave. It seems that all this adventure unfolded there, and that the animals continued to appear in my life, to leap out of the cave to populate my desires.

I enjoyed driving in the hills, no longer thinking about anything, being empty before leaving for Italy. That evening I went back to Clermont-Ferrand for the night, to a hotel that seemed luxurious to me. I deposited Pointel's check in a bank. With that money, I was going to be able to live for a few months. I received a message from Anouk: she told me that Tot had been released, he was coming back to France, he knew everything, he was looking for me. I went to pay a visit to Guy the Cobra, who was living alone in a little house on the edge of Lake Guéry, without electricity. He let me sleep in the adjoining cabin, where I stayed for three days, just enough time to make sure, before isolating myself in Italy, that this type of solitude pleased me, and to read all of *The Golden Bough* leaning against a pine tree.

And then one evening, I went south. Like Aeneas, I had my fetishes, my lares and penates, with me in the trunk: the swallow, the red cookie box with the manuscript, and my papyri.

I drove through the night. I kept driving, trembling with joy. At dawn I stopped at a service station, at the exit of the town of Aricia. I had some coffee and I asked for directions to Lake Nemi. I just had to take the via Diana, the one that wound through the forest—it leads directly to the lake. To hear someone say that name electrified me. I was going to follow the road of Diana.

I drove around the lake. The little road, in places, became thinner between the thorn bushes and the reeds, full of potholes, and it very quickly became no more than a path of stony earth, a footpath that was lost in the brush through the oaks, and which forced you to turn around.

I found a place where the edge of the lake was accessible. The water sparkled, throwing off jewels of bright silver sparks. The sky was reflected in turquoise sheets. I stopped the car and headed through a clump of olive trees. The air was perfumed by orange trees, and right after a myrtle bush, on the edge of the lake, where the water came to lap the banks in a delicious slapping, an old oak tree allowed its leaves to hang over the water. I thought that behind that oak tree, the King of the Wood had once stood, full of glory, worried, waiting for his successor with his sword in hand. I imagined him biting into a lemon at dawn, his mouth carried away by an acid cool, contemplating the immutable expanse of the lake where Diana, it was said, secretly came to bathe.

On that vision I superimposed the one of Actaeon, covered with the skin of a deer, moving quietly between the reeds and hiding behind that tree, contemplating, erect, the nakedness of Diana surrounded by her nymphs, the beautiful Diana of the Woodland Glade whose legs open to the waves, and whose mother-of-pearl breasts reflecting on the water gave the hunter the irrepressible orgasm which is the *true source*.

I called Léna. It was 6 a.m., but I needed to tell her that I had arrived. Her voice was sleepy, a bit thick, full of sweet joy; she sent me dreamy kisses, and in a murmur I told her I loved her—that I was waiting for her.

I undressed and went into the water. The coolness invaded my body. I cried out with joy. That swim is still going on. It will never end. Each morning, after writing pages of this book all night long, I reach the lake by the stony path. I leave my clothes on the banks and, naked, I go into the lake. The water caresses me, the light begins to shimmer, the sky opens up with little blue sparks. I listen, smiling, to the sound of the water in the silence of the dawn. I listen to the noise of the gravel. I'm waiting for Léna. One morning, I hope, she will take off her clothes on the banks of the lake and join me.